## Praise for *Rock Bottom*

"Everything a great thriller should be—action-packed, authentic, and intense."

—#1 *New York Times* bestselling author Lee Child

"A compelling new voice in thriller writing. *Rock Bottom* will keep you in its spell from beginning to end. And I love how the characters come alive on every page."

—*New York Times* bestselling author Jeffery Deaver

"Erin Brockovich continues to fight the good fight, now as a writer of fiction. *Rock Bottom* is a story Erin Brockovich lived. The heroine is brilliant and feisty. Tension and turmoil mount in a high stakes adventure with dire consequences. Nobody could tell this story better."

—*New York Times* bestselling author Steve Berry

"With strong character development and a fast-paced plot, this excellent first novel leaves readers anticipating further exciting adventures with AJ Palladino."

—*Library Journal*

"Readers will love AJ Palladino and her son, a bright, precocious nine-year-old with a crippling disability he uses to his advantage. With highly engaging characters, heart-stopping scenes and a sensitive topic, *Rock Bottom* is one great rollercoaster ride that will not be stopping anytime soon."

—Book Reporter

"Activist Brockovich teams up with bestseller Lyons on a fascinating and intense thriller about relationships, environmentalism and the lengths people will go to protect a secret. The story is fast-paced, dark and dangerous."

—*Romantic Times Book Reviews*,
Top Pick Designation, 4 1/2 stars

"This is a character-driven, environmental-family drama that grips the audience from the opening gunshot until the final confrontation. With several tense subplots that tie together into a powerful taut thriller, fans will demand more similar tales from Erin Brockovich."

—Harriet Klausner, *The Mystery Gazette*

"*Rock Bottom* is an intense, emotional thriller of a debut. From the moment the first page is read, the story catapults the reader into a world of greed, subterfuge and passion. Brockovich has created a compassionate, endearing fire-cracker of a heroine in *Rock Bottom*. To elevate this massively engaging novel, the story climbs the edge of intensity with unwavering precision. Concise language, mastery of dialogue and a surprisingly authentic love story emerge as the reader becomes entranced in the pages of this killer debut."

—*National Examiner*

# HOT WATER

Also by Erin Brockovich

*Rock Bottom*

# ERIN BROCKOVICH

## WITH CJ LYONS

# HOT
# WATER

A NOVEL

Vanguard Press

A MEMBER OF THE PERSEUS BOOKS GROUP

Published by Vanguard Press
A Member of the Perseus Books Group

Designed by Linda Mark
Set in 12 point Adobe Caslon Pro

Library of Congress Cataloging-in-Publication Data
Brockovich, Erin.
Hot water / Erin Brockovich with CJ Lyons.
p. cm.
ISBN 978-1-59315-684-8 (hardcover : alk. paper)—
ISBN 978-1-59315-685-5 (e-book)
1. Women environmentalists—Fiction.   2. Single mothers—
Fiction.   3. Nuclear facilities—Accidents—Fiction.
4. Families—Fiction.   I. Lyons, CJ, 1964– II. Title.
PS3602.R6325H69 2011
813'.6—dc22
2011020811

Vanguard Press books are available at special
discounts for bulk purchases in the U.S. by corporations,
institutions, and other organizations. For more information, please
contact the Special Markets Department at the Perseus Books
Group, 2300 Chestnut Street, Suite 200, Philadelphia, PA
19103, or call (800) 810-4145, ext. 5000, or e-mail
special.markets@perseusbooks.com.

10 9 8 7 6 5 4 3 2 1

*We dedicate this book to the victims of
the 2011 Japanese earthquake and tsunami as well as
the hard-working and self-sacrificing rescue workers
who came to their aid during their time of need.*

He who has a mind
to meddle must have
a heart to help.

RALPH WALDO EMERSON

# ACKNOWLEDGMENTS

Dear Reader,

Thanks for joining AJ on another adventure!

Turns out that nuclear energy is a touchy subject to research. When we interviewed several experts in the field we stressed that we did not want to use any scenarios that could potentially happen in real life—after all, our job is to entertain and explore new ideas through our stories, not to empower potential terrorists.

Unfortunately, writers sometimes have too-good imaginations. We discovered that our scenarios actually *could* happen—and in two cases they were things that the experts had never considered before (nuclear engineers not being prone to thinking like devious, cunning thriller writers).

So instead of setting *Hot Water* in a conventional nuclear facility we created an unconventional, fictional design that is a hybrid of several experimental reactors in Sweden, France, and Russia as well as emerging technology in "micro-reactors" from Oregon State University. However, for our contamination breaches we did use real-life contamination events that occurred in the past and have already been well documented in the public media.

The medical isotope shortage is also real. Currently the needs of patients in the United States are being met from the Chalk River facility in Canada, but it is scheduled for closure in a few years. Chalk River has been closed several times in the past, forcing the United States to rely on the Maria reactor in Poland for its isotopes. New methods of isotope production are being tested in the hopes of resolving this crisis.

We'd like to thank our nuclear experts (who declined to be named) for their patience—and we apologize for any gray hairs we caused with our wild imaginations. The men and women who work in the nuclear field have our respect and admiration for their profound attention to the public's safety.

Thanks also to our technical advisors, Bob Bedard and Melody Von Smith, to Toni McGee Causey for sharing her alligator wrestling expertise, and to Rebecca Forster for her help in researching the child welfare statutes as well as the amount of power and variability in interpreting those statutes that a judge could potentially wield. We also drew upon the knowledge and experience of several law enforcement officers from the Crimescene Writers loop, including Wally Lind, Kathy Bennett, Steven Brown, Robin Burcell, and MA Taylor.

As always, we very much appreciate the efforts of our publishing team at Vanguard Press/The Perseus Books Group, including Roger Cooper and Georgina Levitt; our editor, Kevin Smith; as well as our agents, Mel Berger (Erin) and Barbara Poelle (CJ), and our first readers, Kendel Flaum and Carolyn Males.

We'd love to hear from you! You can contact us through www.CJLyons.net.

Thanks for reading!
Erin and CJ

# ONE

Summer in the mountains of West Virginia has a magic of its own, like a fairy tale come true. For me, it was a fairy tale paid for with blood.

It was August. After five months back home in Scotia (population 864) I'd just about gotten used to folks looking away from me and mumbling about how I'd gotten the man I loved killed and almost got my dad and son killed and just about drowned the entire valley in toxic sludge.

"That's AJ Palladino," they'd say, crossing to the other side of the street as I passed, in case I rubbed off on them. "Yeah, *that* AJ Palladino."

I ignored them. Didn't much care what people said about me as long as they didn't take it out on my nine-year-old, David. And, I have to admit, Scotia did treat David like the hero his dad had once been. They embraced him despite his two disabilities (or abilities, depending on your point of view): having cerebral palsy, which left him mostly wheelchair-bound, and being a genius.

Despite the town's acceptance of him, David still wasn't so sure about Scotia. He was hit hard by the death of his dad. I tried everything, even enrolled him in some online courses. Stuff I didn't understand but he was interested in, like the *Phonology of Ancient Egyptian Hieroglyphics* and *Einstein, Oppenheimer, Feynman: Physics in the 20th Century*. He'd bury himself in them, working like a fever, finishing a semester's worth of material in a few weeks, and then would promptly slide back into boredom and despair.

Given my family's tendency for obsessions—addictions, really, holding on too hard, too long—I was more than a bit worried.

My friend Ty Stillwater, a sheriff's deputy K-9 officer, and his partner, Nikki, a beautiful Belgium Malinois, finally broke David free from his mourning.

Ty somehow found a way to make wheelchair accessible every mountain adventure that a boy could love. He and David would leave at first light and show up again for dinner at my gram's kitchen covered in battle scars. Once, Ty took David rafting down the New River, and they came back half-drowned, sunburned, and sporting matching black eyes that they refused to tell us how they got. They would burst into laughter every time they caught sight of each other.

I loved hearing David laugh but couldn't help but worry each time he left. For too many years I'd raised David alone, and it was difficult getting used to sharing him with others who loved him as much as I did. Not to mention the fact that I was and am a total control freak, especially about David. But I suffered in silence—David hates it when I try to rein in his independence.

Besides, I was busy enough with work to take my mind mostly off David's scrapes and bruises and poison ivy. My new business partner, Elizabeth Hardy, the legal half of our consumer advocacy firm, turned out to have a gift for negotiation, so our first few cases ended quickly and happily for our clients and were profitable for us. All in all, summer felt enchanted, magical.

Even the weather cooperated. The storm clouds that gathered every afternoon remained empty threats. They'd scowl down at Scotia, then scurry away to dump their rain elsewhere.

But sooner or later, the storm has to break and you're going to get soaked.

Which was how I came to be yelling at the man in the Armani suit.

◆

I knew it was an Armani suit because I'd dealt with enough of them when I'd worked in D.C. Not sure how they did it, but it seemed as if every suit jacket had an attitude sewn into the lining: money can buy anything.

Well, it wasn't buying me.

Elizabeth and I hadn't risked everything—including our lives— to start this advocacy firm just to be dictated to by a guy who happened to have enough money to indulge his taste in designer suits.

Armani guy's name was Owen Grandel, and he'd flown all the way up from South Carolina to consult with Elizabeth and me. He was in his late thirties, trim in that personal-trainer executive way, with a shaved head that focused your attention on his dark eyes and spray-tan complexion.

He had *not* come to Scotia to be abused. Or so his expression informed me without bothering with words.

"We aren't in the business of whitewashing a corporation's dirty laundry," I continued, in the mood for a fight and quite happy that Grandel was obliging.

He said nothing. Simply crossed his arms over his chest, leaned his shoulders back, and smiled. The kind of smile you give a precocious kid who's acting out and you're tolerating his behavior just because you know how wrong he is.

David hates it when I smile at him that way.

Thankfully Elizabeth stepped between us before I tried to wipe that smile off Grandel's face. We were in the living room of her house—which doubled as our office space—and she had just brought coffee on a tray. "I'm sorry, Mr. Grandel, we're out of cream. Will milk do?"

I rolled my eyes as she almost curtsied. Then, while Grandel busied himself mixing and stirring his coffee, finally taking a seat in the Queen Anne chair beside the fireplace, Elizabeth glanced over her shoulder at me with a glare that could have sparked tinder.

*Play nice,* she mouthed at me, as if I were the one making trouble. She sat down across from Grandel, smoothing her skirt and crossing her ankles like a lady before reaching for her own cup of coffee.

This is why I usually let Elizabeth handle the suits. I'm more of a field person—get me out there with the regular folks and I'll get to the truth of what's what and who's who and figure out a way to fix things. Then it's up to Elizabeth to cross the legal "t's," negotiate a workable solution for all parties, and collect our paycheck.

So far it's been a pretty good system. Until today.

"I'm not sure that you understand exactly what we do, Mr. Grandel." Elizabeth leaned across the table to snag a sugar cube, her sleeve brushing against his knee.

I barely contained my snort. It was very obvious Grandel didn't understand anything except what his money could buy.

"Oh, but I do, Ms. Hardy." He leaned back and crossed his legs, watching her through half-shut eyes.

When I worked in D.C., I knew men like him. Smooth, charming. Sociopaths. Women would fall all over themselves to do whatever they wanted. Poor sod, he had no idea who he was up against. Elizabeth wasn't like that.

"Which is why I'm willing to pay extra. Above your customary fee schedule." With an elegant flourish of his manicured fingers, he slid a check from his pocket and placed it in front of her.

Elizabeth has a pretty good poker face, but I could tell the amount on the check rocked her. She took a sip of coffee and set her cup down beside the check, ignoring it.

"That's half," he persisted when she didn't leap at his offer. "You get the same when you finish."

"And who decides when the job is finished?"

I stepped forward, unwilling to believe she was even considering. She glared at me and I froze.

"You do, of course." His voice was a low bedroom purr.

Her mouth twisted as she considered. Then she stood in one graceful movement, taking the check with her. "We need to consult about this."

"Of course," he said with a gracious wave of his hand, as if it were his house, not hers. "Take all the time you need."

I know my mouth dropped open because I felt it snap shut again when she took my arm and dragged me out of the room and across the hall to our shared office in what used to be the dining room. She closed the door behind us, then sagged back against it.

"Holy shit, AJ."

The check dropped from her fingers, flitting through the air on the sultry August breeze wafting in through the open windows, and curled up on the hardwood floor, face down. I picked it up, turned it over.

My face went cold as I read the amount. Counted the zeroes. Five of them. My mind did a back flip—no, that figure *couldn't* be right—then sloshed right side up as I looked again.

Half a million dollars. Which meant a million for the entire job if we took it.

Enough to send David to any college he wanted, to bankroll our company for the next decade, to be able to work on projects that really mattered. Freedom, security, opportunity.

All I'd have to do was betray everything I believed in and let myself be bought.

# TWO

Elizabeth liked feeling the solid oak door at her back. It reassured her that this wasn't a dream. Made her feel as if her father and his father and all the generations of Hardys who had lived here in this house stood behind her, ready to support her even if she might be making the wrong choice.

She knew as soon as she'd heard Grandel's pitch that he would be hard to say no to, but a million dollars? For what basically amounted to a public relations stunt?

Small change to a man like Grandel, but for her and AJ. . . . The lace curtains fluttered at the windows and she inhaled the crisp mountain air. So very different from hazy, hot, and humid Philly, where even eight stories up in an air-conditioned fortress of a law office the heat still weighed you down. The thermometer told her it was almost as hot here in Scotia, eighty-two in the shade, but somehow it didn't feel so bad. Her house here didn't even have air conditioning; the breeze took care of that.

"We can't do it." AJ didn't sound so certain as she stared at Grandel's check. Elizabeth knew she was thinking of everything that money could buy for David. Unlike Elizabeth, AJ had never had money. Elizabeth wasn't sure if that made the decision easier or more difficult.

"Why not?" Elizabeth asked, squaring herself for a battle. Even though this house was paid for, she hadn't been able to sell her condo in Philly, and their cases so far had barely covered the mortgage she owed. "I'm tired of counting pennies and thinking twice about everything I want to buy. If that makes me shallow, so be it. But damn it, I didn't leave my entire life behind to come here and constantly worry. I thought we were meant to be making a difference, changing the world one case at a time, isn't that what you said?"

AJ looked surprised. "Isn't that what we're doing? We've been getting paid—"

"Two thousand from Reverend Morley's church. Didn't even cover the lab costs of testing their groundwater. And the eleven thousand from Energy Alternatives went straight to pay you and cover our expenses."

"I thought we were splitting the profits," AJ murmured, grinding the toe of her cowboy boot into the floor.

*Whoops.* Even though both of their names were on the office door—capitalizing on AJ's reputation as an environmental activist—Elizabeth was in charge of the finances. "There haven't been any profits to split. Not yet. That's okay, it's how any business is when it starts up. And my dad's life insurance is covering things so far. But—"

AJ jerked her chin up at that, face flushed with wounded pride. "No. We're partners. You shouldn't be paying me and not yourself."

"I don't have a kid. And a grandmother who needs my help. Not to mention your family . . ." Elizabeth stopped. AJ's parents were a sore subject, one they usually avoided—just as AJ did her best to avoid them in person. It was a fine juggling act since AJ's son, David, wanted to get to know his family, even the crazy side of the family. Elizabeth had no idea how AJ managed everything, but somehow she did. But it took its toll on her, and Elizabeth could see it.

Thank goodness Elizabeth and her ex, Hunter, had never had children. She couldn't imagine how warped they'd be, caught in the middle of Hunter's narcissistic infidelities and her escaping him by fleeing to the office and indulging in over-working. No kid deserved that.

"How could we?" AJ finally ventured, staring at the check once more. "I mean, what he's asking—we don't have any experience with that kind of thing. He needs a PR specialist, not an advocacy firm. Besides, we're supposed to be working for the people, not the corporations."

"Tell you what. How about if we go back and listen to him— really listen. No interrupting to debate the environmental impact of nuclear waste."

"But he—"

"I know you don't like him." AJ was prone to making snap judgments about people—something she said she was working hard to change.

"I never said that—"

"Face it, AJ, you're a reverse-snob."

"I like you, don't I?"

"Not at first. At first you thought I was just another stuck-up lawyer out to make a buck."

That coaxed a smile from her. "Maybe."

"You decided the same thing about Grandel as soon as he walked in with his Armani suit and two-thousand-dollar shoes. How about if we give him the benefit of the doubt and listen without judging? Then we can decide. Together." Elizabeth pulled the door open. "Sound like a plan, partner?"

AJ rolled her eyes but plastered on a smile and strode back out to where Grandel waited.

"We're willing to listen." Elizabeth leaned against the mantel, looking down on Grandel, giving him her best hard-assed negotiator look.

Grandel didn't blink. His smile was slow and wide, as if she and AJ had already agreed. "Look. We're all adults here," he began. "We know that if we put AJ Palladino's name and face on an environmental problem, people are going to understand that we're taking it seriously."

"I don't care how much money you're offering," AJ said, pacing on the other side of the coffee table, her boot heels clacking against the oak floor. "I'm not a PR shill."

"Not asking you to be one. I could hire a good PR firm at half the price. But I need more than good press. I need the community to publicly support me."

"But your problem is with possible radiation leaks from your plant. I don't know anything about investigating that kind of environmental contamination."

"Got plenty of investigators. Between the NRC, the Department of Energy, and my own group, the investigators are tripping over themselves. What I need is someone who will talk to the community—someone who speaks their language, not scientific mumbo-jumbo about microsieverts and isotope degradation."

AJ nodded, shoving her hands into the back pockets of her jeans and rocking on her heels. Slowing down long enough to think about it.

"I don't need you to solve the plant's problems. I need someone to interface with the community."

Elizabeth swallowed a chuckle when AJ's eyebrow tweaked at "interface."

Grandel was smart enough to notice and hurried on, "Someone folks can trust. If you say everything is being done, they'll believe you. If you say that it's safe, they'll trust you."

"Mitigation," AJ said. "That's what the lawyers call it."

Grandel shrugged and didn't look abashed. Instead he met AJ's gaze head on. "I'll be honest with you. That's exactly what I need. Mitigation. To reduce the impact these accidents have had. Someone to get the public off my back long enough for us to get up and running at full capacity. My company's future depends on this plant's success. I'm putting everything I have on the line here."

AJ tensed up, began pacing again, and Elizabeth was certain he'd lost her.

But then Grandel continued, "Remember, Colleton Landing is the only medical isotope plant in the United States. And with Chalk River in Canada closing down, it's going to be the only place in the entire Western Hemisphere where doctors and patients can get the nuclear isotopes they need. Do you have any idea how many patients we can help? Millions. But I can't do it if the locals shut us down because they're afraid."

"You think they're ignorant?" AJ asked, scorn coloring her tone. She was proud of her small-town, self-taught roots. "Small-town fools?"

Elizabeth braced herself, ready to wade in and do damage control. To her surprise, Grandel didn't take offense.

"Then I'm a fool right along with them. My brother and I were raised just down river from Colleton Landing. That's why we chose it for the plant. A chance to give something back. But after what happened in Japan, I guess everyone's paranoid when it comes to a topic like radiation. That's why I need you. The townsfolk need to understand that there's no real risk—and they need to know what we're doing so they can see how hard we're working to keep them, to keep everyone, safe."

"I won't say anything unless you can prove it to me first. No scripts or spin. I get full access to your research and findings. You lie to me or make me lie to them and I'll go public, I swear I will."

"Wouldn't expect anything less." He was smart enough to hide his smile.

"And if I find anything that leads me to believe that there is something wrong with the reactor, I'm not holding back. No confidentiality clause."

"Done." He stood and held his hand out to AJ.

She glanced at Elizabeth, who gave her a nod, then took it.

Grandel shook. "Welcome to the family."

# — THREE —

We moved into the office. Elizabeth began drawing up a contract while Grandel unrolled a sheaf of blueprints across the dining table.

"You know how a conventional nuclear plant works, right?"

Wrong. I wiped my palms on the back of my jeans, hoping he didn't notice. Everything I knew about nuclear power could fit into a sewing thimble, with plenty of room left over for my thumb. But I *would* know everything once I got home and David had a chance to bring me up to speed. One of the perks of living with a nine-year-old genius who has an insatiable curiosity about everything.

"Why don't you walk me through it," I suggested. "Just like you would for the people in your community."

"Good idea. Sometimes I get too wrapped up in the technical specs. Okay, well, in a conventional nuclear power plant you have the uranium fuel ready to go into fission but you keep it just under critical mass with control rods. When you're ready to generate energy, you raise the control rods so the uranium can mix together, beginning the fission process, which releases heat. That heat in turn boils the water flowing through the reactor, which produces steam, which turns a turbine, generating electricity."

I nodded. "Not much different from how a coal plant works—except for the whole nuclear meltdown potential."

Elizabeth shot me a stern glance, so I shut up. We were here to learn about Grandel's plant, not to debate sustainable energy.

"More than electricity, Colleton Landing generates radioactive atoms—isotopes—that doctors use to diagnose and treat disease. And even you'd agree that nuclear power is less toxic to the environment with no $CO_2$ emissions and no need to mine the coal."

Professional that I am, I didn't ask him how long it would take the nuclear material left over from his plant to decay to safe radiation levels and how he intended to protect the rest of the world from it. He didn't have the answers—no one did. That was the problem. Same with coal or gas or oil. Everyone worried about what they needed here and now without thinking about the future.

Instead I pointed to the artist's rendering that graced the front page of the blueprints. "It looks different than the plants I've seen."

Colleton Landing looked, well, I hesitated to use the word aloud, pretty. Compared to traditional plants like Three Mile Island with their massive cooling towers and large buildings housing turbines and the nuclear facility, Colleton Landing looked like a Disney theme park. The drawing showed a large central building with a dome-shaped roof flanked by two graceful wings, sitting on the banks of a wide river and surrounded by forest.

Grandel smiled and nodded, not at me but at the drawing, like a proud father. "Fifteen years of my life went into this design. I won a DOE competition—that's how I got the money to build, finally." He caressed the outline with a finger. "Colleton Landing *is* different." He flipped the page to a cutaway view of the plant's interior, which resembled a clock face. "Instead of one large containment vessel holding the uranium, we divide it into four separate hot cells placed in a ring bathed by coolant on all sides. This allows us to harvest M-99 from the cells at different times—around the clock, so to speak."

He chuckled at his inside joke and Elizabeth joined in. I didn't. "A hot cell is like a small reactor, right? So you have four reactors instead of one? Does that mean you have four times the chance for an accident?"

"Of course not," he scoffed. "That's the beauty of my design. We have less chance of an accident than any other plant on the planet. Think of it like a submarine—in fact, our micro-reactors are partly based on the reactors the Russians used in their subs—layers upon layers of airtight doors that can protect the rest of the sub if there's a breach. If anything, we have four times *more* safety built in." He tapped the walls separating the hot cells. "Each cell has its own high-pressure containment vessel for the core, then we surround all of them in water nestled within a secondary stainless-steel containment housing. All this sits within an outer concrete chamber strong enough to withstand a direct hit by a 747."

"But if you have workers accessing four hot cells to harvest the isotopes, doesn't that multiply the chance for error?"

Now he looked smug. "Not humans. Robots."

"Robots?" Elizabeth asked.

"Robots. Because we're partnered with the DOE, we were able to access robotic prototypes the military was working on. All high-risk areas are manned by robots remotely monitored by humans. Not only are the robots more precise and less likely to make mistakes than the humans, but they're the only ones directly exposed to any possible contamination."

"So where have the accidents occurred?"

His good humor and pride fled, replaced by a glimpse of fear that was quickly masked. He pointed to some lines on the blueprints. A tangle of pipes streamed between the central dome and the wings on either side. "The first was here. A leaky seal on a containment drain line released a small amount of contaminated water into the ground between the reactor building and the turbine annex before the sensors detected it."

"The robotic sensors?" I couldn't resist nettling him. Juvenile, I know.

"Yes. We're equipped with state-of-the-art sodium iodine detectors. The DOE inspector's report said they detected it far earlier than any human system would."

I resisted the urge to roll my eyes. I liked people, wasn't comfortable around machines. Especially not machines smarter than I was. "And the second accident?"

"Simple human error. A crapped-up piece of metal got thrown into the recycling. But our sensors caught it before it left the facility perimeter."

"Crapped up?"

"Contaminated."

"So your sensors caught it inside the plant?"

He studied the map as if it held the answers. "Well, no. We caught it here." He pointed to the inner perimeter fence. "In the recycling truck."

"Didn't that contaminate everything in the truck?"

"Yeah. Very low level, though. Nothing dangerous."

I was beginning to wonder at his definition of "dangerous."

"The third accident," he stressed the last word, "was totally unrelated to the first two. A valve stuck and a small amount of water overflowed from the coolant tanks."

"Overflowed where? Into the river?"

"Oh no. Nothing like that. It backed up into a drain—left standing water on the floor, and a few workers had their shoes exposed."

He frowned again—more than a frown, a scowl. As if he were being singled out unfairly. Or rather, his plant was. "Since it's the first of its kind, Colleton Landing has come under more scrutiny than any other plant in the nation. Unlike other places that have *real* problems—like Indian Point, which lost 100,000 gallons of coolant before anyone noticed. Or Vermont Yankee, which has leaked not just tritium but also cesium into the groundwater. And don't get me started on the mess up in Washington State—workers repeatedly finding new caches of plutonium that the government forgot existed, hundreds of gallons of uranium, plutonium, strontium, and cesium dumped into the Mohawk River. Yet, we're the ones in the spotlight."

Wow. Guess I hit a sore spot. But Grandel's passion was the first thing I'd liked about him since we met. "The investigations have cleared you each time?"

"Yes. In fact, in the first two, both the DOE and the Nuclear Regulatory Commission congratulated us on our prompt and early response and interventions." He gave his head a small shake, as if wondering at the state of the world. "Of course, the press never mentions our commendations or the part where the DOE calls us a model facility. All they talk about is how negligent we are and the risks to the community."

Finally he ran out of steam. Both Elizabeth and I were staring at him. He blushed slightly—guess underneath that corporate raider exterior he was human after all. It was nice to see.

"I'd like to learn more about those other incidents in other plants," I said. "It will give me context."

"No problem. I have reams of incident reports. I brought them with me." He nodded to his bulging brief case. "You can read them on the plane."

"Plane?"

"Sure. I have our Gulfstream waiting."

Elizabeth and I exchanged glances. "Seems like you were pretty sure we'd help you."

"Pretty desperate is more like it. I'm involved in very sensitive negotiations with foreign investors. If we don't prove that we can successfully meet the isotope demand with Colleton Landing and that our plant design poses no public risk, I'll be ruined."

"Not to mention all those patients who won't get the care they need," Elizabeth added.

"Of course. That's always a priority. But now you understand why this is so urgent. Any more shutdowns—even if it's only for a day or two to investigate another mishap—and we'll be so far behind schedule that we'll never catch up."

"I understand and I sympathize," I said. "But there's no way I can leave for South Carolina today."

"Why not?"

He'd never understand. But I had to be honest. "It's my son's birthday on Saturday. I can't miss it."

Grandel flushed. He wasn't a man who people said no to, I could tell.

"Saturday? Today's only Wednesday. How about if you come now and I'll fly you back Friday? Just give me two days—see what you think. You can keep that retainer whatever you decide. Surely your time is worth a quarter of a million a day?"

He paused and I just stared, not sure if I should slap him for assuming I could be bought at any price or hug him for not walking away from a deal that could secure our future.

Before I could say anything, he continued, "I'll even sweeten the pot with a bonus—a savings bond in your son's name. He can use it for college. How's ten thousand sound?"

The air left my lungs so fast my ears popped. I hated that Grandel *could* buy me—or use David to do it . . . but. . . . Elizabeth stood behind Grandel, mouthing "one million dollars."

It was our future—the firm's, David's, my entire family's and Elizabeth's. How could I refuse?

◆

Pea gravel cracked beneath the crutch's rubber tip as David leaned his weight onto it. The noise sent a startled squirrel darting up a nearby hemlock, turning to make an accusatory skittering sound as if reprimanding David for being so loud.

"How far is he?" Gram Flora asked from a few yards below him, one hand shielding her eyes from the sun as though she wasn't almost totally blind.

"Only to the first bend," her personal care assistant, Jeremy, answered.

"David, that's far enough," she called. "Ty, go fetch him back."

Ty said nothing. Which was why David liked him so much. The sheriff's deputy rarely said anything unless it would make a difference, and Ty knew full well that David had his mind set on getting to the top of the mountain, all the way up to the lookout at the wishing stone.

David had been working all summer for this, the perfect birthday present. It was his birthday coming up, but he wanted to do something special for his mom. After all, she'd almost died giving birth to him—a fact he'd only learned about recently. All his life Mom had sacrificed and worked hard to take care of him. Now he wanted to give her something that would let her see how far he'd come.

He was going to the top of the mountain. But not in his wheelchair. Oh no. He was *walking*.

With a little help from his crutches, for sure. But still. He was walking to the top.

The sun sizzled off the sweat covering his face. A slight breeze—a tailwind, that was good—helped to keep him from feeling too hot despite his exertion. One foot, then the other. It was painfully slow going, but he couldn't stop. Not with the image of Mom's smile of pride when she saw him make it to the top on Saturday floating before him. No way he would quit, let her down.

The second turn of the switch-backed path had him looking back down the ridge to Gram Flora's house and the smaller cottage known as the summerhouse, where he and Mom had lived ever since they arrived in Scotia a few months ago. Funny. It didn't seem so long when you looked at the calendar, but it felt like he'd become a whole other person since he'd left D.C.

Guess he was. He'd found and lost a father in the space of a few days. Almost died himself. Met Ty and Ty's K-9 partner, Nikki. Moved in beside Gram Flora and Jeremy. And was starting to get to know his mother's parents—but not his father's, not as much as he'd like. His dad only had a father left, Old Man Masterson. That's what his mom called his paternal grandfather, usually accompanied by a sour look on her face like she'd forgotten to check the date on the milk before taking a drink but was too polite to spit it out.

Forget being a whole other person. He'd entered a whole new world. A strange and wondrous one filled with mountains and trees and birds and animals and all sorts of adventures he'd only read about before coming to West Virginia.

He paused and leaned on his crutches, looking down the mountain. Not because he was tired. Oh no. He just liked the view. The big old white framed farmhouse with its wraparound porch—Flora called it a veranda—and red tin roof, faded from the sun. And the three people watching him from the back steps. Gram Flora, his great-grandmother, in her seventies and blind but still smarter than most people he knew. Jeremy, around his mom's age, black, with a constant smile and an endless repertoire of bad puns.

And Ty Stillwater. His mom's best friend growing up and now David's. Ty had taken David all over these mountains this summer—it was the first time ever that David had tan lines.

A cloud shielded him from the sun for a moment, suddenly chilling him. He waved to the grownups and turned to resume his toil up the mountainside. When he thought about Ty and all the adventures they had this summer, he almost forgot about his dad dying.

Almost.

With a sigh, he heaved his foot forward, sweat puddling between his sock and plastic ankle-foot orthotic. He turned his face up toward the wishing stone and kept on going. Mom was going to be so surprised come Saturday.

He couldn't wait.

# FOUR

I left Elizabeth and Grandel discussing tactics and stumbled out to my bright blue Ford Escape hybrid, staggering under the weight of the reports and manuals and articles Grandel had provided. Not that I'd be reading them myself—ever since a car accident left me in a coma ten years ago, I've had a hard time reading. Wish I could also blame my impulsiveness, temper, and knack for leaping before looking on that as well, but I can't.

David would be doing the reading for me—we made for a good team that way. He'd be way more interested in all this technical stuff than I'd ever be. All I wanted to know was how it impacted the people.

Grandel said my way of approaching things—from the effect back to the cause—was exactly the kind of "reverse social engineering" he'd been hoping for. I think he meant that as a compliment; he was smiling, but his smile was like the smile of an alligator or politician—you never knew if it meant they were happy or hungry.

I piled the stack of reading material into the back seat and then pulled away from Elizabeth's house. Driving through downtown

Scotia was the same summer or winter—empty houses, empty store fronts, empty parking spaces.

Empty hopes and dreams—that was Scotia.

The only new jobs the town had seen lately came from the demolition team tearing down the old school. Once that was done, it would be back to unemployment and welfare, a never-ending cycle that trapped so many in the valley.

Folks around here made do like they always did, with help of friends and family, helping out others when they could in turn. Government assistance would be taken grudgingly but also with a sense of entitlement, seeing as how so many generations of Scotia's men had lived and died in the coal mines, providing energy to the rest of the country even as they were abandoned and forgotten by the outside world.

Ten thousand dollars was more cash than many of these families would see in a year—and Grandel tossed it at me like a bone for a clever dog that had just been taught a new trick.

I felt dirty taking the money, but when I thought about it, I wasn't sure why. It was for David, not me. And Grandel had promised I'd be home in time for David's birthday. So where was the problem?

The fact that I didn't have an answer only made me feel worse. I left town and drove the three miles up the twisting mountain roads to Gram Flora's farm. It wasn't until I got out of the car and breathed in the vista unfolding below me that I was able to untwist the knots between my shoulders.

Flora's farm—which included twenty acres of apple trees, her house, and the small summerhouse David and I lived in, as well as all the land to the top of Hightower Mountain—looked out over Scotia and the mountains surrounding it. It was a view that inspired and humbled.

Ahead of me stood fold upon fold of green. It was as if God had unfurled a roll of Astroturf that smelled of pine needles and crisp, clean sunshine.

It had taken me ten years of exile in D.C. before, faced with the prospect of being homeless, I'd returned to Scotia. I hadn't come home for me. It was for David that I'd swallowed my pride and crawled back to the town that had kicked me to the curb ten years ago when I was alone and pregnant. To put a roof over his head.

With the move came unexpected complications—including my parents and David's father, Cole, and *his* father, Kyle Masterson, who owned most of the land around here along with the coal beneath it.

Now Cole was gone, leaving me to navigate some pretty rough waters between all three of David's grandparents without either David or me being caught in the rapids. Thank God for Gram Flora. She was an oasis of calm in the turmoil.

A Sheriff's Department Tahoe was parked near the summerhouse. Ty Stillwater and Nikki were here. Finally a genuine smile warmed my face. I'm not sure I could have made it through the past few months without Ty's help. He seemed to speak nine-year-old boy as effortlessly as he brought comfort to me without saying a word.

I handle the world by never stopping or slowing down long enough to let anything hit me. Guess I always figured I was a harder target if I just kept on moving. But even I couldn't dodge the feelings brought on by Cole's death or David's almost being killed a few months ago. Ty taught me the value of sitting still long enough to simply feel . . . simply be.

Still smiling, I climbed the steps to Flora's veranda. Voices filtered through the screen door and open windows—excited, happy, overlapping, swirling around me and inviting me inside to join my family.

◆

The voices came from the large wide-open kitchen that took up the rear of the house. Jeremy mixed a pitcher of lemonade with mint leaves crushed into it while David, Ty, Flora, and Nikki sat waiting at the table. Nikki was between David and Ty, but relaxed, in her "off-duty" posture, her chin resting on Ty's thigh, ears perked high as David scratched behind them.

When they saw me they all got sneaky looks on their faces—even Nikki. I plopped the stack of binders onto the stout table that could seat twelve hungry farmhands. "What's up?"

"Nothing," David said. Quickly.

His face was flushed and his shirt stained with sweat. I had to restrain myself from checking for fever. Old habits. But he'd never been healthier. When I took him to his neurologist's appointment at Children's National last month, everyone had *oohed* and *aahed* at how much he'd grown and at his progress. Me? I was already missing my little boy, the one I could carry and cuddle, and wondering at this stranger with his independent streak and stubborn refusal to let me play Mom.

Guess it's been coming a long time, but still.

"We were just talking about Saturday," Flora said.

"How's the planning coming?"

Flora had decided to take charge of David's birthday celebration since she'd missed so many of his past birthdays, and she refused to let me help.

"Just fine. Nothing for you to worry about." She waved a hand and sent an enigmatic smile in my direction.

Jeremy brought the lemonade to the table and began filling glasses. David fished an ice cube out of his, looked to Ty for permission, then tossed it to Nikki, who acted like it was the best invention since the can opener, skidding it between her paws and crunching it eagerly.

"What's all this?" Ty read the cover from the top of my stack.

"*Nuclear Regulatory Commission Report on Safety and Health Concerns at the US DOE Hanford Nuclear Facility.*"

David reached past him to grab the binder, almost knocking his lemonade over in his eagerness. "Hanford? I read about that place. They like poisoned five hundred square miles with plutonium. It's where they made the fuel for the atomic bomb back in 1945."

I sank into the empty chair beside Ty. "Good. Maybe you can explain all this to me."

David kept leafing through the stack. "You have a report on Idaho Falls? The reactor that had a complete meltdown? A few people even died. I thought this was all classified, hush-hush. And the incident aftermath report on Japan's Fukushima disaster—that was just released. Wow. Is this for a new job?" He rocked his chair. He loved getting involved with my work—took a proprietary interest in all my cases. "Cool. What's it about?"

"A new kind of nuclear plant in South Carolina has had a few accidents. Nothing serious—in fact, the government investigated and commended them on their handling of everything."

"So why do they need you?" Jeremy asked. "I thought you guys took on the big corporations, forced them to take responsibility when things go wrong. Sounds like these guys are already on top of things."

"They are." For the first time I felt good about working with Grandel. "At least according to the Nuclear Regulatory Commission and the Department of Energy. But people in the community aren't seeing it that way. They're protesting the plant going into full production, and any further delay could actually cost lives."

"Cost lives?" Ty looked up at that, his protective instincts on alert. Even off-duty, you could spot him as a lawman. The way his gaze never settled for long, the alert-yet-relaxed, ready for anything posture. I was never sure if he resembled Nikki in that or if she had learned it from him. Either way, they made for quite a team.

David, now devouring Grandel's promo brochure, answered, "Colleton Landing is going to take over production of medical isotopes for the US? So we won't have to get them all the way from Poland or Canada? That's great."

Gram Flora chimed in, "I read an article in the *New York Times* about people not able to get the care they need because there's an isotope shortage. Seems like doctors use them for everything from seeing if you had a heart attack to treating cancer."

We all stopped. Looked at Flora, then exchanged glances. One seventy-three-year-old blind woman and a nine-year-old kid, better informed than the rest of us adults.

"What?" Flora felt our scrutiny on her. "Just because I'm old doesn't mean I don't keep up."

"Glad you guys approve, because there's just one little hitch."

"You have to go to South Carolina," Ty guessed. Two steps ahead of everyone else, as usual. No wonder he and David got along so well.

"After my birthday," David said, banging the front wheels of his chair on the floor—his personal exclamation point.

"No. They need me there now. Today. But," I added when David opened his mouth to protest, "they promised to fly me back on Friday. So I'll be here for your birthday."

He and Flora assumed identical expressions of disapproval.

"I promise," I said. That relaxed David. He knew I didn't promise anything lightly and always came through.

Flora didn't look so certain. "Can't Elizabeth go? You could join her later."

I couldn't really tell her that Grandel was paying a boatload of money to have my boots on his ground solving his community relations problems. "Elizabeth isn't experienced in this kind of thing." Not like I was, either. Again that sinking feeling swamped me, like I was jumping in way over my head. "Are you guys okay helping out with David? Elizabeth is going to move into the summerhouse, but she'll need backup."

"Mom," he protested. "I don't need a babysitter."

"Don't even go there, David. It's not up to you."

His face twisted into a pout. "I can take care of myself. I don't want a girl moving in, treating me like a baby."

*Girl?* Elizabeth was three years older than me. But I could tell from the flush that turned his ears pink that he was actually most embarrassed about that "girl" being Elizabeth—he'd had a bit of a crush on her ever since they met.

"Elizabeth won't treat you like a baby. But it would make me feel better having someone here."

"Maybe I could come with you?" he asked. "Colleton Landing isn't far from the ocean. You've always said we'd get to the beach someday. For a real vacation." Other than a few day trips to the Maryland beaches, David had never visited the ocean. "Plus, it's near Savannah, it could be like, educational." How well he knew my weak spot—always a little embarrassed about my lack of formal education, I'd stop at nothing to make sure David had every opportunity. Including taking a bribe from Grandel in the form of a ten thousand dollar bonus.

"David, I'll be working all hours. And I have no idea what the living accommodations are like."

"So I'm stuck here because I'm a cripple."

I blew my breath out, trying to control my response. I'd raised David to not think of himself as handicapped and to never use it as an excuse. Not sure if it was the whole preadolescent hormonal thing or just because of all the changes he'd been through, but lately he'd been testing me, flinging his disability in my face when he didn't get what he wanted.

"You know that's not true. Let me check things out and if I need to go back after this week, we'll talk."

Perfectly reasonable logic. You'd think an almost ten-year-old genius would understand. He banged his chair against the table leg as he pushed back.

"Right. Then you'll find some other excuse to do what you want and leave me stuck here." He wheeled past me, out the screen door leading to the back porch, letting it bang shut. "Grownups." His final salvo was delivered in a tone of disgust—the effect slightly marred by his voice cracking.

I stood, poised to chase after him, but then stopped. I'd drawn the line and had to respect that—otherwise he never would.

"Boy's as stubborn as his mother," Flora said. "Best let him come to his senses on his own. That's what always worked with you."

I hated to admit it, but she was right. As usual.

# FIVE

Packing wasn't easy. For our last two cases, I didn't need to travel or worry about impressing anyone, so my usual outfit of boots, jeans, and T-shirt had been fine. After that, Elizabeth had insisted on replacing my heavy-metal and political T-shirts with polo tops that she'd had embroidered with the company logo. I didn't even know we had a logo.

Two days. Three Hardy & Palladino shirts (I tend to get things dirty) went into my scuffed Eagle Creek travel pack. Ditto with jeans, pairs of socks. I hesitated, then called Elizabeth.

"Think he's gonna trot me out for the cameras?" I asked, even though I already knew the answer.

"That's what he's paying for. I know you don't like it—"

"No." I opened my closet. "It's okay. I'm just trying to figure out what to pack."

It had been four years since I left the law firm—was fired, actually—after winning the case that made me famous. I'd kept some of my "power" suits but hadn't worn them since. Now I eyed them suspiciously. I'd lost weight—not intentionally. My diet had consisted of worry about David, no money, and waiting tables while juggling two other jobs.

I don't recommend it. Pulling one of the navy blue pantsuits from the closet, I held it up to the mirror in front of me. Made me look like a whole different person. A woman I no longer recognized. Did I want to go back to being her? I wasn't sure. Sighing, I folded it into the suitcase.

"It's the South." Elizabeth read my mind from three miles down the mountain and across the hollow. "They'll expect you to act like a lady."

"The things I do for a million bucks." I hung up and added the matching skirt and pumps to the case. I don't wear nylons for anyone, but that brought up the problem of underwear. I tossed my usual cotton panties and sports bras into the bag, then hesitated, scrounging into the far recesses of my underwear drawer. Found a pair of black silk panties and the matching underwire bra with lace inserts. I held the bra up. It had been four years since I'd worn it to court the day the judge ruled in favor of our case against Capitol Power. One of the best days of my life.

"Lucky man," Ty's voice interrupted my memory love-feast. "Do I know him?"

My face burned. I wadded the bra up and threw it into the case. "Know how to knock?"

"I did. You didn't hear me. Guess I know why." He nodded to the wad of lace and silk sitting on top of my jeans.

"Don't be ridiculous. How would I have time to meet a man, much less think about dating?"

He leaned against the door jamb and stared at me for a long hard moment, like I was being particularly ornery about something. Which I was. And it had nothing to do with my lack of a social life.

Ty didn't want me to leave David. I didn't either, but what choice did I have?

An entire debate ensued in the space of two blinks. Ty and I were like that, ever since we were kids. We knew each other well enough to see through to the end of an argument faster than we could get the words out.

Usually we didn't need words. But this time, for once, he didn't back down first. Instead, he took things to the next level, asking, "When did your priorities get so screwed up?"

That got my attention. "Who the hell gave you the right to have any say over my life?"

I stood up straight but still wasn't able to meet his gaze head on since I'm only five-five and Ty's at least six foot two. A very muscular and handsome six-two. Ty combines the best of all the races contributing to his heritage: Scots-Irish, Cherokee, and African American.

We've been best friends all our lives. Suddenly, I wasn't quite sure what we were. Which meant that right now he was one more complication in my life.

Lately I'd been fantasizing about him becoming more than a just a friend. Only late night, under the covers imaginings, because how could I ever ask anyone to put up with my crazy world of constant juggling and worry? Not to mention the fact that I need all the friends I can get and I wouldn't want to risk losing him.

But if there's one thing I can't bear, it's when people try to judge me and tell me how to live my life. Which was usually the last thing Ty would ever do.

He glowered at me, something else he usually never did. Shrugged one shoulder hard and sharp—I was surprised it didn't gouge the doorjamb—and spun on his foot.

Ty and I never fought. Debate or argue, sure. Even the occasional stewing in silence. But actual someone-could-get-hurt-here fight? Never. Just goes to show how much this case had already gotten under my skin.

Before he could leave, I took the two steps I needed to reach him and touched his arm. "Ty, I'm sorry. I'm nervous about this case and about leaving David."

He turned back to me. "Usually your gut instinct is right on target. I don't see why you should ignore it now. Maybe it's trying to tell you something. Maybe you shouldn't go."

I pulled away. "I have to. It's important."

"Just don't forget what you promised David."

That stung. As if I'd ever forget a promise I made to David.

Before I could snap back with some kind of clever rebuttal, he was gone.

I finished packing, threw my bag in the car and found David to say good-bye. He was in Flora's front room, furiously drawing in his sketch pad. He shut it and shoved it into his backpack before I could see what he was working on. I knew better than to ask.

"Here's how this is going to work," I told him, using my "don't try to find any loopholes" voice. "You're going to listen to Elizabeth and do what she asks you to do without talking back. You're going to shower every morning without her needing to remind you."

He squirmed at that. For some reason personal hygiene had become a sore topic lately—he'd go days without showering or changing his clothes. Then when I bought him deodorant—well, you would have thought I was asking him to commit social hari-kari! Flora says his behavior is normal for boys David's age. I'm not sure about that, but it's not normal for my David. Heck, he used to love showers so much I'd have to restrict him to only two a day, max.

"You *will* pick up your clothes and do your laundry and not wear the same thing every day," I continued, pushing my luck. An eye roll and shoulder shrug were his only answer. "And," I pulled him into a tight sideways hug-slash-headlock, "you will remember that

I love you very, very much and I'm coming home just as soon as I can. Okay?"

He squirmed free, but not before I landed a loud kiss onto his head.

"Whatever." His tone verged on adolescent ennui, but a smile creased his face and suddenly my baby boy was back. "Did you invite grandma and grandpa to my birthday? And Mr. Masterson?"

It wrenched my heart every time he called my folks "grandma" and "grandpa"—much less when he mentioned Cole's father with no term of endearment since they were still virtually strangers.

Masterson had met with David twice under my supervision at his mansion. I'd sat right outside the study door while they'd talked, trying hard not to flashback to the last time I'd stepped foot in Masterson's study—ten years ago when I'd told him I was pregnant. We'd argued, and on my way home a coal truck had run me off the road and into a retention pond. I'd almost died, David as well.

David and Masterson's talks felt more like job interviews— David dwarfed by the twelve-foot-high ceilings, his head barely reaching the top of Masterson's massive walnut desk that sat on an elevated dais so he could look down his nose at everyone.

At least that's how I saw it—I'm a bit prejudiced.

"You did remember to invite them, didn't you?" David repeated when I didn't answer.

Actually, I'd been hoping he'd forgotten about inviting them. I just knew that any event that combined my folks, Masterson, Flora, and me was certain to end in disaster.

"Mom . . . please, it's my birthday. I want them here."

"Okay. I'll ask them." I snuck in another kiss and quick hug before he could escape. "Bye. Love ya."

He waved absently as he wheeled himself back out into the sunshine, ready for his next adventure.

I sighed and headed in the opposite direction. It was going to be a long couple of days.

My folks live in a house that's almost a century old and filled with junk. Seriously. After my big brother, Randy, died, my mom's already obsessive tendencies turned to hoarding in a desperate effort to preserve Randy's memory.

From the outside it looks like a normal house. White siding, Cape Cod, two stories, gables, shutters hanging a little crooked, paint a bit faded.

Walk inside the front door and if the doors to the other rooms are closed—which they always are—everything still seems normal. Maybe even a bit Spartan with Randy's black-rimmed photo the only personal item in the foyer. My father makes sure the steps are kept clear. He also put in new doors to block the other rooms from view. Enabling Mom and drinking his way into denial are his two main passions in life.

Open one of those closed doors and you unleash an eruption of worthless junk. Comic books, soda bottles, sporting equipment, model airplanes, toys, clothing, ball caps—it's enough to fill five Dollar Generals five times over.

But never enough room for me. Or David.

I knocked and waited for Mom to answer. She's Old Man Masterson's bookkeeper and works from home, using my old room as an overstuffed office. Dad is a foreman at the mine, so he was at work. In the spring, after I accidentally entered my childhood home and discovered Mom's "little secret," they'd both made it clear that I was no longer welcome without an invitation.

Of course, I refuse to let David anywhere near the place until they clear out at least the first floor. Five months later and I don't think they've done anything except rearrange the piles of junk into new piles of different junk.

"Angela Joy," Mom said when she opened the door. "What

brings you here?" She glanced past me—probably to make sure I hadn't called Adult Protective Services. Not that I hadn't been tempted after she and Dad refused any help or counseling. But when I'd talked with a caseworker and Elizabeth researched it, we discovered that since there were working bathroom facilities and exit routes, my parents were in no imminent danger.

So said the law. I disagreed. But, as usual in my family, no one paid any attention to what I thought.

"I'm leaving for business. Going to be gone a few days, and David wanted me to remind you about his birthday party."

"A business trip?" she said in disapproval, leading me inside. She kept on walking up the steps, never looking back to see if I was following. "Do you think it's wise? A single mother leaving her son alone? In my day—"

"He won't be alone." What did she think I'd done the ten years I'd raised David on my own in D.C. as a single mom? Lock him in a closet while I was at work? I didn't ask—my folks never did get my sense of humor, and sarcasm was lost on them. "Elizabeth is going to stay at the summerhouse, and Jeremy and Flora will be watching him as well."

She made another noise, clicking her tongue against the roof of her mouth, but I ignored it. The second floor hallway was barely negotiable, a tight passage etched out between piles higher than my head, precariously stacked against both walls.

"Don't touch anything," she snapped. She hadn't forgiven me for stepping on a bobble-head toy and breaking it the last time I was here.

We entered her office, weaving our way past stacks of document boxes, paper files, and several cheap filing cabinets. She took the only chair at the TV tray that held her laptop. I stood, holding my arms tight to my sides and trying not to breathe too deeply for fear of coughing up dust and setting off an avalanche.

"Where are you going?"

"Colleton Landing, South Carolina. It's just north of Savannah."

"South Carolina?" she said in alarm, swiveling her chair to face me. "You can't go there. They've got alligators and sharks and swamps and isn't that hurricane still out in the Atlantic and—"

"Don't worry, this job is inside a plant, not out in the field." I didn't tell her it was a nuclear plant that produced radioactive medical isotopes. In addition to OCD, Mom also plays at being an amateur hypochondriac—she's always healthy but thinks up the worst possible diagnoses for anyone else who makes the mistake of revealing a symptom. "Most I'll be facing is mosquitoes as I walk from the parking lot."

Wrong thing to say. Her eyes grew even wider. "Mosquitoes? We're talking West Nile and Eastern Equine Encephalitis and maybe dengue fever. I'll have to look that up."

I blocked her path to the computer. "Mom. I'll be fine." Took a deep breath, bracing myself. Over the years not only had my mother's hoarding and hypochondria blossomed but she was pretty near agoraphobic—had only made it over to Flora's once in the five months we've been here.

"You and Dad are coming for David's birthday." She stared at me blankly. "Saturday. At Flora's."

Her gaze darted away from mine as if answers lay in the stacks of documents surrounding us.

"Mom. David's expecting you. It's important."

"Well . . ." Her voice trailed off as her gaze sharpened, snagged by some doo-dad out in the hallway. "We'll see. Your dad and I are so busy, you know."

Before I could say anything, she darted past me and began rummaging through a pile of boxes from Amazon and QVC, some opened, some still sealed, a few bent and smashed by the weight of junk covering them. A football rolled past her grasping hands, followed by a Game Boy and a lava lamp. Any of which her grand-son would most dearly appreciate. Instead, they were gathering lost memories of another boy, long since dead.

"I ordered this for your brother," she muttered as she dug deep, her head buried in the pile.

Randy had died fifteen years ago. His room was a shrine, frozen in the past. My old room was the present—her job with Masterson, no trace of her only living child.

And the rest of the house? As the pile of junk shifted and swirled beneath her movements, my mind flashed to a gruesome future—she and Dad buried alive.

"Mom—" I started, then bit back my words. I'd tried to get her into counseling, had tried cleaning things myself—both of which had been disasters. Dad had threatened to cut me and David out of their lives forever if I didn't stop "interfering." If it was only me, I would have walked away. But I couldn't deprive David of his only family, no matter how mixed up they were.

"Found it," she exclaimed in delight, emerging from the shuffle of junk, holding a slim box aloft. "I'm sure your brother won't mind if you borrow it. You might need it down there in South Carolina."

She thrust the box into my hand. It was a four-inch fixed stainless-steel SOG knife. Nice one with its own nylon sheath. I started to give it back but stopped. Ever since a killer had caught me empty-handed and defenseless, I'd been carrying the small folding Buck knife I'd had since I was a kid, but I could definitely see the potential intimidation factor in this one. It looked like something a Navy SEAL would carry. With that sheath it would fit perfectly in my boot.

"Manners, Angela Joy," Mom chided when I didn't say anything.

"Thank you," I mumbled. My head was splitting and Grandel was waiting. At least flying on a private plane I wouldn't have to worry about getting the knife through security. "I have to go now. But you'll be there Saturday, right?"

Too late. She was already on her knees scrabbling through the pile, searching for more buried treasure. She waggled her hand at me without looking and I left.

As I closed the door behind me, the house seemed to sigh. Whether happy or sad to see me go, leaving my mother trapped inside her memories, I wasn't sure.

## — SIX —

"You're late," Elizabeth said as I pulled into her driveway. She hopped into the passenger seat before I could turn the engine off.

"Had to deal with my mother." I resisted the urge to sigh. "What happened to Grandel?"

"I sent him on ahead in his hired car. Figured this would give us a chance to talk."

"Sneaking around behind the client's back. Wow. This case is off to a great start."

My sarcasm wasn't lost on Elizabeth. "Welcome to the real world. Look, I know this case isn't our usual area of expertise, so I called a friend."

"A friend?"

"Well, a guy I kinda dated once or twice. He's a radiation oncologist at Penn. Super-scary-smart."

"So why'd you stop dating him?"

"It was a blind date, right after Hunter and I divorced. Larry's a great guy but he's pretty intense. OCD, you know what I mean?"

"Oh yeah, I know about OCD." Now I did sigh, thinking of Mom. "So Larry knows about nuclear plants and all this stuff?"

"Some of it. Theoretical stuff, mostly. He gave me an earful about how important having a US source of isotopes is. Said they're used in PET scans and diagnosing heart attacks in addition to treating all sorts of cancer."

"Okay, I get it. Grandel's saving lives with his plant. Not sure how knowing that is going to help me make sense of what's going on down there."

"Hey, my specialty is family law, divorces and prenups, and custody—not like I have a bunch of nuclear physicists on my speed dial. Anyway, I e-mailed you Larry's contact info in case you need advice."

Finally I got it. Elizabeth wasn't buying Grandel's *GQ* act either. He wasn't in this to save lives; it was all about the bottom line. "Wait. You mean in case I don't like what Grandel is telling me, I can double-check with Larry, see if he's pulling a fast one?"

"Something like that."

"Distrusting our own client. Feels like I'm back in D.C."

"Hey, never forget the first rule of law."

"Trust nobody—"

"Assume nothing."

Elizabeth nodded. "I also did some research on Grandel's foreign venture capital partners that he's worried about. Turns out they're from Japan."

"Japan? After what happened with the earthquake and tsunami and those plants going into meltdown, I'd think they'd be the last country to want a new nuclear plant."

"The plants damaged by the tsunami were forty years old. And given the amount of rebuilding they need to do, they need energy, fast, and can't import enough oil without crippling their economy. Apparently almost a third of their energy supply came from nuclear power before the accident and the government still thinks investing in new, safer nuclear technology is its best option."

"But after the accident, the Japanese public—"

"Is not too thrilled with the idea of new nuclear plants. So of course Grandel's potential investors are seeking a fool-proof, weather-proof, god-proof technology. They're apprehensive about public opposition and hypersensitive to any hint of scandal or cover-up. They're coming to tour the plant next week to make their decision."

"Hence the worry and the tight deadline."

"Exactly."

"So I'm supposed to educate the population about a new kind of nuclear reactor, calm their fears, get them to actually support the plant, and stop their opposition—all in a week? Elizabeth—"

"I know, I know." She smiled—her best "it'll be okay although I have no idea how" smile. "But if anyone can do it, you can."

◆

We pulled into the parking lot of the general aviation airfield outside Smithfield, the county seat, about half an hour over the mountain from Scotia. It wasn't a "real" airport—no terminal, just a few fiberglass hangers and a dozen small planes lined up in a field. On the tarmac waited a sleek, small jet.

Elizabeth helped me with my bags—the travel pack and a messenger bag that held my laptop.

We approached the jet. Another plane, a small single prop, revved its engines, preparing for takeoff.

"I forgot to call Masterson." I stopped and grabbed my cell phone.

"Why do you want to talk to him?" Elizabeth shouted over the noise.

"Promised David I'd invite him to his birthday party on Saturday." I dialed. I didn't bother about the noise—it would give me an excuse to cut the conversation short. "Mr. Masterson, please. AJ Palladino." His secretary put me on hold. A minute later Old Man Masterson was on the phone.

"AJ, what do you want?" Typical, curt and to the point. Masterson blamed me for his son's death, so our conversations tended to be undercut by anger.

Not too hard to understand, since I still blamed myself for Cole's death as well. Intellectually, I knew it wasn't my fault—but emotionally, well, that was going to take some time.

"David asked me to invite you to his birthday party on Saturday at Flora's."

"Boy sent me a written invitation. I have it on my schedule." His tone softened when he spoke of David.

Even I couldn't ignore the fact that Masterson was smitten with his grandson—proud of his accomplishments, determined that David would be his legacy. He wanted David to take his father's name, carry the Masterson surname. I told him it would be up to David, not me, once he was old enough to decide.

Unfortunately, you give a man like Masterson an inch and suddenly he's camped out in your living room, proclaiming squatter's rights. His response had been to bring suit, requesting permanent visitation rights whenever he wanted.

Elizabeth was doing everything she could to stall the proceedings. I hadn't told anyone else about it yet, hoping it would all magically go away, but sooner or later I'd probably have to face Masterson in court—with my son the prize.

"What's all that noise?" he asked before I could hang up.

"Airplane. I'm leaving for business."

"How long will you be gone? Maybe the boy should stay with me—after all, I am family."

I choked back my response, forced myself to remain civil. "No thanks, I've got everything worked out. Gotta go."

I hung up before he could pry into David's living arrangements further. I hated the way Masterson was always trying to insinuate his way into David's life—but I couldn't keep David from his grandfather. He was part of David's family. For better or for worse.

"Hey, relax," Elizabeth said, prying the phone from my clenched fist before I could smash the wretched thing. "I'll keep an eye on David."

"Thanks."

She surprised me with a quick hug. Grandel appeared at the jet's hatch and waved me on board. I grabbed my bags and jogged over, turning back at the top of the steps to wave good-bye to Elizabeth. The mountains behind her were arrayed with a golden halo shining down between a cluster of gray-blue-white clouds.

Grandel closed the hatch behind me and I felt homesick already.

◆

*Swish, swoosh.* The skip of his fly dancing on top of the water was the only foreign sound on this part of the river. Bob Hutton kept casting, maintaining a steady, even rhythm with his G. Loomis 8-weight, enjoying the way his mind emptied of everything except the gentle gurgle of the river.

For a man in Hutton's business, it wasn't often that you could let your guard down and totally relax, so every minute spent on the river communing with the gods of fishing was a minute spent in heaven.

Until his phone buzzed and the hell that was the world outside exploded his calm oasis. He jerked his rod, debated for a split second to ignore the mechanical summons, but decided against temptation. He knew who was on the other end of the line, and it would be dangerous to provoke one of his oldest clients. Dropping his rod into the boat, he picked up his phone.

"Hutton here." It was a point of pride that he didn't fear using his real name on an open line. In fact, that was the only time he used his name—any other time, any place in the world and people would know him by another, disposable name. But Hutton understood the marketing advantages of branding himself, so he used his name, cemented it in the minds of his clients—along with his accomplishments and what he would do to them if they ever betrayed that name.

Branding, it was all branding. Just like Coca-Cola or Campbell's soup.

The man on the other end of the line didn't appreciate such subtleties—although he did appreciate Hutton's unique talents.

"It's time," he said. "When can you get here?"

"Good afternoon, Kyle," Hutton replied, hoping his use of Masterson's first name would agitate him as much as having a peaceful afternoon of fishing interrupted.

Usually Hutton picked the time and place for his jobs, but this one was different. More of a long-term contingency planning type of thing. Didn't matter; he knew the subject and was good to go. "So we're finally moving forward?"

"Things have changed. I need to get my grandson out of that environment before it's too late."

Masterson was always yammering on about his precious grandson and what a terrible mother the kid had. "You want me to move on the mom, then?"

"No. I'll tell you what I need when you get here."

"You know that's not how I work." Hutton leaned back against the gunwale, tracing the progress of a hawk circling overhead with his finger, taking imaginary aim.

"It is when you work for me."

Hutton bristled at Masterson's imperative tone but held his silence. Far better to let men like Masterson think they were in charge. Didn't matter. Hutton knew who really held the power in this relationship.

"I'll be there in a few hours."

"Come prepared to travel."

Great, he'd have to burn a vehicle—just like with phones and aliases, he never used a vehicle more than once. "Travel costs extra—more risks."

"Like I give a good goddamn. Haul your ass up here, time is short." Masterson hung up, obviously assuming that Hutton wouldn't hesitate to obey his orders.

Hutton packed his gear and headed back to his small cottage. He hated leaving the river with its peace and quiet behind, but even when working with a client as odious and lacking in finesse as Kyle Masterson, he had to admit, he loved his job.

Already adrenalin hummed through his veins at the thought of how he would once again outwit, outsmart, and outmaneuver any-one who stood in his way.

Not that there would be much competition, not in a tiny back-water mountain town like Scotia, West Virginia. It'd been a long time since he'd been there—and, if he did his job right, no one except Masterson would ever know he'd been back.

Hutton was a ghost—and he liked it that way.

# SEVEN

The inside of the jet was smaller than I'd expected—of course, what did I know about private jets? It was also noisier. There was a table with seats facing it on both sides. No flight attendant. But the flight was short, Grandel reassured me, as he ushered me into a window seat on one side of the table and took the seat beside me.

Once we took off, he spread out the plans of the plant on the table and I studied them. "Show me where each of the incidents took place."

He pointed out the leaky drain pipe, the area where the contaminated tool had been used, and the stuck valve.

"Nothing in common," he finished. "I know what you're thinking—sabotage. But the government eliminated that idea."

"How?"

"For one thing, the only people with access to all three areas are myself and Morris."

"Morris?"

"My older brother. He's my plant manager." He waved a hand in dismissal. "Plus, the company who made those pipe seals has had problems in the past—out of several thousand seals used in a project this size, having one leak isn't unheard of. And the worker admitted that he laid the tool down while unpacking a crate—it simply got mixed in with the packing materials he was disposing of."

"And the stuck valve?"

He shrugged. "Wrong place, wrong time. Just about any other location and we would have had an alert sounded before any damage was done. Of course, now we've gone back and added additional sensors even to noncritical areas. Despite the fact that the DOE and NRC don't require them. Make sure you tell folks about that."

"What other safety measures have you installed?"

He jabbed his finger at the plans. "Two levels of outer perimeter security, both secured by armed guards, as well as large volume sodium iodine detectors—state of the art. If anything, they're a little too sensitive. Once inside the plant we have two more layers of security plus portal detectors for anyone entering or leaving the operational area. We go above and beyond all regulations," he finished with pride. "Colleton Landing is my life's work. I'm not going to let anything tarnish the reputation of my plant. Especially not a few badly timed minor mishaps."

He turned to me, staring into my face as if judging me. "Besides, those aren't the real problem. It's these damn protestors and bloggers and everyone in the community trying to destroy us. They need to understand that if I go under, the entire town will as well."

Gee, paranoia and narcissism combined. Grandel's grandiose beliefs explained why he'd waited so long to reach out for help— probably thought it would all go away if he just wished hard enough.

The pilot announced our descent into Savannah. After stowing the plans and buckling his seatbelt, Grandel pointed out the window where the blue band that was the Atlantic could be seen past yellow and green marshland. "I thought you might want to stay at our executive suite on Hilton Head Island. I'll have a driver pick you up in the morning."

"How far is it from the plant?"

"Forty minutes."

"I'd rather be near to the plant. And have a car. Surely there are accommodations closer? I don't need much. I won't be spending a lot of time in my room."

He frowned. Elizabeth would have been proud—I almost reminded him that I wasn't here as his paid spokesperson to trot out whenever it suited, but I held my tongue.

"I suppose we can arrange something," he muttered.

Grandel's driver met us in a black Yukon and hauled our bags into the back while Grandel waited inside the air conditioning and I stood outside on the tarmac, trying to readjust my eyes to the bright sunshine, unfiltered by trees or the shadows of mountains. Of course, I'd forgotten my sunglasses.

Flat, it was so flat. My gaze kept roaming farther and farther, nothing to stop it except for the Gulfstream building beside us and the Savannah Airport terminal at the other end of the runway. A commuter jet rumbled past as it landed and taxied to the terminal.

It was hotter here than back home, muggy with no breeze, although beneath the smell of aviation fuel I thought I detected a whiff of ocean. Maybe that was wishful thinking since the only trees I could see were palm trees and a few seagulls circled overhead.

I joined Grandel inside the Yukon. He was on his cell making arrangements for a car for me and a room close to the plant.

"You're going to wish you'd listened to me and stayed in Hilton Head," he said once he hung up. "Our place there is second row, has an ocean view, only a few feet from the beach."

"Thanks, but I'm here to work." Although I had a feeling he was right. A fleeting image of me walking on the beach, blissfully alone, dolphins frolicking in the surf, warm sand between my toes, sped through my brain. I've never taken a vacation—not a real one. The only times since David was born that I'd been without work weren't exactly voluntary.

He shrugged. "Okay. I had to put you up in the Landing. It's a motel, caters to families of Marines at Parris Island who can't afford to stay in Beaufort. Some of our people stay there as well. Pretty much a dive, but it's the closest to the plant."

"I've stayed in worse."

"Suit yourself. The car will be dropped off later."

"Can we see the plant now?"

He looked irritated. Clearly a man who liked to set his own pace and call the shots. "Of course," he said, but his voice didn't hold the cordiality it had earlier when he was busy trying to charm Elizabeth. "Whatever you want."

I had the feeling what he really wanted to say was: We'll do whatever *I* want.

Almost wished Elizabeth was here so I could tell her "I told you so."

◆

Elizabeth drove AJ's SUV back home and began packing. She sighed, carefully selecting and folding her planned wardrobe for the rest of the week into her suitcase.

She'd never lived alone until she left Hunter, but since then she'd surprised herself by how much she enjoyed it. The peace and quiet. No one moving her things around. Everything in its place, where it should be.

She liked that stability—maybe security was a better word? Whatever it was, it felt comfortable. She didn't need to worry about what anyone else thought or wanted or was doing. It was her space to do with as she pleased.

Now that she had her father's house all to herself, that feeling had intensified to the point where she was actually dreading giving up her freedom to spend a few days with David.

And she liked David. As kids went, he was by far the easiest she'd ever encountered. Old enough to take care of himself and carry on an intelligent conversation, young enough to listen to her and do what she asked him to do.

She stopped at her bureau, comb and hairbrush in hand, eyes caught by a photo of herself and her parents when she was about David's age. In the photo, there was a definite physical divide between her and her parents—as well as between themselves. If they hadn't all been captured in the same frame, you would have never assumed that the three were family. The photo was taken just a few months before her parents divorced, so that made sense. Except the distance between parents and child had never improved.

Good thing she and Hunter never had kids, that was for sure.

She added the comb and brush to her toiletry bag. The doorbell rang. She dropped the bag into her suitcase and dashed down the steps to answer it. It rang a second time before she could get to it.

Nobody local, then. They'd all wait before leaning on the bell again so soon.

She opened the door. A man stood on her porch, half turned away, poised to leave, as if the eight seconds it'd taken her to reach the door was too long to wait. He was tall, six-three, with sleek dark hair, wearing an expensive tailored suit just a shade lighter than his hair. He held a black leather attaché case in one hand.

As he turned to her, his features chiseled out a smile that revealed perfectly straight, perfectly white teeth in a perfectly formed face.

"Hello, Elizabeth," he said in a friendly drawl that made her skin cringe.

"Hunter." She resisted the urge to slam the door in his face. "What the hell are you doing here?"

# EIGHT

We drove up I-95 for a short while, then turned onto a four-lane highway that seemed almost as crowded as the interstate. Tourists going to Hilton Head, Grandel told me. But they kept going straight while we turned onto a secondary road that was marked Parris Island/Beaufort.

It was a pretty drive from there. Out my window we passed a few farms surrounded by white picket fences, horses grazing in the fields. There were also gnarled, sprawling trees dripping Spanish moss, palm trees, tarpaper shacks leaning away from the wind coming off the sound, rusted cars parked in front lawns, and people rocking on porches, their bodies the nearest thing to a straight vertical line to be seen.

My eyes were still trying to adjust to the lack of a horizontal horizon. There were plenty of curves—graceful, genteel undulations, not the hairpin mountain switchbacks I was used to—but no hills. Occasionally we'd get to an especially flat area where water, gleaming blue and gold as it reflected the afternoon sky and yellow marsh grass, crept right up to the edge of the road. Once, I saw an alligator in the mud between the road and the water, shaded by one of the thick-trunked trees that Grandel told me were called live oaks.

I didn't like the look of the alligator. Even though his posture was relaxed, his attitude seemed superior, arrogant, as if he knew I was just a visitor and a potentially tasty one at that. I decided I wouldn't be doing much walking while down here.

We crossed a small bridge over an inlet of shimmering bright blue water, passed a Quonset hut labeled "Marina" surrounded by pickup trucks and a few empty, sagging docks, and then turned onto a two-lane road before reaching a paved lane that seemed barely wide enough for one-way traffic. The trucks and cars parked along the shoulder didn't help any.

"They're at it again," the driver muttered, the first words I'd heard him say.

"Idiots," Grandel replied.

We rounded a curve and I saw that the lane was choked with protesters. A few in tie-dye shirts carrying "NO NUKES!" signs, others more conservatively dressed as if for church, reading from Bibles. Still more in work clothes, looking worried, including several women carrying babies and trailing toddlers tugging at balloons reading "Children First, Safety First, Profits Last." Others carried crosses and shouted "Repent!" A strangely mixed bunch.

And my problem to solve. Along with the media—although thankfully there didn't seem to be any reporters here today. Maybe they'd lost interest. That would make my job easier.

Grandel's phone rang. "Yes." His face grew even more livid. "I don't know how the hell they knew. No, that's not the answer. Tell the board to calm down. We'll smooth things over before the Japanese get here."

He hung up, sputtering in fury. "Someone leaked it that I'd gone to hire a PR firm to solve our problems instead of staying here to fix them." He slammed his fist against the dash. "Now the board wants my head. Why can't they understand that there are no real problems at the plant? Our only problems are these crackpots who are too ignorant to see the good of what we're doing."

I hoped none of the "crackpots" could hear him through the car doors. The driver said nothing, simply edged us past them carefully. Grandel calmed down to merely fuming and I hazarded a question. "What do they want?"

"What do you mean?"

"I mean, what do they want? I saw at least three different factions out there. Some anti-nuclear—they won't be happy until the plant is closed, no matter how safe it is. And nothing I find or say will help that. Others seemed religious—"

"Goddamn holy rollers. They think the plant means the end of the world is coming. Their leader, Richard Vincent, runs a nightly revival and revs them all up, sending them to convert us 'damned heathens' before the rapture or some such malarkey. The man's a charlatan but his followers don't care."

"Okay. Probably not going to sway them. Plus, it sounds like their leader is using you as an easy target, so he probably doesn't want the plant to close—but he'll also enjoy the additional sense of fear that any mishap at the plant, no matter how minor, contributes to his message."

He slit his eyes at me. "You don't know the half of it. Vincent is a greedy sonofabitch, that's for sure. Go on."

"Seems to me, your biggest problem is the last group. Those moms and the other locals who truly believe their homes and families are at risk. They're the ones we need to convince."

"And how do we do that?"

"Like I said when we began. Give me access to everything and let me verify the safety record and safeguards, then we'll talk with them."

"You mean like invite them to coffee? I don't think so."

"When you approached the government for funding, how did you do it?"

"I went to D.C., scheduled some meetings, then followed up with a few dinners and—"

"Exactly. You treated them with respect because they had something you needed. Now we do the same with the community."

"So what? You want me to go door to door, kissing babies?"

"How about if you start with appreciating the fact that these are the hard-working people who keep your plant going? And stop with the wisecracks—they aren't nuts or crackpots or idiots. They're moms and dads concerned about their livelihoods and their families' safety."

He made a little noise as he sank back into the leather seat, one hand twisting the platinum ring he wore on his pinky. "So, just talking? Simple as that?"

"A little respect goes a long way, in my experience."

He said nothing, but nodded as if he was already convinced. I knew it couldn't be that easy. Plus, I first had to prove that the plant was safe—and everyone knows it's impossible to prove a negative.

◆

Hunter didn't answer Elizabeth. Rather he simply stood there, looking. She had to fight an all-too-familiar urge to squirm and glance down, break eye contact. It didn't help that he was so much taller than her. Or that he wore Saville Row while she'd changed into khakis and a sleeveless cotton blouse since she was on her way to David's.

But somehow she found the strength to meet his superior, smug, smarmy smirk. As he raised an eyebrow, taking in her attire and surroundings, she remembered why she'd left him. Funny how much harder it was to remember why she'd ever loved him.

"So. This is the bustling practice that seduced you away from Philadelphia. Charming."

"What do you want, Hunter?"

"Thought I'd serve this in person." He handed her a sheaf of legal papers. "Notice of appearance."

She skimmed them as he sauntered to the porch swing and took a seat, making himself at home.

"Masterson hired you? But why?"

"Maybe he was impatient about how slowly things were moving with his hometown team." He shrugged, the fabric of his jacket falling flawlessly back into place, and stretched his legs out. "Or maybe he cares enough about his grandson to hire the very best, no matter the cost."

"The whole case is ridiculous and you know it. Look at the precedents on grandparents seeking visitation. *Troxel v. Granville*, for starters."

"There's no West Virginia precedent. And won't it be fun setting one?" He slipped his Gucci sunglasses on and stood in one fluid motion. "Just like old times, right, Elizabeth?"

She stared at him, her stomach churning in a familiar rumba of anxiety. It took everything she had not to flinch when he bent down and kissed her on the cheek.

"See you in court. Judge Mabry wants us there ten o'clock tomorrow."

He sauntered to his Mercedes and was gone. Still she stared after him, speechless—without any idea of how the hell she was going to defeat him in court. Because the only time Hunter Holcombe had ever lost a fight was when she'd walked out on him.

And she knew damn well that he wasn't going to let that go unpunished.

# NINE

Once past the protestors we stopped at a security checkpoint. Beyond it was a parking lot surrounded by a twelve-foot-high fence topped with razor wire. We were waved through and continued to follow the road as it wound around the outside of the parking lot and continued to follow the river, only now the view to the water was a bit obscured by the security fencing.

The zigzagging road itself was also a security measure, artfully disguised. Much nicer than a gamut of concrete barriers.

I spotted another alligator lounging in the mud against the other side of the fence, as well as several beautifully graceful birds. Herons, cranes, egrets—I wasn't sure. They all had long legs, slim necks, and carried themselves like ballet dancers, seemingly unafraid of the gators as they waltzed through the water. We passed beneath some trees, rounded a curve, and stopped at the second security post at the inner perimeter fence, where I caught my first glimpse of the plant.

It wasn't anything like I'd imagined, not even after looking at the schematics Grandel had shown me. Instead of the concrete bunker I'd expected, it was all chrome and glass, laid out hugging the contours of the land as the river curved behind it. The rooflines were also curved, but in an old-fashioned way like a conservatory, not jarring like Disney's Epcot Center. There was a large central dome with branches coming off either side—one side for the turbines, I remembered from the plans, the other for the reactor coolant pumps.

The lawn surrounding it on three sides was filled with plants. A field of lavender mingled with yellow wildflowers lay to the side of the walkway leading from the parking lot, roses clustered closer to the front entrance—almost hiding the third security checkpoint—and flowering trees with bright purple, pink, and white flowers were scattered throughout.

"Welcome to Colleton Landing," Grandel said, the pride returning to his voice. "With each fence there are radiation detectors," he continued. "Three perimeters in total—the last at the entrance to the facility."

I nodded appreciatively. It wasn't often you saw security and beauty so nicely interwoven.

"Beyond the glass, the containment area is built to withstand a major earthquake, a direct hit by a jet, or even an F-5 tornado." The driver parked the car and opened the back door for us.

"What about hurricanes?" I asked, remembering something on the news that morning about a storm meandering across the Atlantic, defying all efforts by the meteorologists to predict its course or landfall. They'd made a joke about the fallibility of weather forecasting even in this day and age of computer models, but now that I was here near the coast, it didn't seem quite so funny anymore.

"If it wasn't for security issues, we'd be designated a storm shelter," Grandel said. "Safest place to be would be here."

If I lived here and a storm hit, I think my first instinct would be to run away from the four nuclear reactors in my backyard, not toward them. Which gave me some insight into how to approach the community. "Have you told people about that? Is there a way to give them a tour of the safety features?"

"Not without compromising security."

"Maybe just a few select community leaders who could help spread the word?"

He frowned. "Maybe. It would take some arranging, clearances and extra security."

I understood that security was a hot topic these days, but he couldn't expect public support without giving them some glimpse behind the scenes. "Think about it."

We turned toward the entrance when a man came running through the doors. He was gaunt, as if he regularly forgot to eat, with the same chiseled features Grandel had except accompanied by an unruly shock of dusty brown hair and a tan that appeared genuine. He wore rumpled khaki pants and a white dress shirt with the sleeves rolled up, and he clutched a leather messenger bag slung across his chest.

"Is this her? Is this her?" he asked, beaming first at Grandel, then at the driver and security guard, and finally at me.

"Yes, Morris. This is her." Grandel managed to sigh twice in as many sentences.

"AJ Palladino." Morris pumped my right hand in both of his. "I am most pleased to meet you." His voice was tinged with a definite southern accent, unlike his brother's. "Welcome to Colleton Landing."

"Thank you." I rescued my hand before he could mangle it. Gaunt but strong.

"I can't wait to show you everything." His face clouded as excitement and confusion warred. "What first? The control room or isotope retrieval or maybe the turbines, everyone always loves seeing the turbines—"

"Morris, calm down. AJ isn't interested in the technical aspects of the plant. She just needs—"

"Oh, but I am interested," I said—mainly to contradict Grandel. I didn't like how he treated his brother, and Morris's enthusiasm was definitely catching. "I'd like to see it all."

The driver hustled around the car, holding a radio to his ear. "There's a disturbance at the front gate," he reported to Grandel. "A woman's down."

We piled back into the SUV—Morris as well. The driver didn't take us back along the road, though; instead the guard raised a barrier blocking the path that came directly from the parking lot, without curving around beside the river. I spotted a small jitney tram sitting behind the guard shack and realized that employees must be shuttled from their cars along this path. It was as wide as a single lane of road, but not meant to be driven at the speeds our driver was using.

We bumped past the middle gate and into the parking area, then out to the first gate. The crowd of protestors had contracted into one writhing mass of humanity, their signs forgotten on the ground, an occasional head or hand raised high as they bent over someone on the ground, hidden from sight by their bodies.

The driver honked his horn, trying to scatter the crowd. I didn't wait but hopped out of the car and began to push my way through. The heat hit me again. For a moment it felt hard to breathe, as if the air was too hot and heavy to drag into my lungs, but I ignored the sensation.

"Make a path, give her some room," I shouted as I kicked and shoved my way past people standing around doing nothing except making things worse. To my surprise, Morris was on my heels, following me, while Grandel and the driver and security guards worked to move people back.

I made my way to the fallen woman. She wore a tight-fitting ankle-length black dress with long sleeves and a high neck buttoned up to the top. She was pale, sweaty, not moving except for one hand grasping at her throat. As I knelt beside her someone jostled me, kicking me so hard that I almost fell on top of her.

"Back off," I snarled over my shoulder.

Gradually, the crowd receded, except for a few others dressed conservatively like the woman—they'd been the ones carrying the end of the world signs earlier. Reverend Vincent's people, I guessed.

The woman's pulse was fast, skipping along under my fingertips. Her skin was hot—too hot. Because of David, I knew a little more first aid than most people. This looked like the kind of heat exhaustion he used to get when he was younger. With that black dress fastened up so tight, this woman—I looked again and realized she was younger than me, this girl—might as well have been buttoned into an oven.

"Anyone have some water?" I asked as I began to undo her collar buttons.

"Stop! Don't touch her with your filthy hands!" One of the men with her grabbed my arm, but Grandel's security guy hauled him off me.

Morris crouched opposite me and handed me a bottle of water from his bag. "It's not very cold, I'm afraid. I prefer my water at twenty-one degrees Celsius."

"That's fine, don't worry." I poured some water over her hair and clothing.

She was awake, watching me, although she still remained silent, but she nodded her head in thanks as I raised her head up with one hand and held the bottle to her lips with the other.

"You fainted," I told her. "Probably the heat. Have you been drinking fluids? How long have you been out here?"

She swallowed hard but pushed my hand away when I tried to unbutton another button on her collar.

"I'm fine. Thank you." Her voice was a soft murmur, but the man who'd yelled at me before heard her.

"Don't you talk to my sister! Get your hands off her, you heathen whore!"

The woman broke eye contact, her cheeks flushing.

I bent close, pretending to steady her as she sat up, and whispered, "Don't worry, I've been called worse."

"The ambulance is coming," Grandel said. "How is she?"

"I think she'll be fine once she gets some fluids in her." I looked around. The heat shimmered off the blacktop and stuck my jeans to my skin. I'd only been out here a few minutes—what must it be like to be out here all day? I turned to Grandel. "You need to have your people bring water out here for everyone. And a canopy to shelter them from the sun—"

To my surprise, Morris chimed in, "How about an evaporative cooler? I can easily rig one—"

"Morris, shut up." Grandel jerked his head to the side, summoning me.

I didn't like his imperative manner, but the woman was fine, so I waited a moment—just to piss him off—before joining him on the side of the road. We were on the side near the river, standing beneath a branch draped in more Spanish moss than a Christmas tree had icicles.

"What are you thinking?" Grandel's voice was controlled but angry. "We're not going to give these people water and air conditioning while they try to destroy my reputation."

"It's not your reputation, it's your plant's," I reminded him.

"My future depends on this plant running smoothly without any more mishaps. Which is what I hired you for." He didn't look too happy about that employment choice right now.

"My point is, that reputation depends not on how good you are, but on how good you are perceived to be." I tried to translate basic human nature into concepts he could understand—power, control, deception. "Treating these people with respect and common courtesy will go a long way to cementing a good impression of Colleton Landing."

His face twisted as he looked out across the mud and water. The tide must have been out because there were about ten yards of mud between us and the water. Something moved in the mud under the shadow of a tree close to ours. Another alligator.

My nerves skittered with primeval flight or fight, but I forced myself to stand still. The gator didn't care one way or the other. He merely oriented himself to keep us in sight, gave a shudder to splash more mud over his scales, and went back to his nap.

Grandel made up his mind, smiling and clapping me on the shoulder as if mugging for the cameras. "Okay, we'll do it your way. But in the future, you come to me first. Don't go shouting things out in public like that."

"Of course." All the better for him to grab the credit—but that's what he was paying me for, so I held my tongue.

◆

After dinner, alone in the summerhouse with Elizabeth—now David knew what a volcano felt like. Or the inside of a nuclear reactor like the kind his mom was getting to visit. So unfair.

His skin felt hot and stretched so tight he thought his feelings would burst right through it. His heart kept galloping away, and with it his ability to look at Elizabeth without his throat closing tight, threatening to choke him to death. He couldn't speak. Not without his voice emerging high-pitched like a little girl's and cracking.

It was torture sitting in his chair pretending to work on inking Captain Awesome's latest adventure—saving a nuclear plant from meltdown—while Elizabeth curled up on the couch, surrounded by legal documents, her teeth nibbling at her lower lip as she flicked her pen back and forth. God, she was so pretty. What could he say to make her notice him?

"Interesting case?" he finally asked. Idiot. How lame was that. Of course it was interesting if it had her so absorbed.

"Huh-huh," she made a noise without looking up at him.

"What's it about?" His mom shared all her cases with him.

She glanced up at that, her brown hair falling into her face at the sudden movement. He wished he were close enough to touch her hair, maybe tuck it behind her ears like the cool guys in the movies always did. They never had to say anything, the girls just knew, and next thing they'd be together, kissing and hugging.

Not that he wanted to kiss Elizabeth. Well, maybe. No, probably not—from the movies and TV it looked complicated, like it would be so easy to mess it up if you didn't know what you were doing.

"Sorry," she said, answering a question he couldn't remember asking. "Confidential."

His face lit on fire so fast he was astonished his eyebrows weren't singed off. "Oh. Of course. Sorry. I knew that."

Lame, lame, lame. He sounded like a stupid little kid. Elizabeth was so smart, so beautiful. Of course she'd never notice him.

Then came the *coup de grace*. She smiled at him—not the good, "I like you" smile that he wanted to see, but more the "that's okay, you're just a child" smile that his mother sometimes gave him and he despised.

She went back to her files and he melted into his chair, completely demolished.

All he wanted to do was talk with her—but how?

He couldn't ask Ty. He'd seen Ty around women and he wasn't exactly smooth. Especially not around David's mom. Ty would usually just stand there watching, waiting for a chance to take action. Besides, Ty might tell his mom.

Jeremy. Jeremy would know. Jeremy was one of those guys who could talk to anyone. Within five minutes you felt like you'd been best friends for life.

"I'm going up to the house, say goodnight to Gram Flora," he announced, cringing as his voice cracked.

Elizabeth didn't even look up. "That's nice. I'll be here, ready to tuck you in when you get back."

Tuck him in? She did think he was a baby. Not even his mom tucked him in anymore.

He needed help. Desperately. Jeremy was his only hope.

# TEN

By the time the ambulance arrived, the woman was fine and re-fused transport—or rather the men with her refused for her. I was about to intervene but she warned me off with a glance that said she'd end up in more trouble if I made a fuss, then she signed the papers the paramedics gave her.

The rest of the crowd had pretty much dispersed—some were enjoying cold refreshments under a bright blue awning that Grandel's security guys had conjured up while the rest had driven off. Grandel had dropped his suit coat, rolled up his sleeves, grabbed a lemonade, and began working the crowd with the charm and zeal of a politician running for office.

Morris ended up at my side, watching his brother from the shade of a live oak—on the other side of the road from the river and its alligators. "I'm sorry I wasn't able to show you around the plant today."

"That's okay." Grandel had the crowd laughing. Morris nodded his head, beaming like a proud parent. "Are you older or younger than he is?"

It was hard to tell Morris's age—his face was creaseless, his hair hung thick and full with the overdue for a haircut swing of a college student. And he seemed so much more relaxed than Owen.

"Older. By three years. But we watch out for each other."

I squinted in the bright sunshine slanted low through the trees as the sun began to set, reappraising Morris. "Your brother said you run the plant?"

"Yes ma'am. But without Owen everything around here would fall apart."

Owen certainly made it clear that he agreed with that sentiment. "Is that because Owen designed it?"

Morris looked down, shuffled his feet in the red clay dust. "Actually, I designed it. But Owen got it built. Without him, this place would just be some sketches on the back of napkins."

Now I really didn't like the way Owen treated his older brother—taking credit for his work, acting like Morris was some kind of charity case that he'd given a job to. It was clear that Morris was different—not Asperger's, not exactly, more like socially inept and uncomfortable. He kind of reminded me of me, in fact.

It was also clear he was absolutely devoted to his younger brother—something I was certain Owen manipulated as easily as he had manipulated me into taking this job.

"Morris, do you think I could get that tour tomorrow?"

He turned to me, startled, his face lighting up in a way that made me think of David. I had the sudden urge to call home and check on him, see what adventures the day had brought—if he was speaking to me again.

"I would love to give you a tour, AJ."

Morris headed back to work. A guard drove up with another dark SUV—this was my car to use for the duration, he explained as he had me sign forms in triplicate before giving me the keys. He'd also drawn a map to my accommodations and transferred my luggage to the rear of the SUV.

"Here are your security badges for re-entry. They will only get you to the front gate, then you'll be given an entrance pass. No cell phones, electronics, or recording devices of any kind are allowed past the entrance. Mr. Grandel is expecting you tomorrow morning at ten o'clock."

He was gone before I could thank him. Grandel was still entertaining the masses, embracing his new role as gracious host. I decided I'd get out of the heat and my sweaty clothes, clean up, wade through the reams of research Grandel had given me, and call it a day.

◆

David rolled into Flora's kitchen without knocking—they were family, and family didn't need to knock, she'd taught him. Which was kinda weird because he still knocked when he visited his grandfather, Mr. Masterson, and his mom always knocked at her folks' house and her mom or dad would come out on the porch to talk, never ask her inside. But when they went to visit Ty's mom, they'd walk right on in just like at Flora's.

As much as David had spent his whole life wishing for one, sometimes having a family was very confusing.

The kitchen was dark except for the red-tinged light from the setting sun streaking through the lace curtains over the sink. David turned on the light. Flora's kitchen was the heart of the house, taking up the entire back half of the first floor. There was a huge fireplace at one end, flanked by two comfortable overstuffed rocking chairs and tables. Most nights that's where Flora could be found, knitting and listening to an audio book, while Jeremy read nursing journals or worked on his laptop.

The room was empty. The dinner dishes sat in a sink filled with water—even though Jeremy had started them over an hour ago when he'd shooed Elizabeth and David away, saying he'd clean up.

A hollow echo began to drum through David. Jeremy was a total neat freak—a product of being a nurse and living with a blind woman—and he'd never leave the dishes half done.

"Hello?" David called. His voice bounced back from the walls without any answer.

He rolled forward. A gallon of milk had been left out on the kitchen counter alongside Flora's insulin bottles. The insulin belonged in the refrigerator—which stood ajar, cold air from it coaxing goose bumps from David's arms despite the hot night.

"Jeremy? Gram Flora?" He was yelling now, not caring who he disturbed.

The dining room was also empty. If David couldn't find them downstairs, he'd have to go get Elizabeth—the steps up to the second floor were too steep for him to try himself.

He wheeled through to the living room—the parlor, Flora called it. Jeremy lay half on the sofa, half off, one arm flung over his face as if hiding. He was snoring. An overturned bottle lay on the floor beside him, empty. David wrinkled his nose and spotted a puddle of vomit staining Flora's prized rag-rug below Jeremy.

"Jeremy, Jeremy, wake up!" David tugged at his arm; it flopped to Jeremy's side. He made a groaning noise, the kind David made when he wanted to sleep past the alarm before school. "Jeremy, where's Flora?"

No response except another snuffled snore. Jeremy stank of liquor—which was strange because David had never seen him take a drink, not even beer. Yet, here he was, passed out drunk.

But where was Flora?

# ELEVEN

David grabbed his cell phone from the knapsack that hung on the back of his chair. In case of emergencies, that was what the phone was for, times like this. He dialed the summerhouse.

"Good evening, Palladino residence," Elizabeth answered in a formal tone like she was their secretary or maid. Any other time and David would have laughed.

"I need help," he said, fighting to pause between words so they didn't crash headlong together. "Something's wrong with Jeremy. And I can't find Flora."

"I'm coming." She hung up.

He dared to leave Jeremy and crossed out of the room into the foyer. And found Flora crumpled at the bottom of the stairs. Was she breathing?

Using the banister to balance on, he left his chair and knelt beside her. She was breathing, but slowly. Her pulse was racing, hard to feel, impossible to count. She was clammy—from the heat or . . . he thought. Insulin. Flora had bad diabetes, "brittle," they called it.

The front door pushed open and Elizabeth rushed in, turning on the light.

"Oh my God," she gasped, freezing with her hands half up like she was getting ready to surrender, her gaze darting from Flora to Jeremy and back. She knelt down and looked like she was about to straighten Flora's body.

"No. Don't," David told her. "She could have hurt her neck."

Elizabeth snatched her hands back. "Of course. You're right." She got back up to her feet. "I'll call 911."

She started toward the kitchen where the phone was. David was going to hand her his cell but figured it was better to use the landline.

"Grab her blood sugar monitor," he called. "It should be in the drawer beside the fridge."

He heard Elizabeth talking to the emergency operator. Her voice sounded unnaturally loud, like she was the one in shock. Beneath his fingers, Flora made a moaning noise.

"It's okay," he whispered, one hand on her forehead to keep her still in case she was waking up. "We're here, everything's going to be okay."

Jeremy took that moment to roll off the couch, landing face-down in the puddle of vomit. Then he began puking some more.

"Elizabeth! Hurry!"

Elizabeth returned, carrying the phone receiver in one hand and Flora's machine in the other. "I don't know how to use it."

"I do. Help Jeremy before he chokes."

She did a double-take, made a gagging noise herself, and put the phone down before reaching to tug Jeremy's collar, trying to haul him up without touching the vile fluid running down his chin.

At least he was out of danger of choking. David focused on Flora, using the machine to test her blood sugar, just like Jeremy had shown him. He winced at the *clack* of the lancet snapping out to pierce her skin and then waited impatiently for the machine to give him a result.

*Danger. Low Blood Sugar.* The way the letters bounded off the screen, if the machine had a voice it would be shouting.

Elizabeth had her hands full with Jeremy, so David hauled himself back into the wheelchair and pushed through to the kitchen. What had Jeremy said? Low sugar, low sugar . . . icing. He had small tubes of icing that would bring it back up. David rummaged through the drawer that held all of Flora's medical supplies and found the pack of icing.

Wait? Was it safe to give her something by mouth when she was unconscious? There was something else, what was it, glucose—no, that wasn't it—glucagon.

David searched again and grabbed the bright red emergency kit. Inside was a bottle of powder, a syringe with liquid, and some alcohol swabs. He quickly plunged the needle into the bottle and injected the liquid to dissolve the powder.

He wheeled himself back to Flora, shaking the bottle as he went. It turned clear and he drew it back into the syringe. His hand shook so bad he could barely read the markings on the syringe. What if he was wrong? But he couldn't wait—Flora could go into seizures and die from low blood sugar. He leaned back and glanced into the living room, hoping Jeremy had miraculously recovered and could tell him what to do.

No such luck. Jeremy was now sitting on the couch, head dangling between his knees, holding it as if afraid it would fall off, and vomiting onto his shoes.

It was up to David. Hands shaking, he turned to Flora. Her color was worse, more faded than the thin cotton housedress she wore.

Now or never.

◆

The Landing Motel was just as much of a dump as Grandel had promised. A single-story strip of rooms marked by dingy white doors and faded gray siding, it boasted a small café-slash-souvenir shop whose claim to fame was homemade cherry cider and candied pecans. I hauled my luggage inside my room and turned the AC on high. While the window unit sputtered and spit out tepid air that felt about body temperature, I regretted not taking the beachfront accommodations Grandel had offered. But this wasn't a vacation.

I didn't bother to unpack more than the basics, hoping that I wouldn't be here long enough to get to the bottom of my bag. I plugged in my cell after noticing that there was barely one bar and reached for the landline to call home. I was already missing David and wishing I hadn't come—suddenly all the money in the world seemed meaningless compared to sitting at Flora's big table having dinner with my family.

David. This was all for him. So he could have a real future instead of fighting for mere existence like I had.

No answer at the summerhouse, even though it was after eight and getting close to David's nine o'clock bedtime—which I was certain he'd conned Elizabeth into postponing. I tried Flora's. Elizabeth answered.

"I'm glad you called," she said, her tone anxious. "Something terrible has happened."

# TWELVE

I stood up so fast the base of the phone flew off the nightstand and clanged to the floor.

"Elizabeth? Are you there? What happened?" My voice sounded very loud and shrill, but that was the least of my worries.

"Calm down. Everyone is all right."

Hard to calm down when the sound of an ambulance's siren broke through her words.

"David? Is he okay?"

"He's fine, he's fine. It's Flora. Her blood sugar went too low and we had to call an ambulance. But she's okay—they gave her a shot and some IV fluids and she was already awake and joking with the medics as they carried her out."

"If she's so fine, then why are they taking her to the hospital?"

"Precaution. Said she'd probably be there a night or two."

Her calm tone only riled me up. These kind of things weren't supposed to happen—not to my family. "Where was Jeremy during all this? Why didn't you call me sooner?"

"Flora made me promise not to call you," Elizabeth said.

"Like hell she did. I'm coming home."

"No. She's fine. Really. And so is David."

"How did this happen?"

"The paramedics said Jeremy must have mixed up her long-acting insulin with her short-acting—so when he gave her the shot that was supposed to last all night, it all went to work at once. If David hadn't found her—"

"David found her?" This couldn't be happening. Not after David watched Cole die. "You're sure he's okay?"

"Okay? AJ, he did great. Stayed calm, took control, knew exactly what to do. He reminded me of you."

"Where was Jeremy through all this?"

Long pause. "Passed out. Drunk. Couldn't remember anything."

No. That was wrong. Very wrong. "Elizabeth. Jeremy doesn't drink."

"That's what he told the cops, but they arrested him anyway."

"Why? On what charges?" No, this couldn't be happening. Could Jeremy have been lying? Had he fooled us all into believing he was someone he wasn't? It was like I was listening to a soap opera in another language, one that made no sense.

"AJ, if he was drunk and caused Flora's accident, then it's a criminal matter."

"No. You have to get him out. This is all wrong. Make them do a blood alcohol and a tox screen." I twisted the phone's cord around my thumb so tight it went white. Didn't feel any pain. "I'll talk to Grandel. I'm coming home."

"What good would that do?" Worst thing about having a lawyer as your friend—they'd argue the sky was fuchsia if you said it was blue, just for the hell of it. "All you'd do is get the cops mad and make things worse. I can take care of Jeremy. David's fine. Flora's fine. You have much more important things to do there."

More important than my family? Never.

But the work I was doing here would secure my family's future.

I paced until the cord stretched to its limit. The future has always been a murky, intimidating concept for me, uncertain, filled with spooky shadows and too many chances to get things wrong. I much prefer the clarity of the here and now.

Only right this instant, my here and now wasn't so very clear. I twisted in a circle, eyes darting from corner to corner, searching for an answer in the dingy motel room. I knew what I wanted to do—but I also knew what I needed to do if I wanted to protect my family.

Elizabeth broke the silence. "AJ. You know I'm right."

I blew my breath out, aiming away from the speaker so she wouldn't hear. There was nothing worse than being trapped here, so far away, helpless to do anything. Except for maybe being right *there*, back home, helpless to do anything.

"You're right. Did you call Ty?" Ty would straighten all this out. He was good at that, making sense of chaos—probably why we were such good friends; the chaos that was my constant companion didn't seem to faze him.

"He's headed into the station to check on Jeremy. Everything will be all right. I promise."

◆

"David," Elizabeth called out. "It's your mom. She wants to talk to you."

David wheeled himself in from the front porch, wishing he could be riding in the ambulance with Gram Flora—lights and sirens and getting all the cars out of the way.

One of the paramedics had given him a shiny plastic fake Junior Firefighter badge. Like David was some kind of kid standing around watching instead of the person who had just saved Flora's life. Not even Elizabeth had known what to do, but he had.

Not that anyone gave him any credit for acting like an adult.

He sighed as he took the phone from Elizabeth. No matter

what he did everyone still treated him like a little kid—and Mom was worst of all. "Yeah."

"Are you okay?" Her voice had that high-pitched sound it got when she was really upset and trying to hold it all together. Putting on a brave face, she called it, but she never looked very brave when she got like that. More like she was gonna cry.

"Mom. I'm fine. I wasn't the one who got sick."

"Right. Of course not." A pause as she took in a breath. "I heard you did good—Elizabeth said you knew just what to do."

"All I did was what Jeremy taught me. How come they arrested him?"

A longer pause and he knew she was deciding whether or not to lie to him. His mom almost never lied to him—or anyone, for that matter—it was one of the reasons he put up with her and her constant questions about what he thought and felt and was doing.

"They think he got Flora's medicine mixed up and that's what made her sick."

No duh. He wasn't six. "You mean the Lantus and the regular Humulin. But Jeremy wouldn't have done that—"

"He might have if he wasn't thinking straight."

"Mom. Stop treating me like a baby and start using your brain. Jeremy doesn't drink. And Elizabeth and I were here for dinner only around an hour before this happened—is it even possible to drink that much that fast? Plus, regular insulin starts acting around fifteen minutes after you take it, so that means Jeremy would have had to be drunk before he gave her the insulin—and Flora never noticed? Gram Flora notices *everything*. So, if he was drunk, why didn't she just come down to the summerhouse? It doesn't make any sense."

This time the silence went on so long that he wondered if she'd hung up and he'd missed the click. "Mom?"

"Have I ever told you how proud I am of you?"

What the heck did that have to do with anything? He rolled

his eyes, glad she wasn't there to see him. They needed to help Jeremy *now*.

She continued, "Did you tell anyone about all this?"

"I never had a chance. The police took Jeremy away and the ambulance guys were working on Flora and—"

"You need to tell Elizabeth. Everything. I'll call Ty and make sure he has someone watching the house."

"I don't want to stay here. I want to go to the hospital, keep an eye on Flora." He looked over his shoulder, thought he saw movement, but it was just the curtain waving in the breeze. "Mom, why would someone want to hurt Gram Flora?"

"It could be that they wanted to hurt Jeremy."

He liked that she didn't try to convince him that he was wrong. "Why? Because he's gay?"

"Some folks have a hard time with that. Did you see anyone around the house today?"

"No. But Jeremy did tell me a few guys tried to beat him up last week when he was over in Beckley."

"Really? Why didn't he tell me?"

"Because you'd try to do something about it and it would only get folks riled up and make things worse. Like the time those guys ran into his truck with their SUV when you were at the Tractor Supply in Smithfield. You almost got arrested; terrorist threats, remember?"

"They were the terrorists. Red-neck thugs—forget I said that," she added hastily. "Okay, you and Elizabeth go to the hospital and stay the night there—or at Elizabeth's house. I don't want you out of her sight, you understand?"

There she went, treating him like a baby. Again. "Mom—"

"Don't 'mom' me. Please. Don't make me come all the way home just to babysit you—"

"C'mon. You're not serious." Now he was getting angry. Again.

"David. You are a very smart and very capable boy. But you need to promise me that you'll let the grownups handle this, okay?"

No, it wasn't okay. What would it take to prove to them that he could take care of himself? But as always, he knew better than to argue.

"Okay. I'll tell Elizabeth."

"Thank you. Tell her to call me as soon as the doctors say anything."

"I will."

"I love you."

He hung up wanting to repeat it back to her, but he just couldn't. Saying stuff like that was for babies.

◆

I stared at the phone. David had hung up on me. The little brat. If I wasn't so worried that I'd shout at him or say the wrong thing, I'd have called him right back and taught him a lesson about manners. Especially after scaring me half to death. Of course, he was probably scared as well, even though he refused to show it.

Which didn't make me feel any better. Instead it made me feel worse, trapped here like a caged animal, sweltering in a box, unable to breathe or move or do anything to help my family.

Instead of hurling the phone out the window like I wanted, I forced myself to dial another number.

"AJ, give me a second," Ty's voice came along with the sound of a car's engine. Then the sound of four-way blinkers, and I knew he'd pulled off the road to talk to me. Ty liked to play by the rules—law and order and all that. "Everyone's okay."

I loved how his simple statement wove its way through the airwaves to engrave itself on my heart as the truth. Like I'd only half believed until I heard Ty—someone I could trust with everyone dear to me—say it.

Yet, I still questioned him. "Are you sure?"

I felt his shrug and eye roll. What can I say? I'm stubborn and skeptical and can't help but question everything. Which he knew and understood without arguing. Unlike my own son.

"I'm sure."

"Jeremy can't have done this."

He made a noncommittal grunt—one of his cop noises.

"What are the police doing to investigate?" I persisted, determined that they wouldn't make Jeremy into a scapegoat. If he was innocent, I couldn't help but add. I liked Jeremy, but how much did I actually know about him? Could I trust my gut instincts about him?

"The guys took a sample of his stomach contents and they're taking him to the hospital for lab work before they book him. But it will all take time before we know anything."

"He was set up."

"Any ideas who would want to hurt him?"

I told Ty about the encounter we'd had in Smithfield and what David had said about the men in Beckley.

"Why didn't you report it?"

"Jeremy wouldn't let me." I hesitated, then confessed, "He wanted to walk away and if we had, everything would have been fine. I'm the one who got pissed off and escalated things. There were witnesses. He was afraid I'd end up in trouble."

"Good to know one of you has some common sense."

"Are you going to check them out or not?"

"I am. But going from a parking lot brawl to framing Jeremy for hurting Flora, switching meds, knowing how to incapacitate him without raising an alarm that Elizabeth or David would have heard—that's pretty darn sophisticated."

He was right. "It doesn't make sense."

"Targeting Jeremy this way—it feels personal. Has he had any recent relationships that have ended badly?"

"There was one earlier this summer that had him upset. But I don't know any names. He's very discreet."

"This case you and Elizabeth are working on. Would she have left anything sensitive at Flora's or at the summerhouse? Maybe this was all a ruse to get her out of the way while she dealt with Flora and everything."

"No. Everything is public knowledge. Except the plans for Grandel's plant—but he's kept those with him at all times, would only let us look at them, not copy them."

"But they'd be worth stealing?"

I thought about it. Grandel had convinced the government that his—or rather Morris's—design was good enough that they'd invested millions of dollars in it, and now he had foreign partners ready to invest. "Yeah, they'd be worth a lot. Millions or more."

He made a small noise. His thinking noise. "It's a long shot, but I'll talk to Elizabeth about it. Any other cases you two are working that might have anything to do with this?"

"Nothing that Jeremy or Flora have anything to do with." Our only other case was Masterson's request for visitation rights. There's no way sending Jeremy to jail or making Flora sick could affect whether or not he saw David on weekends.

"Okay. I'll let you know if I learn anything."

"Ty—"

"As soon as my shift is over, I'll pick up David."

I loved how he didn't make me ask. Just talking to him made me feel calmer. "Do you think I should come home? You didn't think I should come down here in the first place."

"I think I can't tell you what to do. Other than to trust us to take care of things here. Including David."

"Did you hear what he did? How he saved Flora?"

"He's a pretty resourceful young man." The pride in his voice matched my own.

"He thinks I'm over protective and treat him like a baby."

No answer. Then, "Maybe he's right. Give him some space."

"Right now he's got about five hundred miles of it. And it's driving me crazy."

That made him chuckle. A warm noise, like the sound of a trout jumping in the river catching the sun as it leapt. "You'd be just as upset if you were here, only you'd be driving us crazy as well. Relax. We've got it covered."

"Call me—"

"I will." Another pause. This one felt awkward, like neither of us wanted to be the first to break the connection. The sound of the police radio crackled in the background. "I have to go. Bye."

He was gone. Suddenly five hundred miles felt like the other end of the universe. And I was all alone.

Hutton watched from the shadows on the porch. The kitchen windows were open, so it was easy to eavesdrop. The woman, the lawyer, she seemed more in control finally. But the boy—he was impressive. The way he'd handled the two downed victims, the way he pieced everything together so quickly.

Bright kid. No wonder Masterson wanted him under his control instead of ditzy AJ Palladino's.

Hutton remembered AJ from way back when. She'd been a wild child, hanging around with one of the Stillwater boys and Masterson's son—the son she'd gotten killed a few months ago when she returned to Scotia. He hadn't liked her then and he hadn't liked her when she was splashed all over the news as a champion of the people when she'd won that big case against Capitol Power.

There was a price to pay for being cocky. AJ had fallen hard. Come crawling back home.

The lawyer turned the kitchen light off, leaving Hutton in a deeper darkness.

For a hit man who specialized in making his jobs appear as accidents, it was all about the thrill of the hunt. No messy explosions, no collateral damage. Hutton prided himself in his precise surgical strikes—so precise that he'd never appeared as even a blip on any lawman's radar.

Some in his business would say he was wrong to target the old woman, that taking out the gay guy would have done the job. Masterson sure as hell would have preferred it that way—he hated the idea of his grandson having anything to do with a man like Jeremy Miller. But, the way Hutton figured, the old had already had their chance. Best to give the young a break. Which is why he'd left Jeremy alive.

Flora, he'd thought for sure she was a goner. But the kid had saved her.

That would teach Hutton not to be too cocky—something he tried always to guard against, but when you outsmarted everyone with every job you did, it was difficult to remain humble.

He listened as the kid and lawyer made their way out of the house and down to the cars. At first he hadn't been too interested in Masterson's assignment, but now, thanks to the kid, this job was getting interesting.

# THIRTEEN

My first instinct was to get in Grandel's SUV and hit the road, head on home. But that wouldn't solve anything.

I couldn't clear Jeremy's name; only Ty and Elizabeth could help him. I couldn't help Gram Flora; she was in good hands with the doctors. And David had made it clear that he didn't want me there to worry and fuss over him.

All I could do was stay here and finish the job I'd started. The job that meant my family's future.

The logic was simple. That didn't mean I had to like it. I couldn't bear the thought of sitting in solitary confinement, waiting to hear news that wouldn't come for hours, so I decided to take a walk.

As soon as I opened the door, the night unleashed a black-fisted punch of heat that almost forced me back inside. I realized I wouldn't be making it very far. Not that there was anywhere to go. The motel sat by itself—the only other building in sight on the lonely road was a gas station that had gone out of business, about a quarter mile away. I hadn't even heard a car drive past since I arrived.

The sun had set but somehow the temperature was still rising, so the night offered no sanctuary from the heat. Instead of heading out to the road, I turned my steps toward the small café next to the motel office, hoping it was open.

As I walked, I noticed that there was one other car parked in the guest lot—a rental. I pushed open the door to the café. There, sitting at a small lunch counter, surrounded by bags of pecans, jugs of cherry and peach cider, and a bunch of South Carolina–themed knick-knacks—most of them featuring alligators or pirates—was a short man with a simmering gaze, enjoying a bottle of beer.

"AJ Palladino, as I live and breathe," he called out, raising his bottle in a welcoming toast. "I had a feeling you might show up around here."

I was surprised to see that he was wearing the same plain white shirt and black trousers as the protestors I'd met earlier. Last time I'd seen Yancey he'd been wearing a fancy suit and pitching a TV show to Hollywood execs.

"What are you doing here?" I asked, taking a seat beside him. "What happened to your all-girl eco-militia?"

He heaved a sigh, but his eyes glittered with avarice. Yancey had reminded me of Charles Manson the first time we met—now more than ever, despite his newly acquired homespun demeanor. "When the show got canceled, the money left and so did they. It's just me on this gig."

Yancey—it was just Yancey, no first name that I knew of—was a media activist. Groups hired him to gain them more publicity and funding. Which, come to think of it, was exactly what Grandel was paying me for. No wonder this job made me feel slimy. "You're working with—"

"The First Church of the Redeemer." He stood, his voice dropping in timbre as it rose in volume. "The end days are near and that reactor is going to bring down the Lord's wrath in a cataclysm that will destroy the world."

A man showed up from behind the bar—a small corridor connected the café to the office. "We're closed," he said, "but since he," he nodded to Yancey and the six pack that sat on the counter beside him, "brought his own, you're welcome to sit awhile."

"Thanks, that'll be fine."

He nodded again and left, seemingly unworried about leaving two total strangers in the middle of his treasure trove of pecans and plastic alligators.

"So does your church want to end the world? Or do you want to stop the reactor?"

Yancey chuckled and took his seat, handing me a bottle of Sam Adams. "Honestly, I'm not sure. Both, I think. It gets a bit confusing, and if you press them too hard, they start speaking in tongues and hallelujahing so loud I can't think." He shrugged, wiping beer foam from his lips with the back of his hand. "Don't really care one way or the other as long as they pay the bills. But it does make for a challenge getting the crowd behind us."

"Sounds like they're just scared."

"Maybe. Aren't most people? Especially when they don't understand what's going on?" He stared at me over the rim of his bottle. "You could help with that."

"Had a feeling you were going to say something like that. I already have a client."

"Owen Grandel, right? If so, then maybe we can work together." He slid me a sly glance. "You know it has nothing to do with religion, right? Grandel already tried to buy off Reverend Vincent— he's the head of the church. Vincent's response was to hire me to 'raise a ruckus,' as he put it."

"And Grandel's reaction was to hire me to restore his 'ruined reputation.' Sounds like what they really both need is a time-out."

He finished his beer and glanced at the clock. "What are you doing tonight? Why don't you come with me, meet them? They're not so bad as they sound—or as Grandel makes them out to be."

Yancey didn't have me fooled—he wanted something from me, that much was clear. But I followed him out, figuring that it never hurt to check out the competition.

◆

David pushed his wheelchair onto the hospital's visitor elevator ahead of Elizabeth. He quickly swiveled and found the button to hold the doors open for her. She smiled at him, but it wasn't her usual smile. This one was a smile that was polite but otherwise absent, barely making it past the worry lines that had appeared around her lips.

His mom got those lines sometimes. Like when the bill collectors were calling or when they'd got kicked out of their apartment. But somehow Mom always figured out a way past the worry and things worked out just fine.

He wished now that he hadn't acted like such a jerk on the phone with her. Sometimes he just couldn't help it—she'd say something or not even say it, just imply it with her tone, and he'd react before he could think.

He wished now that he had told her to come home. Not that he needed her or anything. But somehow when Mom was around and bad things were happening, he felt better. Like she could make things right again.

Of course, she couldn't. Wishful thinking like that was stupid. She was just an ordinary mom, no one special—which was why she couldn't save his dad.

That was the heart of his anger. Losing his dad after waiting so long to find him. And Mom couldn't do a damn thing about it.

"David?" Elizabeth was reaching past him to release the doors and push a button. "I said Flora is on the third floor."

"Oh. Sorry." The doors closed and they started up.

"Are you okay?"

"I'm fine. Just don't like hospitals," he lied.

Despite his many visits to hospitals, he usually liked them—as long as he wasn't too sick. The nurses would come and take care of you whenever you pushed a button and were always smiling, willing to find you the red Jell-O instead of the yucky yellow stuff or wheel the big videogame console down if you were stuck in bed. And you could learn all sorts of cool stuff in a hospital— last time he had surgery on his tendons, the resident taking care of him told him all about her research into nerve regeneration. She even let him watch her PowerPoint presentation—really neat, made him want to learn how to work miracles like that, help people.

That was almost two years ago. Now he was torn between forensic archeology and quantum mechanics. Both a form of time travel—one to the physical past and one to the subatomic never-never land. Yet, they were both strangely connected in theory: that there was more than one reality. The reality that we perceived and took for granted was recorded in history books or by our senses. But there was also an alternative reality, just as valid but never measured or preserved for examination.

If people could just open their minds to all the wonderful possibilities surrounding them. . . . The elevator lurched to a stop. David wheeled out and waited for Elizabeth, who was still moving at a speed slower than normal. She glanced at a slip of paper in her hand. *Room 307.*

She turned—the wrong way. David waited and she turned back after two steps. She let him lead the way until they reached Flora's room.

By the time they got there, Elizabeth was as gray as the dingy linoleum beneath their feet.

"You don't like hospitals," he said, feeling sorry for her. She looked worse than she had when dealing with Jeremy puking.

She shook her head. "It's the smell. I'll be fine."

"Don't worry. You'll get used to it. Try breathing through your mouth."

"Thanks."

It felt so weird, the way Elizabeth let him take charge. A good kind of weird. Like she trusted him. Believed in him.

So unlike Mom. Mom didn't trust anyone.

Elizabeth knocked on the door, cracked it open. David could see Gram Flora lying on her bed, sleeping. The other bed in the room was empty. Elizabeth pushed the door the whole way open and they went inside. It was way past visiting hours—any of the nurses at Children's would have kicked out anyone who wasn't a parent long before now—but the nurses here didn't seem to care. They'd only seen one since they came on to the floor and she was headed the other way, into a patient's room.

Flora looked so frail—so very, very old, like an Egyptian mummy all hollowed out and empty. David swallowed his fear, trying to keep it from his voice.

"We can stay with her, can't we?"

Elizabeth's legs wobbled and she sank into the chair beside Flora's bed. She looked like she wanted to be anywhere but here. But they couldn't leave Flora alone—what if something happened and her nurse was too busy to notice? This little hospital was nothing at all like Children's, where there was always a buzz of activity. This place felt abandoned, like there weren't enough people to remember everything.

David was beginning to understand why his mom never trusted anyone—especially in hospitals.

Plus, what if he was right and someone had done this to Flora on purpose?

"Please, Elizabeth." He sounded like a baby whining, but he didn't care. He held Flora's hand—the one that was free of the IV and pulse-ox monitor. His hand covered hers easily. He'd never before realized how tiny she was; her bones felt so thin beneath his fingers, like he could snap them without even trying.

"Okay." Elizabeth gave in just like he knew she would. "We'll stay."

# FOURTEEN

I insisted on driving—no way did I want to be at Yancey's mercy in case he got distracted and ditched me while he went skirt-chasing. He directed me down the highway, and then we wound our way through a series of unmarked back roads lined by large tracts of unoccupied land and the occasional shack or rusted trailer interspersed with woe-begotten FOR SALE signs. It was a clear night, and occasionally I'd catch a glimpse of the river through the thickly leaved trees and their tattered curtains of Spanish moss.

We rounded one more bend and came to a clearing beside the river. The river was wider here, and without the thick foliage to obscure it, it seemed endless. Rows of cars were parked in a field in front of a large circus tent lit up by spotlights that waved through the sky as if beckoning the faithful. Or in my case, a no-longer-believing heathen, calling to those long ago fallen from grace.

Children raced through the field of cars, unsupervised as they squealed and ran, giddy with freedom. Adults milled around the open walls of the tent, some talking earnestly, a few clustered together holding hands or kneeling in prayer, others alone, staring out over the stars reflected in the water as if weighing a decision.

We emerged from the car, and for the first time since arriving in South Carolina I breathed a lungful of salt air. "We're close to the ocean."

"About half a mile that way." Yancey pointed. "But look over there." He placed his hands on my hips and rotated me to look directly past the revival tent, across the river.

A blue-white glow filled the horizon. Colleton Landing, I realized. "It's beautiful."

He shrugged as if taking credit for the light show. "You can see why it's such a powerful focus for Vincent's group. Something that beautiful can't be neutral, it has to be good or evil. Or, in Vincent's case, both."

"I don't understand."

"That's the beauty of it. You don't have to. Listen."

We stood at the rear of the tent, beside one of the large supporting poles. At least a hundred people were crammed beneath the canopy, all leaning forward to hear the man pacing the stage above them.

He was tall—around Ty's height—with hair so blonde that it sparked white in the glare of the spotlights. Classic Nordic good looks accompanied a voice pitched just low enough to mesmerize as it enticed you to attend each word.

"Brothers and sisters," he was saying, pacing so close to the edge of the stage that I was afraid he'd fall. He kept going back and forth, back and forth, as if revving himself up for a spectacular explosion of words. "Brothers and sisters!"

A handful of *Amen*s and *Hallelujah*s greeted him.

"We live in a fallen world."

More shouts of agreement.

"A world fallen into Satan's hands. Corrupted by sin. And what must we do with corruption when we find it amongst us?"

"Purge it! Purge it!" the audience chanted back.

"That's right! We must purge corruption. And how do we do

that? By embracing God. By embracing his plan for our lives. By relinquishing our hold on this world and preparing for the next!"

"Amen!"

Still Vincent was pacing, faster and faster, now pumping his fist into the air as he spoke, his other hand holding a Bible to his heart. The crowd was swaying in time with his pacing, heads nodding with each fist pump.

"In Second Corinthians, Paul says that this life of affliction lasts but a moment. He says that we are all on an eternal path to glory. That we can find our path by looking at the things not seen by man but only seen by God. That unseen world is eternal. It is God's gift to us if we can only forsake this corrupt world, the world of the seen, the world of the mundane."

"Forsake it!"

"Instead, we must embrace our destiny. And what is our destiny? What awaits us in God's kingdom?"

He stopped. Center stage. His audience, whipped to a frenzy, suddenly found themselves off balance and out of breath as they caught up with him and focused. He stood, head bowed, both hands cradling the Bible.

"What is our final destiny?" His voice was a whisper, yet it carried effortlessly to the back of the tent.

Everyone there leaned forward, eager to hear the answer. Silence heavier than the humid night air filled the space.

"What is God's plan for us?" He jerked his head up as if he too were listening. Then his eyes went wide and he seemed to grow taller.

He alone had the answer from on high, his posture shouted. "We must embrace that which is unseen and eternal. The divine spark that is God's and God's alone. We must use it to end this corruption and bring forth God's kingdom here on Earth!"

Now he was shouting as the crowd thundered in response, clapping and stomping and praising God in a whirlwind of voices.

The lights came up behind him to reveal a choir and small band. They began singing and playing music, something about an unseen world beyond this one, as ushers passed an offering basket and asked for anyone who wanted to receive a "healing blessing" from Reverend Vincent.

Soon there was a line of people waiting for the healing. The ushers expertly culled the herd and shepherded to the stage a frail old woman, spine crooked, hands knotted from arthritis, leaning heavily on a walker. Two assistants joined Vincent on stage and supported the woman on each side.

Vincent prayed. At first silently, with his lips moving, then louder and louder until he laid hands on the woman so powerfully that she was pushed back away from her walker. The walker flew to the side—it would have appeared propelled by God's hand except that I caught the dexterous kick one of the assistants applied. The audience gasped, holding its breath. Waiting.

"I give him high marks for showmanship," I whispered to Yancey.

He nodded and winked. "Hush now, the man's communing with the Almighty." A southern accent had crept into his voice—even though I knew full well he was from California.

The old woman stumbled. She was caught by the two assistants. Her face was twisted in fear, but Vincent bent down and whispered something in her ear and she nodded slowly. He waved off the assistants, who gingerly let go. She faltered. The crowd inhaled, a sound like the wind stirring the candle flames surrounding Vincent and the woman.

Then she stood. Unassisted. And she walked. One step, then another.

The crowd went wild. Hands raised to heaven, dancing in the aisle, women fainting, people chanting and speaking in tongues. Vincent rushed to the front of the stage—nicely timed to mask his assistants behind him catching the woman as she fell and hustling her out of sight beyond the curtains.

"Guess I don't have to ask how a church can afford your fees," I muttered to Yancey as the collection baskets began down the aisles once again.

"They don't care about money," he said, a hint of wonder in his voice. "They truly Believe with a capital B. C'mon, I'll introduce you." He tugged me through the throng until we were face to face with Vincent as he came down the stage steps flanked by his two assistants. One of them was the angry young man from the protest earlier today.

Up close, Vincent was a lot younger than I'd thought—around my age, late twenties. His hair was matted with sweat and his shirt clung to his body, revealing a nicely toned musculature. Guess all that pacing and ranting made for a good workout.

Yancey made introductions. "Reverend Vincent, this is AJ Palladino."

"Charmed, I'm sure, Ms. Palladino." He bent his head over my hand as if bowing.

"Quite a show," I nodded to the stage.

"All in the name of the good Lord."

"Don't mind her, Rev," Yancey said. "She's an unbeliever."

"Fine with me, Brother Yancey. They make for the best converts. Look to St. Paul."

His polite words and fine manners weren't working on me. I'd met too many snake charmers like Vincent before. But he did remind me of someone—Owen Grandel.

"How much do you charge to cure someone?" I asked.

Yancey raised an eyebrow at my impudence but Vincent merely smiled. "How much would you pay for salvation? To not just believe but *know* you were destined to sit at the right hand of God come the Judgment? Faith is priceless, Ms. Palladino."

One of his assistants, the guy from the protest, appeared ready to intervene, to whisk him away before I could further contaminate their holy-roller Kool-Aid.

Vincent shrugged him off. "I sense that you're troubled, child," he said, touching my left shoulder and pressing down, hard. "Let me take your troubles away, let me carry your burden. Rest, child, give it all to Jesus."

It might have worked—if I didn't understand what he was doing. "Nice try, Reverend Vincent. But Jesus and I haven't been on speaking terms for a long time."

He blinked as if surprised I hadn't handed over my wallet along with my soul. Most folks—especially ones who already more than half-believed, like his audience—are susceptible to the tricks of persuasion. Too bad for him, the first lawyer I worked with taught me all about how a well-placed gesture, certain key words, and intonation can literally hypnotize a jury . . . or an audience.

To my surprise, Vincent let out a hearty laugh.

His left-hand assistant—the same man who had yelled at me when I tried to help the woman at the protest earlier today, blanched. His hands fluttered as if he was forcing himself not to make the sign of the cross or trying to ward off an evil spirit: me.

"Paul, would you escort Ms. Palladino to my office? I believe we should get to know each other better."

"But, sir—" Paul looked aghast at Vincent's request. He slid a fancy touch-screen phone from his pocket and tapped at it, using it as a shield between him and me. "Sir, we have scheduled—"

"Forget the schedule," Vincent interrupted, glowering at Paul, who in turn glared at me, as if it was my fault, disrupting the Lord's work.

Yancey intervened, smiling brightly. "I'll take her, Rev. I know the way."

"Good. Liam, you go with them." He nodded to his right-hand assistant, a stony-faced brick wall of a man who could have given the Buckingham Palace guards lessons on masking expressions.

Vincent's smile softened the fact that he didn't trust Yancey and me alone in his office, but I didn't take it personally and I knew Yancey was used to worse slights on his character.

Liam walked us through the crowd, which was now singing a gospel song about Heaven's wrath. People didn't just make room for Liam, they got the heck out of his way fast, giving him a wide berth, eyes wide with fear. I had the feeling that of everyone crammed under this tent top, Liam was probably one of the few true believers, a fanatic who would do anything Vincent told him.

My fears were confirmed when Yancey made the mistake of trying to start a casual conversation. "Hey Liam, tell her how you got those scars on your hands."

I glanced at Liam's hands. They were covered with twisted scars clustered in unusual patterns.

"These two were rattlesnakes," Liam said, his voice as expressionless as his face. "And these copperheads. Not sure what kind of snake this one was—but the good Lord wasn't ready to take me that day."

"Vincent said you've walked over coals to show your faith."

Liam shrugged. "Reverend Vincent asks, I do. That's how faith works."

Seemed to me he was confusing faith with hero worship, but I wasn't about to contradict three hundred pounds of muscle and sinew.

"I don't suppose Reverend Vincent has ever asked you to do anything to maybe mess things up at the Colleton Landing facility? Anything that might make them shut the plant down?" I asked.

"Now why would I do that?" Vincent's voice carried a fake-jovial edge as he walked up behind us, clamping his hands down like vice-grips on my shoulders. "Without that plant, my work here is done. And I like it here. Tons of heathens who need my intervention to save their souls."

"You mean heathens like me." I stood my ground, refusing to acknowledge Vincent's invasion of my space.

Liam raised his eyebrows—I guessed that was anger, or as close as he came to registering anger. Of course, if he didn't show his emotions, kept them bottled up inside, that didn't bode well for anyone he unleashed them on.

Vincent finally released me—I was sure I'd have bruises in the morning. Any other time and place and I might have drawn the SOG sheathed in my boot. But I wasn't among friends here, I was vastly outnumbered, and I had the feeling that violence was exactly what Vincent expected of me. I hated it when folks stereotyped me before they got to know me.

We arrived at a large RV parked in the shadows behind the tent. Liam unlocked the door, opened it and looked inside, then nodded to Vincent, who bounded up the steps past him. Yancey and I followed.

Inside was a cramped living/dining area with two large leather recliners parked in front of a wide-screen TV.

Yancey plopped down in one of the leather recliners, breaking the tension. "We're all heathens here. Vincent, where's the beer? I'm parched."

Vincent nodded to Liam, who grabbed two beers from the refrigerator. He handed one to Yancey.

"No, thank you." I not only wanted my head clear, but there was no way I was about to drink something that came from Vincent.

Liam didn't change course, his look of scorn making it clear that he hadn't intended the beer for me to start with. Vincent took the beer and settled himself in the second recliner, leaving Liam and me standing. Liam crossed his arms and leaned against the wall, looked like he could stand there all day and night without moving except to blink.

Lacking the powers or patience of a gargoyle—which was exactly what Liam reminded me of—I sat down on the edge of the banquette even though it meant I had to crane my head to make eye contact with Vincent and Yancey. It also put me a tad lower than them, and when Vincent gave me a look that brimmed over with satisfaction that I was in my place, I realized he'd manipulated me.

Talk about your men with control issues. Instead of bouncing back up to my feet, I lounged back and curled my legs up so I was sitting Indian style. Much more comfortable and a posture that looked anything but submissive.

"So, Reverend Vincent, what did you want from me?" I asked.

He chuckled again—I was really beginning to hate that smarmy half-laugh, it was even worse than his smirk. "Nothing, my dear. I want nothing from you. Except your soul."

# FIFTEEN

I decided to play along. "Who says I haven't already sold my soul?"

"Well now, that would be most unfortunate. Because I believe you can help me with a problem. Something that would be mutually beneficial."

"I'm already getting paid by Grandel."

He took a long sip of beer. I'd never seen a man drink beer from a bottle so delicately. As if it were a vice he savored in secret. Given the conservative leanings of his congregation, maybe it was. Yancey guzzled his and motioned to Liam for another. Liam waited for permission from Vincent—a simple nod—before retrieving it.

I sat there and watched. More than one power-game was being played out here, but I didn't know enough to put any of them in context.

Vincent lowered his bottle, licked his lips, and sighed appreciatively. It was just Yuengling, for chrissakes, I wanted to shout. But for once I stayed silent. I could play the waiting game, too.

"I'll double whatever Grandel's paying. All I need you to do is report back to me. Share a little information, that's all."

"What kind of information?" Could Vincent and his people be behind the incidents at Colleton Landing? Maybe they'd found a way around the security and had fooled the investigators into labeling the radiation leaks as accidents.

"Just the date of their next isotope shipment. It's a matter of public record—or it will be. I'd just like a little advance warning, that's all."

Right. A little advance warning that could lead to people dying if a shipment of medical isotopes went astray. I kept my face friendly—it took an effort. Men like Vincent and Grandel who played games with people's futures made me furious. But I played it cool—must be Elizabeth's influence on me.

"I'll think about it," I said, getting to my feet.

Liam blocked my way for one hard moment. But Vincent gave the nod and he stepped aside, even opened the door for me, well-trained Neanderthal that he was.

◆

Elizabeth finally bribed David into taking the other patient bed by allowing him to stay up reading. Of course, his reading was different than any other kid's she'd known. Or most adults, for that matter. David shared Flora's fondness for audio books. He'd fallen asleep listening to Steven Hawkings's *A Brief History of Time* while reading *Godel, Escher, Bach*—a book Elizabeth had once attempted to read in order to impress a guy she'd dated in college but had quickly given up on.

David was almost the entire way through the eight-hundred-page book—and he'd just started it the day before.

Spooky, having a kid so smart around. Like the way he'd breezed through all the research material Grandel had left. During dinner he'd given them an impromptu lesson on the history of nuclear disasters, including several that had happened here in the

US that she'd never heard of, probably because they were in government installations.

She shifted in her "sleeping" chair—the most uncomfortable piece of furniture ever devised. And supposedly designed to allow loved ones to grab some sleep while holding vigil? Not likely. The most she could achieve was a light doze, and as soon as her body relaxed, one of the infernal chair's wretchedly placed springs would poke her awake again.

The nurses came in every few hours to check Flora's IV and blood sugar, but other than that, they left her alone. Finally, after the last one pricked Flora's finger and left without even acknowledging Elizabeth's presence, Flora stirred.

"Jeremy? Where—"

"Shhh," Elizabeth sprang to her side and took her hand. "It's Elizabeth. You're in the hospital."

"Hospital?" Flora pushed herself up on her pillows. "Oh yeah, I forgot. Whatever did they keep me for? I feel fine. Except for a headache. And my arm's cold from this damn thing." She wiggled her hand with the IV fluids flowing through it.

"What happened?" Elizabeth asked. Although Flora had been awake at the house and fairly coherent, she hadn't explained her view of the events. If Elizabeth was going to help Jeremy, she needed to know everything—even if it was the worst.

Flora frowned, her entire face folding in an attempt to concentrate. "I fell asleep in my chair. Woke up feeling kinda funny, so I headed up to bed. Made it to the stairs when I got dizzy and everything went black. I don't remember anything else."

"Do you remember Jeremy giving you your evening insulin?"

"But he wouldn't have—the doctor changed the schedule since I've been eating dinner later. Now Jeremy comes up when he goes to bed and gives me the last injection right around eleven."

"So Jeremy wouldn't have been giving you a shot around eight-thirty?"

"Not unless I missed my dose at dinner. But I didn't—he gave it to me right on time. You were there." Flora's blind gaze sought out Elizabeth's. "Why all these questions about Jeremy? What happened?"

"We found him with an empty bottle of Southern Comfort. The police arrested him."

"That's preposterous. Jeremy doesn't drink. And even if he did, why would they arrest him?"

"Someone gave you an overdose of insulin, Flora. The police are blaming Jeremy."

Flora sank back against the pillows. "That's the craziest damn thing I've ever heard. You go tell them they're wrong."

"I'll get him out on bail tomorrow."

"Bail, schmail. They need to find who *did* do this. Stop wasting their time accusing an innocent man."

"Right now all the evidence points to Jeremy. Flora, isn't it possible—"

The old woman slashed her hand through the air, demolishing Elizabeth's question before it was even asked. "No. It's not possible. I'll tell them I gave it to myself before I let that boy end up in jail."

"But if you didn't and Jeremy didn't, then who did?"

Flora pursed her lips in thought. Then she patted Elizabeth's arm. "Guess that's up to you to find out."

◆

Later, as I drove Yancey back to the motel, I asked him the question that had been bothering me all day. Goes to show how desperate I was that I was asking Yancey for answers.

"Why is Grandel engaging in a pissing match with Vincent? I know he's worried about the plant's reputation, but nobody would take Vincent's group seriously. No offense," I quickly added.

He chuckled. "None taken. But you'd be surprised. Besides, it's not about Colleton Landing. Grandel explained his design to you, right? The modular construction?"

"Yeah. Four reactors in one, safer, more efficient, yada yada . . ."

"Grandel's company is poised to take that design and modify it for power production. Since the NRC fast-tracked the isotope production plant because of the national shortage, he can now leap-frog over the biggest names in the field. His design is so compact that instead of the long and expensive process of manufacturing and assembling a custom, large-scale nuclear reactor, Grandel can transport a complete micro-reactor in a standard-sized cargo container. Imagine, being able to have unlimited electricity no matter how remote you are. Cheap, abundant electricity. It could topple governments, redraw the map—"

"Change the world." Visions of barren fields in the Sahara springing to new life with water pumped by Grandel's generators, swamp land reclaimed, clean water filtered and flowing to every home no matter how remote. . . . "That's why Vincent won't take the money Grandel offered. He wants in on the bigger payoff."

"You nailed it. If there's one thing Vincent is, it's a big-picture kind of guy. And of course that big picture paints a target square on Grandel's forehead—Vincent's true believers see Grandel as the anti-Christ, the other energy companies are scared they're going to lose all their municipal and government contracts; hell, even Third World dictators are gunning for him. Or they will be, once the word gets out."

"So this isn't public knowledge?"

He shook his head. "Vincent only learned about it because he's an investor in Grandel's company and actually read the fine print in his prospectus. When he heard about possible foreign investors, he put two and two together. Originally he was looking for ways to manipulate the stock price, make some fast money, but he realized his best bet was to keep buying all the shares he could and put pressure on Grandel to cut him in on the action. And so the First Church of the Redeemer was born."

"And you're helping him? Isn't that illegal? SEC violation or something?"

"How the hell should I know? I don't own any of the stock—the price is too rich for me now with Colleton Landing going online. Besides, my job is simply to clarify the Church's message to the community and buy Vincent some free publicity. Nothing illegal about that."

I snorted. Yancey's definition of "legal" was vague to say the least. I'd learned that firsthand when I met him five months ago.

"So I guess I'm the competition," I said. "Since my job is to clarify Grandel's message to the community and discredit the Church."

"In my experience once you bring religion into the mix, the more you try to discredit anything the more firmly and vocally people believe. Just remember that, AJ."

"But that's the problem, isn't it? What's between Vincent and Grandel has nothing to do with religion—they're both just manipulating the public to get what they want."

"Doesn't matter. The true believers will never give up. Vincent has stirred up a rattlesnake nest and not even you will be able to calm it down." He turned and grinned at me. "Not alone, anyway."

"You think we should work together." He'd mentioned that before.

"Why not?"

"Maybe because your boss wants my client brought to his knees."

"But not really. Both of them want the company to succeed and the foreign investors to buy in, big time. It's just that Vincent wants a bigger piece of the pie than Grandel is willing to share with him."

"So, if I talk to Grandel about Vincent, will you get the protestors to tone things down? At least until the deal with the foreign investors is signed?"

"You first." His grin reminded me of a rattlesnake I'd once met on a trail. Same beady eyes as well.

What choice did I have? There was no way I could do my job with Vincent manipulating his congregation—like I'd told Grandel earlier, we had no power with them. Fastest way for me to finish the job, make everyone happy, and get the hell home would be to work with Yancey.

Not only that, but after hearing about the potential good Colleton Landing could do, I realized that as despicable as Grandel was on a personal basis, fighting to save the plant was the right thing to do. Not just for him—for the community, for the people Colleton Landing could help in the future.

We turned into the motel parking lot. I left the car, shouting a hurried goodnight over my shoulder before Yancey could try to take advantage of our forced partnership. As I entered my room— now cooled from broiling to mere sweat-lodge—I felt like I'd just made a deal with the devil.

For the second time today.

◆

Hutton waited until he was sure Masterson would be in bed for the night before calling him with a report. Petty, he knew, but he liked to keep Masterson off balance.

"Good work," Masterson told him when he'd finished. "Nice touch, framing the faggot."

"We aim to please."

"Too bad you didn't kill him, though."

Hutton changed the subject. He figured what two consenting adults did behind closed doors was their own business—live and let live, so to speak. Not that Masterson would ever agree, especially not with the welfare of his grandson at stake. "Have you decided on the other matter? The long distance one?"

"It depends on the outcome tomorrow. But in the meantime, I might need you here for a little touch of arson."

"Arson? Not my area of expertise." Which was a lie. Hutton had completed several successful jobs using fire—all ruled as accidental. But it wouldn't pay to have Masterson knowing that.

"It won't be anything difficult. Believe me, this place is a fire trap; one spark in the wrong place and it will go up on its own."

"Collateral damage?"

"Doesn't matter one way or the other. Either way, I'll get what I want."

It offended Hutton the way Masterson acted as if lives lost were meaningless.

Masterson treated Hutton like Hutton was still the twenty-three-year-old kid he'd hired to "take care of some business." All these years and Masterson still didn't understand the power of finesse. No shades of gray for Masterson, just black and white.

"It'll cost you extra," Hutton replied, not because he really did charge extra but because his pride demanded some form of compensation for having his talents underappreciated.

"Just be ready for my call." Masterson hung up.

Hutton made a mental list of the ways he might consider killing the man. Better than counting sheep, in his experience.

# SIXTEEN

It was too damn hot to sleep—and the AC's spitting and sputtering only made things worse. By morning I wondered if I should borrow a shotgun and put the damn thing out of its misery.

It wasn't just the heat. I was too worried about Gram Flora and too busy trying to unravel Grandel's and Vincent's motives to sleep.

Instead, I spent the time memorizing the layout of the plant and skimming through the DOE investigation summaries. They put the three Colleton Landing incidents into perspective—all three were clearly minor nuisances that were barely a blip on the radar compared to other plants' radiation leaks.

The more I read, the more I realized that nuclear plants and the risks of exposure from them could happen anywhere. Some of the more recent accidents had taken place in the heart of highly populated areas. Like the meltdowns in Japan, or the problems at Indian Point, only twenty-four miles from Manhattan, where several pipes had been found with large holes in them leaking hundreds of thousands of gallons of coolant water. And there was another nuclear facility on Long Island that had leaked tritium.

After reading about the horrors elsewhere, I wasn't surprised when in the end, both the DOE and NRC praised Colleton Landing's unique design for mitigating any potential exposure to the public and commended the plant's personnel for their actions.

Should have made my job easy. But if things were that simple, Grandel wouldn't have needed to hire me in the first place. He was right, in this day of instant Internet information, the court of public opinion would save or crucify Colleton Landing, not the government's rulings.

Despite its poor cell coverage, the motel did have Wi-Fi, so I browsed the web offerings on Colleton Landing. Several particularly vicious blogs and Twitter feeds seemed aimed directly at Grandel and his plant. Their tone ranged from far political right to liberal, covering all the bases, but I couldn't help noticing that the language in all of them sounded similar. Even the ones spewing apocalyptic religious rants had the same syntax and rhythm as the others—something I'm sensitive to since the easiest way for me to read is to have my computer read things out loud using text-to-voice software.

I had the feeling the man behind the Internet vitriol was Vincent. And that it would all magically disappear once Grandel capitulated.

Now I knew how the rope in a tug-o-war felt, only I wasn't sure that I wanted either man to win.

I decided to concentrate on the reason why Grandel said he'd hired me: to educate the public. That was a battle I could fight with passion.

My cell phone was still down to one miniscule flickering bar, so I called home on the landline. No answer at the summerhouse or Flora's, the hospital wouldn't let me talk to her—said she couldn't be disturbed and I'd have to call back later—and Elizabeth's cell went straight to voice mail.

Finally, desperate for news, any news, not to mention a friendly voice, I called Ty, even though I knew he'd just finished his overnight shift.

"It's me," I said when he answered. "I didn't wake you, did I?"

"I'm at the courthouse. Waiting on Jeremy so I can give him a ride home."

That explained why Elizabeth wasn't answering. She was bailing Jeremy out of jail.

"They're still pressing charges?" One thing about having all night to stew—I'd begun to doubt everything, even my initial instincts about Jeremy.

"The DA's got this thing about Flora being a 'vulnerable segment of the population—'"

"He's up for reelection."

"Jeremy's case makes for great publicity—sympathetic victim, gay, black man supposedly drunk, taking advantage of her. So yeah, he's out for bear."

"Was Jeremy actually drunk?"

"His BAC was point-oh-three. Nowhere close to the limit." Blood alcohol concentration, I translated—when Ty was in cop-mode he tended to use all sorts of words and abbreviations he never used at home. "But that doesn't rule out other substances. They did a tox screen but it's not back yet."

"If he wasn't drunk how did this happen?" I wanted to believe in Jeremy—after all, I'd trusted him with Flora's life and David's—but I'd seen too many people in D.C. lead seemingly normal lives until their addictions spiraled out of control. Was he using drugs and I never noticed?

Ty read my mind. "No signs of drug use—we searched his truck and room and he's got no tracks, of course he could be snorting or popping pills." He lowered his voice. Suddenly he was Ty again instead of Deputy Stillwater. "Honestly, AJ, I'm not sure what happened. Not even Flora knows—"

"She's okay?"

"Elizabeth said she was awake and talking. Doesn't remember anything but falling asleep in her chair. Swears up and down that Jeremy didn't give her any extra insulin. Not that anyone's believing her. Jeremy's real torn up over it, though."

I didn't have an answer for that. Nothing made sense. "What about those guys from Beckley who were harassing Jeremy?"

"Alibi—they were in a pool tournament all night long. Dozens of witnesses."

"Did Jeremy think of anyone else?"

"Elizabeth is the only one who's talked to him. I'll ask him on the ride home."

That left me with more questions than answers for now. And nothing to do except worry. "How's David doing?"

"Just dropped him off at my mom's place." David loved visiting Ty's mom—the Stillwater clan was large enough that there were always other kids over there. "He seemed okay—a bit quieter than usual. Except for asking me all kinds of questions about Jeremy's case and forensics and stuff I couldn't answer. I think I pissed him off—he accused me of treating him like a kid."

"Join the club." Still, my long-distance maternal instincts were abuzz with anxiety. "Ty. Do me a favor, will you?"

"Sure. Whatcha need?"

"After you get Jeremy home, would you stay with David? Until Elizabeth gets there?"

"What are you worried about, AJ?"

"I can't help but think it's a pretty damn convenient coincidence that both Flora and Jeremy are incapacitated the same night I leave David in their care."

There was a long pause. "Who would do that? And why?"

I had to admit it sounded far-fetched. Ten years living in some not-so-nice neighborhoods in D.C. had honed my para-

noia to a sharp edge—maybe too sharp. Or it could just be a long
night spent without sleep and with plenty of crazy scenarios
swirling around my brain. Finally I gave in and decided I'd let Ty
judge for himself. "Masterson. He's fighting me for official visitation rights."

It sounded preposterous as soon as I said it. Ty's doubt vibrated
through the line, but at least he didn't scoff out loud.

"I'll watch out for him," he finally said. "You've got my word on
that. But, AJ, I really think you're wrong about all this. Besides, I
know for a fact that Kyle Masterson was in Charleston last night—
addressing the Kiwanis at a fundraiser."

"Still, I feel better knowing you're watching David. I'm going to
wrap things up here and get home as soon as possible." I doubted I
could fully swing the community in Grandel's favor, not with only
today and tomorrow to work with, but I could get things kick-
started and come back after David's birthday.

"Okay. I gotta go. You take care, now."

"Thanks, Ty." He hung up before I could say anything more—
I'm not sure why, but "be careful" was on the tip of my tongue.

◆

The sky was clear, the air heavy as I walked over to the café. Several
Hispanic day laborers were waiting—looked like they were picking
up packed lunches. Nice to know the place did some business. The
counter was staffed by an older gentleman who had coffee poured
for me before I slid into my seat.

"Hope you like it black, we've got no cream."

"Black is perfect, thank you."

He nodded, his eyes drawn to the TV behind him. On it the
weatherman was showing a map of the predicted route of Hurricane Hermes, which had grown to a Category Three but was still

not predicted to make landfall as it churned its way up the Atlantic coast. Colleton Landing sat just beyond the range of computer predictions painted on the map like a wide swath of red. Good. I didn't want any stupid hurricane keeping me here any longer than I had to be.

"Fools," the old man snorted, dragging a dishrag along the countertop. "Anyone can see it's hurricane weather."

Worried, I glanced outside the window where the sunshine was blinding. "Really? There's no signs of any clouds."

"Mark my words. By noon, they'll be changing their story."

A woman poked her head in from the kitchen. "Shut up, Henry, you'll scare off the trade." She bustled in, wiping her hands on her apron. "Don't mind him, sweetheart, he says that every time there's a storm within a thousand miles. Last time we got hit was almost sixty years ago. Now, what can I get you?"

She held a small notepad and pencil handy. I didn't look at the menu. Since I wasn't sure when I'd get lunch, I ordered a protein-heavy meal worthy of a long morning's work: two eggs, sausage, hash browns. She gave me a brusque nod, seemed disappointed in my mundane selection, pocketed her notebook without writing down my order, and disappeared back into the kitchen.

"You all lived around here for long?" I asked as I waited.

The counterman tore his attention from the TV. "Yep."

The woman brought a stack of Styrofoam containers out to the waiting workers, handed them out, then rejoined him.

"How do you like it?" I tried again.

The man stared at me like I was a dolt for asking. The woman answered, "Raised three kids here." She nodded to the photos arrayed on a corkboard below the TV. "Did them just fine."

"Nice looking family." I smiled at a picture of the man, a decade or two younger, pushing a little girl in a swing. Two gangly but handsome boys wrestled off to the side. "They work here, too?"

The man shut the TV off in disgust. "What work? Ain't been no work 'round here since they put in the new highway."

"Guess that hasn't helped business much."

The woman was silent, appraising me. "I know your name sounded familiar. I seen you on TV. You're that lawyer—"

"No. I'm no lawyer," I was quick to correct her. "I used to work for some." I extended my hand. "AJ Palladino. I'm down here looking into the troubles out at the Colleton Landing nuclear plant."

They both shook my hand—a little hesitantly, but I get that a lot.

"Floyd and Noreen Smalls," she introduced them. "What troubles out at the plant? Something new happen?"

"No. But folks seem pretty riled up about the plant going to full capacity. When I was there yesterday, there was a bunch of protestors out front. You have any idea why? Seems to me the plant is the main place where folks around here can get work."

The man spit a wad of tobacco juice into a mason jar. "They pay good, that's for sure."

"What do you think of the Grandels?"

"Owen—don't got much use for him. Same as when he was a kid—all he wants is what's good for him, itching to leave this place 'bout as soon as he could put both feet to the ground and take off running."

His wife chimed in. "You know, when his folks died, the police almost arrested him?"

"Noreen, don't go starting any gossip. You know how I feel about that. Boy was cleared of any wrongdoing."

"They never did figure out what started that fire, and you know it, Floyd Smalls." She hugged her arms around her chest. "I'm sorry, but I just never took a liking to that boy, not at all. But his brother, Morris? He's a sweet boy."

Floyd agreed, nodding and actually daring a smile. The ragged creases lining his face twisted sideways, revealing yellowed teeth. "Smart one, too. Fixed our walk-in without us even asking. Would've went out of business for sure without it. Woke up one morning and there he was, got the compressor in pieces all around him, smiling like a fool—"

"Floyd," Noreen chided. "Don't call him that. Morris is," she hesitated, "special. But he's done a lot for this community, don't you let anyone tell you different."

"No ma'am," I promised. "So the plant doesn't bother you?"

"Navy's had nuclear stuff hidden up and down the coast for half a century. Did you know there is a hydrogen bomb buried right near here, off of Tybee Island? Been there since 1958. Could vaporize us all any old time, if it ever went off," Floyd said. "Why should we be bothered now that we're finally getting some money and jobs back from it?"

"Money? How so?"

Noreen explained, "Morris worked a deal with Palmetto Electric so the plant gives us electricity pretty near for free. A real lifesaver in these hard times, I tell you."

"That sounds nice. So why do so many people want to shut the plant down?" I persisted. They hadn't actually answered my question—not yet.

A buzzer in the kitchen went off and Noreen left to attend to it. Floyd leaned his elbows on the countertop. "They don't really want to shut it down," he whispered. "They just don't got no other choice. What with the economy being so down and all."

Before he could say anything else, Noreen returned with my breakfast. A huge soup bowl of cheese grits topped with plump shrimp.

"But I ordered—" Her glare shut me up. Made me feel like I was back home with Gram Flora. I hated grits—even Flora's. Thinking of Flora made me homesick, so I took a timid taste anyway. A creamy confection of warmth melted on my tongue, rich and silky smooth. I dug in. Finally came up for air.

"These are better than even my gram's," I announced as I reached the bottom of the bowl. Noreen nodded like a proud mama.

"The secret's the milk," she said. "You tell your gram that. Don't use water, you gotta use milk."

"Yes ma'am, I'll remember that. Thank you." I paid the bill and got down from my stool, reluctant to go back out into the heat. Barely eight-thirty and already the parking lot shimmered like a desert mirage.

"You tell that Morris Grandel we say hey—tell him to stop being a stranger," Noreen called after me.

I wanted to be prepared for anything, and it seemed like my stuff might be safer stowed in my car parked at the plant's secure lot, so I quickly tossed everything back in my bags and threw them in the SUV. Then, lowering the visor as far as it would go and squinting against the bright morning sun, I headed east to Colleton Landing.

◆

Bailing clients out of jail hadn't been part of Elizabeth's old job back in Philly. She tried her best to look like she knew what she was doing, following the leads of the other attorneys in the criminal court's arraignment hearings. Just like on the civil side of things, the justice system seemed fueled by an inordinate amount of paperwork and lots of sitting and waiting.

Finally it was her turn before the judge. A deputy led Jeremy to stand beside her. He wore the same clothes he had last night, reeked of sweat and vomit, but other than blood-shot eyes and sagging shoulders, he looked okay.

The prosecutor, a thirty-something white man with an eagle-beagle glint in his gaze, started. "Your Honor, the police found the defendant alone in the house with the victim, obviously in an intoxicated state."

Elizabeth leapt to Jeremy's defense. "First of all, he lives with the victim, so of course he was in the house. And secondly, how do you explain the defendant's blood alcohol level being near zero?"

"Point oh-three to be exact," the prosecutor interjected. "And the police documented the presence of a large amount of vomit reeking of alcohol on the defendant's clothing and the area immediately around his person when they arrived. We are awaiting further toxicology testing to determine if the alcohol was perhaps ingested after the defendant had already become intoxicated with some other substance. If they reveal the presence of an illegal substance, we are prepared to add additional charges when the tests results become available."

Jeez, this guy had an answer for everything—and he'd just left the judge with the impression that Jeremy was some kind of drug addict. Great. "Your Honor, even the victim has stated that the defendant did not give her the extra insulin in question."

"Your honor, we have not been able to interview Mrs. Hightower to verify the defense's contention; however, I would like to point out that Flora Hightower is the very definition of a high-risk, vulnerable victim. She is seventy-three, legally blind, with severe diabetes, and until last night was totally dependent on the defendant for care. Therefore, we ask for bond at $50,000."

Elizabeth's eyes bulged in disbelief. "Fifty thousand? Your Honor, that's outrageous! Mr. Miller has no criminal record, has ties to the community and presents no flight risk—"

"Really? Where will he reside?" the DA countered. "Surely not back with Mrs. Hightower. And if he has no home and no job, then what's to keep him tied to our community? He has no family here—perhaps he has some other special relationship that would keep him here?" He leered suggestively at Jeremy, challenging him to bring his sexuality into the public forum.

*Publicity whore and racist, homophobic pig,* Elizabeth cursed mentally even as she fought to keep her face impassive. "Your Honor, we resent the prosecution's highly prejudicial implication—"

"Save it for trial, counselor. Bail is set at $50,000, cash or bond." The judge's gavel banged. "Next case."

# SEVENTEEN

I turned onto the drive leading into Colleton Landing just before nine. Tomorrow was Friday, so this would be my only full day to solve Grandel's problem.

The protestors were already gathered, which was good because I wanted to talk to them, get some idea why they were protesting, who had organized the protests, and what they wanted. I was surprised to see that the only ones actually picketing were Vincent's people—led by Paul, his assistant. Despite the heat there were more women here today, wearing heavy long-sleeved, high-collared black dresses and walking beside the men dressed in black slacks and white shirts.

The cynic in me wondered if Vincent did that on purpose, was maybe even arranging for media coverage if there was another fainting episode. My suspicions were confirmed when I spotted Liam lurking around the edge of the trees with a handheld video camera.

The other protestors had taken advantage of Grandel's hospitality, sitting on lawn chairs in the shade of the blue canopy, drink coolers stacked around them. There were two new additions since yesterday: twin industrial-sized fans positioned over large galvanized tubs that held bales of hay soaked with water. The protestors looked pretty comfortable, maybe even a bit annoyed when my car pulled into sight, forcing them to their feet to do their job. As soon as I pulled off the road and parked, they sank back into their chairs.

"Morning," I called out as I joined them. "You all are committed, coming out here on a hot day like today."

It was already ninety-two according to the thermometer in the SUV, and the humidity was enough to stick my shirt to me before I walked three steps. D.C. sometimes got like this, an oppressive heat trapped by the buildings. Here, close to the river, with so many trees, it seemed unnatural, like Mother Nature should have figured out a solution already.

Made me glad for the cold air under the canopy when I joined the protestors. Behind us, Vincent's people began singing a hymn as they linked arms across the road, swinging their hands as if playing Red Rover with an unseen enemy.

I looked around. There was no media presence—except for Liam recording their antics. The video would surely be on YouTube and a dozen other sites within the hour. If there was one thing Yancey knew about, it was the power of going viral.

I sat down beside a young couple in their early twenties who politely made room for me at their picnic table and introduced themselves.

"Why are you out here?" I asked. The woman, Elise, was pregnant, barely showing but self-conscious enough that she kept rubbing her belly as if to make sure her baby was still there. "It can't be easy coming out in the heat every day."

They exchanged glances. "It's important," her husband, Nate, said.

"For the baby." The woman patted her belly again.

"You think the plant puts your baby in danger?"

Another shared glance. "Uh, yeah."

"From what? What are you worried about?"

They squirmed uncomfortably. "The radiation?" Elise finally answered.

Nate had had enough. He stepped in front of Elise protectively, lowered his voice. "Look, Miss, we really need this job. Could you please ask someone else your questions?"

Before I had a chance to ask him about his "job" or if their paycheck was signed by Vincent, a familiar voice called out from the road.

"Hey y'all," Morris said, waving and smiling at several of the protestors as if he knew them. Maybe he did because they smiled back. "AJ, did you see the swamp coolers I rigged up? Not bad for solar powered. The fans force an increased evaporative—"

"Nice job," I assured him, not wanting to get lost in the science so early in the day. "What are you doing out here?"

"Oh, I spotted you on my Kermit when you pulled in the drive." He pulled out what looked at first glance to be an over-sized lime-green cell phone with a Kermit the Frog sticker gracing its back. It had a touch screen as well as a sliding keyboard. Morris tapped a few keystrokes and the screen split into several views from security cameras, all revealing my car pulling in and driving toward the plant. "We own the property out to the highway, so we monitor it."

"Then why are the protestors here? You could have them removed for trespassing."

"We'd never do that. They have a right to speak their minds." He slid his "Kermit" back into his messenger bag, leaned close, and whispered, "Besides, Owen says better they're here where no one can actually see them."

"So you came to make sure I made it to the plant?"

He grinned, then fidgeted with the strap on his bag. "Kind of. I thought, if you wanted, we could go in together." He cleared his throat. "If you don't mind me escorting you."

Who could resist those puppy dog eyes? Especially when I no-

ticed Liam sidling closer, scowling when he heard Morris's sugges-
tion. "Of course. It would be a pleasure."

He took my arm like we were prom dates. "Bye now," he called
to the protestors. "Let me know if y'all need anything."

"Bye, Morris," several called back, waving.

I just shook my head. Coming from West Virginia mining country where protests and strikes were often violent confrontations
pitting brother against brother, this polite and cordial Lowcountry
way was nothing less than surreal.

At least Vincent's people maintained their rigid, angry postures—
reaffirming my faith in human nature.

By the time Elizabeth finished with the bail bondsman and his paperwork, cutting him a check for $5,000 and putting her house up
as collateral for the rest, she was running late for Judge Mabry and
their meeting with Hunter about Masterson's visitation case.

Part of the requirements for Jeremy to be released was that he
have a residence to return to, so she'd given her address as Jeremy's
and sent him and Ty to move his things from Flora's house to hers.

So much for having the place to herself. But hopefully it
wouldn't be for long.

She rushed into Judge Mabry's chambers feeling flustered and
not at all prepared to take on Hunter. As soon as the judge was
seated at his desk, Hunter wasted no time in launching his attack.

"Judge Mabry, we are concerned that while the plaintiff and defendant are represented, there has been no advocate appointed for
the child in question. We request that be rectified as soon as possible so that we can move forward with the proceedings."

Elizabeth stepped forward. "Your Honor, my client was hoping
that her son would not need to be dragged into these proceedings.
After all, as you can see by my response to previous motions, there

is ample precedent negating Mr. Masterson's right to mandatory visitation."

"But none here in the state of West Virginia. And if your Honor has read the Supreme Court's decision in *Troxel v. Granville* he'll see that—"

"That six of the nine justices disagreed with each other on the interpretation of the Washington State law," the judge said dryly. "I've done my homework, thank you, Mr. Holcombe."

He rustled a few papers on his desk and looked up over his glasses. "Given that West Virginia statutes state that visitation shall not substantially interfere with the parent-child relationship, I think it reasonable to hear from all parties, including the child. Therefore, I am ordering that a court-appointed special advocate be provided for the minor in question."

"Thank you, your Honor. And now I'd like to amend Mr. Masterson's petition for visitation to one for emergency custody."

Elizabeth jumped. "What? You can't be serious—"

The judge glared at her and she reined in her anger and surprise. "On what grounds, Mr. Holcombe?"

"On the grounds that Ms. Palladino has abandoned her son—"

"She left for a business trip," Elizabeth interjected, "she's only going to be gone a few days and David is under the supervision of capable adults chosen by his custodial parent."

"Capable adults," Hunter implied finger quotes with his tone, "such as the defendant's own attorney, Ms. Hardy. Placing the child in her custody, even temporarily, can provide her with opportunity to exert undue influence on such a young mind."

"I would never—" Elizabeth sputtered, her anger flaring again. Back in Philly she'd been known for her courtroom cool, but Hunter knew all too well how to turn her own words into weapons against her. How dare he make this personal? Especially with David's future at stake. "Your Honor, I resent counsel's implication—"

"He has a point, Ms. Hardy. Surely there are actual family members capable of assuming custody until Ms. Palladino returns?"

"Of course." She opened her mouth and closed it again. Hunter, damn him, knew exactly what her dilemma was and he enjoyed letting her stew in front of the judge. "Ms. Palladino left David in the care of myself, her grandmother Flora Hightower, and Mrs. Hightower's personal care assistant who is a licensed practical nurse."

"A grandmother who is seventy-three and blind and currently in the hospital, placed there because of negligence from her personal care assistant, your Honor. And even if that man was capable of caring for the child, he's hardly a fit custodian. Hence the need for an emergency hearing."

"Go on, Mr. Holcombe." The judge's interest was piqued—always a bad thing in a judge.

Hunter was practically drooling as he dragged out AJ's family's dirty laundry for the judge to examine. "The young man in question is a homosexual, your Honor—"

"Irrelevant, your Honor!" Elizabeth interrupted.

Hunter mercly stood there, face placid except for a slightly tweaked eyebrow that implied all sorts of salacious possibilities if young, innocent David were to spend any time alone with Jeremy. "And he's currently in jail—"

"Incorrect."

"Excuse me. Mr. Miller is out on bail, awaiting trial on charges of medical negligence and assault."

The judge raised both eyebrows and gave a *hurhumph*. "I have to agree. Hardly a fit parental substitute for custodial supervision of a minor. What about the grandparents?"

"Mr. Masterson would happily allow David to come stay with him until the mother decides to return, whenever that may be," Hunter said, as if granting a boon.

"Wait, what about AJ's parents? They have just as much right to custody as Masterson." Too late, Elizabeth realized that she'd opened a door—one that Hunter, damn him, had been waiting to shove his foot into.

"Is their house wheelchair accessible?" he asked. "Mr. Masterson has renovated the first floor of his domicile to accommodate his grandson's special needs. He'd be happy to open his residence to an inspection by the court, if your honor would like."

Elizabeth blanched at the thought of the court sending an inspector to AJ's parents' house. "And Mr. and Mrs. Palladino would be happy to move into David's current domicile so that he would not be forced to leave his home. Much less disruptive for a child, I'm sure you'll agree, Judge Mabry."

The judge paused, and for a sinking moment Elizabeth was certain he would rule in favor of Masterson. Hard to send a kid home to a rickety farm building when you could send him to a mansion where he'd get everything money could buy.

But then the judge nodded in her direction. "Very well. If Ms. Palladino's parents move in with the child and assume care until she returns, that will be suitable. But," he glanced at Elizabeth before she could begin to relish her victory, "there will be no contact between the minor and this personal care assistant. And I'd like Ms. Hardy to minimize her contact to what is required to assist the child's court-appointed advocate in his duties."

"Thank you, your Honor," Elizabeth said. Technically she'd won, but it didn't feel at all like victory. Instead it felt like the prelude to disaster.

Hunter cemented her premonition with his next words. "Your Honor, we'd like to move forward with a formal hearing as soon as possible. My client has no desire to prolong this or to cause his grandson further distress."

"Distress? It's your client's manipulation that's causing David distress—"

"Counselor." The judge shook his head at her. Elizabeth shut up.

He flipped through his calendar. "I have an opening tomorrow, three p.m. I'll see all parties then, ready to proceed."

"Your honor, my client may not be back by then—"

The judge raised an eyebrow. "If she values retaining custody of her child, she will be."

Hunter didn't even bother to hide his snicker as he shut the door behind them. "Just like old times, isn't it, Elizabeth?"

It took every ounce of energy not to slap him.

# — EIGHTEEN —

It turned out Morris had walked from his office. I parked the SUV in the lot near the outer perimeter and we strolled toward the plant. Instead of taking the more direct pedestrian/tram route, he guided me along the road that looped around the outside of the parking lot and curved alongside the river. My polo shirt was quickly drenched in sweat. I wondered how he managed to look so cool. He wore khakis and a broadcloth shirt identical to the ones he'd worn yesterday.

"You and Owen grew up around here?" I broke the silence as we walked on the side of the road, only the chain-link fence separating us from the tidal mudflats. It was a bit cooler here in the shade of the live oaks. I liked the way they curved and twisted—they'd be fun trees to climb.

"Down the road. Small place, not even on the map anymore, not since the last census. Harbinger was its name. Mainly shrimpers and their families, just about all gone now."

"And you both left? Went to college?"

He nodded, a sudden cloud of sorrow hiding his smile. I'd gotten used to seeing his constant smile and regretted asking the question as soon as it fled. "I was already at Georgia Tech when my folks died. Their insurance paid for Owen to go as well."

"Are you both nuclear engineers? PhDs?"

"Not quite. I never got my doctorate—couldn't handle the oral tests or dissertation defense." The smile returned, a shy winking of self-effacement. "I don't do so well around people. Not like Owen. He's a real people person. Got his MBA."

So Owen wasn't even an engineer. We passed the second checkpoint and I stopped for a moment, admiring the way the sun wove through the fields of lavender and wildflowers. "Morris, I know this is none of my business, but did you know that Owen tells everyone that he designed Colleton Landing?"

He looked away, scuffing his boat shoe in a pile of pine needles. "That's okay. We're brothers. We've always shared everything." Morris sounded like he believed that, but I wondered. To willingly give credit of his creation to his brother? "Owen says he needs this win. He's meant for bigger and better things. World-changing things, he says. Not that he ever asks, but I think he'd be better off staying right here. We make a great team. And it's nice, being back home."

Grandel sounded like he had no qualms riding piggyback on his brother's shoulders to secure his own place on the fast track. I made a mental note to ask Elizabeth to do some checking on Owen's background.

"Don't you want some of the credit? You deserve it."

"Nah. Owen poured his heart and soul into this place. He was the one who got the funding, talked to all those congressmen and officials. Without him, Colleton Landing would never have been built." He shrugged. "Like I said, I have a hard time talking to real people—not like you, I mean important people—not that you're not important. You know what I mean. Crowds and committees and boards and inspectors and all. Owen does all that so well."

"Morris, you know Owen is planning to expand the company,

take your design around the world. Your ideas could be worth billions of dollars."

"I already have everything I need right here. And if he stopped to think about it, so does Owen. We can be happy here, just like when we were kids." His smile grew blinding, expanding to fill his entire face. "Owen will change his mind about leaving, I'm sure."

I doubted that. Grandel, with his Armani suits and Rolex watches, didn't seem the kind to stay in a backwater like this longer than necessary. Then I realized what was really worrying Morris. "He isn't taking you with him?"

A strange look twisted across his face, like he'd swallowed the wrong way and had to choke it back down. He looked away and coughed. "Don't worry. It won't come to that. He's going to stay."

Poor Morris. He seemed like such a nice guy to have such a lousy brother. I changed the subject. "Is there a reason why someone would want to know in advance about a shipment of medical isotopes?"

He thought about my question without asking what was behind it. As if it were a logic puzzle rather than a possible security threat.

Nice and naive, despite his obvious genius. I felt a little bad about using him for info, but I didn't want to go to Grandel with my suspicions until I understood more of what was going on.

"The isotopes are extremely time-sensitive," he finally answered. "So if you knew a shipment was going out and you were able to stop it, theoretically the isotopes could decay to the point where they were unusable."

"Would setting off one of the radiation alarms, like the incidents you've already experienced, delay a shipment from leaving?"

"Sure. We'd need to check it for leaks, make sure security was in place—" His face clouded again. "Oh, you think someone wants to steal the isotopes, make a dirty bomb?"

Actually, I was hoping he'd tell me that medical isotopes couldn't be used for bombs. I didn't like the idea of Vincent's followers possibly intervening to bring about the end of the world themselves. "Is that possible?"

"Of course. See, a dirty bomb isn't really about killing or hurting people. There's not enough radiation to actually kill anyone, not unless you're too close to a large concentration that's unshielded. But the idea of *potential* radiation—that causes panic because people don't understand. And that panic is the real danger, what the terrorists really want: to terrify us."

"So the isotopes you ship, they couldn't be used to build a conventional nuclear bomb?"

"No. Atomic bombs are made with plutonium or highly enriched uranium. We start with low-enriched uranium and bring it to criticality, producing Molybdenum-99, which is then extracted and subsequently used to produce the technetium and other isotopes used in medical tests and treatments."

He shook his head. "People have been brainwashed into thinking any kind of nuclear event by definition cannot be survived. But even in the event of a real bomb or nuclear plant meltdown, simply staying inside behind a concrete wall will block the vast majority of radiation unless you're in close proximity." He suddenly ran out of steam, seemed surprised that he'd talked so much.

"Good to know." I wasn't sure if I should confide in him about what Vincent had asked me.

If Vincent was a real anti-nuclear crusader, then maybe he wanted to create a dirty bomb–like event and blame the plant to further his agenda. But Yancey's portrait of Vincent as a greed-driven manipulator looking for an easy score by muscling in on Grandel's company seemed more likely. "Do you have a shipment leaving anytime soon?"

"Sure. Tomorrow."

"I think maybe you'll want to increase security. I was talking to some of the protestors and they seemed interested in the next shipment of isotopes."

He looked truly startled. And a bit frightened, as if the real world didn't often impinge upon his sunshine-filled universe. "Our protestors?" He acted as if they were family. "Really? I don't believe it."

"Just add the security. For my peace of mind if nothing else."

"Sure, AJ. No problem." His mood and smile had returned to normal. "Anyone tell you, you're easy to talk to? I don't think I ever said so much in one sitting my whole life."

◆

By the time Elizabeth finished at court it was lunchtime. But before she could stop to eat anything—she'd skipped breakfast as well, felt like she was back in Philly rushing around and forgetting about everything except winning her next case—she had to convince AJ's parents to move into the summerhouse with David.

When she pulled into their driveway, she saw Frank Palladino's pickup truck parked there. As a foreman at Masterson Mining, one of the perks of working above ground was that he got to come home for lunch every day to his "lovely, blushing bride."

In a way Elizabeth envied the deep emotions that bound Frank and Edna together, but, after seeing how they treated AJ, their only living child, she wasn't sure that the price they'd paid—that AJ paid—was worth it.

Wondering if they'd pass that price onto their only grandchild, she walked up to their front door and rang the bell. Thankfully, it was Frank Palladino who answered instead of AJ's mother. Frank at least tolerated Elizabeth. His wife, Edna, tended to look right past her as if she wasn't there.

"AJ isn't here," Frank greeted her. As if she was a kid looking for AJ to come out and play. He started to close the door, but Elizabeth was prepared and slipped her foot over the threshold before he could retreat.

"I know. She's in South Carolina. David needs your help."

He glanced over his shoulder before stepping outside and closing the door behind him. "David? What's wrong? Is he okay?"

"He's fine." She quickly outlined the events of the night before and the judge's decision. "So you're the only ones left. Unless you want him to stay with Masterson."

She'd added the last hoping it would clinch things, but instead he nodded thoughtfully. "Mr. Masterson has that big house, all that help. He could keep a good eye on David. Better than we could."

Lack of sleep and an overabundance of frustration welled up inside Elizabeth. "You cannot be serious! He's your grandson—I can't believe you can't help out for just a few nights."

The door opened before Frank could say anything and AJ's mother joined them. "Frank, your lunch is getting cold."

Frank turned away as if by delegating David's care to Masterson, he'd solved the problem. Elizabeth could not accept that. "You do understand that without your help, AJ could lose her son. Forever."

Total hyperbole—at least she hoped it was—but given the dirty tricks Hunter and Masterson had already played, Elizabeth wasn't taking anything for granted. If they found any reason to prove AJ unfit to parent David, a sympathetic judge could grant custody to Masterson.

"What's she talking about, Frank?" Edna Palladino asked, still not making eye contact with Elizabeth.

"AJ needs you to stay a few nights at the summerhouse with David," Elizabeth answered her. "One or two nights at most. Just until she gets home."

Edna wrung her hands and glanced over her shoulder at the empty foyer with its closed doors. Elizabeth had seen firsthand what lay behind those doors, but she never thought that a house filled with junk would take precedent over family.

"Leave? Who'd look after the house?" Edna asked Frank. "All our stuff?"

Frank ushered her back inside. He stood on the threshold, turning his head to follow Edna's progress even as he spoke to Elizabeth. "I'm sorry. We can't help."

Then he slammed the door in her face.

◆

The rest of the kids, Ty's nieces and nephews and a few young cousins, were all outside playing in the woods. David had done most of his practice with his crutches on the mountain paths behind Ty's mother's house, but there hadn't been time to drive all the way home to get them this morning, so today he was stuck in his chair.

That was okay. He had his notebook and pencils and laptop, and the house had a good Internet connection, so he parked himself in a quiet, shady corner of the side porch of the hundred-year-old log cabin and went to work analyzing Jeremy's case.

Years ago, when he was a little kid, he'd devoured Sherlock Holmes, but now that he was learning more about science, he realized that you couldn't rely solely on pure logic and deduction. You had to throw a little imagination into the mix as well. What Einstein used to call his thought experiments.

David began with a simple timeline scrawled onto a blank page in his notebook:

*Dinner finished, 6:45, Flora fine.*

*Me and Elizabeth left for the summerhouse around 7:10, Flora fine.*

*Returned to find Jeremy smelling of alcohol and Flora passed out at 8:35.*

Which left an hour and twenty-five minutes for someone to drug Jeremy and overdose Gram Flora. Flora said she'd fallen asleep right after dinner, when Jeremy had begun washing the dishes. But the dishes hadn't been finished, so the attacker, call him Mr. X, must have interrupted Jeremy in the kitchen. Somehow surprised him and incapacitated him so fast that he didn't make enough noise to wake Flora.

David frowned at what he'd written. He drew a line down the middle of the page and made a new column for questions:

*Why didn't Jeremy remember anything?*

*What skills were needed to incapacitate Jeremy so quickly—he was a big guy, in good shape.*

*How did Mr. X know about the insulin?*

That one was easy—everyone around town knew about Flora's diabetes.

*What had Mr. X given Jeremy to make him pass out?*

Hmm . . . he drew a line connecting this question to the first and opened his laptop, doing a quick search on "amnesia, drugs." Wow. There were a lot, mostly called "date-rape" drugs. Rohypnol looked most promising.

Okay, but how had Mr. X (he drew a quick sketch of a bad guy with a black cape and mask in the margin) incapacitated Jeremy in order to give him the drug?

Another quick search and he quickly narrowed it down to variations of choke holds. That or a Taser-type of weapon, but best he could find, that should have left a mark somewhere on Jeremy.

So Mr. X knew where Jeremy and Flora lived, had counted on the door being unlocked—most of the people around here never locked their doors, something that still amazed David after growing up in D.C.—snuck in, and waited for his opportunity. Premeditated.

David chewed on his pencil, not liking the answers he was getting. The attacker could have been there watching them all through dinner. That was spooky—and not the good kind of spooky. More like creepy serial killer stalker spooky.

He adjusted his drawing of the attacker, morphing him into more of a ninja-type. Mr. X could have snuck up on Jeremy while the water for the dishes was running, choked him until he passed out, carried him into the living room and dosed him with Rohypnol or one of its variants, then poured the booze down his throat.

Which was bad news for Jeremy, because unless the hospital tested for it specifically, Rohypnol was almost impossible to detect once it was metabolized.

Maybe some would be left in the vomit. Gross, but it was something.

Back to the timeline.

*Mr. X chokes Jeremy, drugs him, say five minutes.*

*Once Jeremy's out of it, forces the booze down his throat. What, maybe ten minutes? Glug, glug, glug, yeah, ten minutes.*

*Leaves Jeremy on couch. Finds insulin, overdoses Flora, sets up kitchen to make it look like Jeremy had done it in a drunken stupor . . . another five to ten minutes.*

*And leaves. Twenty to thirty minutes tops.*

Which still left the fifteen to twenty minutes needed for the insulin to start to make Flora sick.

If it wasn't for Jeremy reacting to the alcohol and drugs and vomiting most of it up, he could have died of alcohol intoxication or maybe even aspirated. If it wasn't for David arriving to find Flora, she could have died as well.

David gripped his pencil hard as he scribbled out the masked figure, adding layer on layer of black until his pencil snapped. He leaned back, feeling out of breath and shaky and empty and sick all at once.

Why, why, why? Who would want Jeremy or Gram Flora dead?

Because whoever Mr. X was, he didn't care if people died. People David loved.

And no one was looking for him. No one even believed he existed. No one except David.

# NINETEEN

Morris led me to the front entrance of the plant and we walked inside. I'd been expecting something like a military installation, but instead the main lobby felt like an upscale hotel: the domed ceiling with the sunlight coming in through the glass panes, steel pillars, marble floors, a steel-and-wood open staircase leading up to offices situated above us in a horseshoe configuration. People in business attire walked along the second-floor promenade, carrying folders and looking important.

The security officer at the main desk greeted us. Unlike his compatriots outside in their uniforms, he wore a suit and tie, making him look more like a concierge than a deterrent to would-be terrorists. Of course, that was Grandel's goal. To relax prospective investors without scaring them with thoughts of security.

"Welcome, Ms. Palladino," he said with a smile that appeared genuine. "Please place all your personal belongings in here for safekeeping." He slid a plastic bin across the desk toward me.

I dropped my car keys and cell phone inside. "For security, right? So no one takes any pictures?"

"Actually, it's not so much about security as safety," Morris said.

"Some embedded controllers in the auxiliary diesel generator control rooms have EPROMs which have been known to be erased by camera flashes in the past, triggering a generator trip—"

I had no idea what he was talking about, but it didn't sound good.

"Plus, we wouldn't want anything to get crapped up," he finished with a smile.

I stared at him. "That's not going to happen, right?"

"Oh no, of course not. We're not even going anywhere near—I was just joking. Owen says I never know when to shut up. Sorry, I didn't mean to make you nervous or anything."

It was clear I was the one making him nervous. "No, that's fine. Just checking."

He seemed relieved. The guard gave me a coat-check receipt, and Morris led me to yet another checkpoint beneath the stairs. It looked like a metal detector. I remembered the knife in my boot—maybe I should have left it with the guard? But I was already feeling uncomfortable, dressed in my Hardy & Palladino polo shirt and jeans. I hesitated, watching as Morris stepped inside the unit, put his hand on a small pad, then turned and put the other hand there.

"It's a portal detector," he explained. "To make sure no one is coming in with a high count."

"You mean radiation?"

"Sure. Step inside, it's painless. That's right. Just put your palm there. Hold it. Now spin around and put the other hand there. Perfect. See, nothing to it."

I guess you'd get used to it if you had to do this every time you went in or out, but I was kind of freaked, holding my breath, waiting for an alarm klaxon to sound and a red siren to go off as everyone screamed and ran for cover. Instead it was just a bored technician reading a computer screen.

"You're clean," she said, waving me through and handing me a lanyard with a small plastic bob that resembled a pedometer hanging from it.

"What's this?"

"Personal dosimeter," Morris answered, flipping a similar device that he wore clipped to his breast pocket. "See the screen? It's just reading background now. It will change if there's any radiation. If it gets too high that red light will blink and an alarm will sound."

Great. I was glad they were so careful, but it was certainly a bit nerve-wrecking. Morris opened one of a pair of frosted glass doors and held it for me. I stepped into a glass-walled corridor.

"The observation deck," he explained. "You can look into the control room where it's all happening without disturbing anyone."

The control room looked pretty much right out of the movies. Four curved workstations, each staffed by two technicians, filled with flashing buttons, computer terminals, keyboards, and a ton of switches. Surrounding them along the outside wall were large monitors showing every aspect of each reactor: primary coolant levels, pump flow, secondary coolant, emergency coolant, status of control rods, reactor core temperature, time until isotope extraction, and a lot of other things I had no idea about. In between each computer screen were old-fashioned analog dials, presumably revealing the same information.

"What happens if the electricity goes out?" I asked, fascinated by the power any one of those tiny buttons held, yet also thinking that it all looked very, very boring.

"Unlikely, since we not only generate our own but also have backup generators. Plus, we have two sets of manual controls for everything. One inside here and a second inside the containment area. Redundancy on redundancy, that's the key to safety."

Safety definitely seemed to be paramount. There were signs everywhere—I even spotted one at the exit from the control room reminding people to tie their shoes. Of course, trip on your laces, fall and push the wrong button in here and you might unleash a nuclear holocaust.

"So, how does a meltdown happen?"

He smiled. "You're thinking about what happened in Japan. Those reactors were forty years old. With today's technology, there's no good reason for a meltdown—especially not with my design. Redundancy, remember."

"But in theory?"

"In theory, you'd have to somehow let the reaction chamber reach critical mass and then fail to control the ensuing reaction. This would lead to overheating—thus the term meltdown. All that heat and pressure would need somewhere to expand beyond the containment chamber, and that would lead to an explosion." He shook his head. "Never happen. Not here. You'd need the control rods to fail as well as both the primary coolant pump plus the secondary plus the emergency coolant."

"In all four reactors?" I was still fascinated by the idea that somehow four reactors were safer than one. "Or would just one failing cause a chain reaction?"

"But see, that's the problem—if any one of those highly improbable things occurred, we'd simply scram the affected reactor—"

"Scram?"

"Dump the control rods into the core. That stops all fission in about five seconds flat and lets the reactor cool down. Problem solved before it starts."

I looked at the operators, staring at their gauges and monitors and dials and readouts. Maybe it was as simple as Morris said.

I wished I had as much faith in humans' ability to mess with nature without leading to tragic consequences as he did.

A woman entered the glass doors behind us. "Ms. Palladino?" she asked in a bright voice. "Mr. Grandel will see you now."

Owen Grandel's office was on the second floor, so I had to go through the portal detector again—sighing in relief when I was pronounced "clean" once more—and then up the lobby stairs. The room looked like any other chairman of a prosperous company's would: modern furniture, nice paintings on the walls, fresh flowers in vases, and a large picture window behind the desk. Only, Grandel's view was into the control room.

Grandel nodded to one of the leather chairs across from his desk as he finished typing something on his computer. His assistant brought me a glass of iced tea without asking—and somehow managed to get it just right, not too sweet.

"I met Vincent last night," I started, wanting to see how Grandel took the news.

His face filled with distaste. "Bastard is blackmailing me with that cult of his. Wants to take over my company or a large chunk of it."

"So I heard. He asked me to find out when the next isotope shipment is scheduled for. Made me wonder if he was planning something."

"Or if he asked you because he knew you'd tell me and we'd delay the shipment—which we can't afford to do—or waste time and money on new security measures." He tipped his chair back as he considered the angles.

"Could Vincent be behind the accidents?"

"Believe me, I thought of that. But we rechecked all our personnel, there's no one with ties to him, no one showing any sudden influx of cash that he could have bought off—I don't see how he could have orchestrated it. But I do think he's behind the false alarms."

"False alarms? You never mentioned those."

"Radiation sensors are extremely sensitive—especially the ones on the perimeter. A few weeks ago we began getting a barrage of alarms but when we checked with handheld units, there was no trace of actual radiation triggering them. Morris recalibrated the remote sensors and they all now send any alarms to his handheld first so he can verify them. It seems to have solved the problem, but I still can't help but wonder if Vincent was behind it."

"Maybe testing your responses—but why? He doesn't really want the plant shut down, that would defeat his purposes. He just wants to inconvenience you enough so you'll give in to his demands."

"Which I have no intention of doing. I'll burn this place to the ground and start over before that happens."

I didn't believe that for a moment, but Grandel's fists were clenched so tight that I thought he might well burn Vincent's place down. Then I remembered what Noreen had said about Grandel's parents dying in a fire.

A shudder ran through me before I could stop it. Both Grandel and Vincent were dangerous men playing a dangerous game, and I was caught in the middle. "What could he or anyone have to gain by causing false alarms?"

"I have no idea."

I considered my next words carefully. I needed to give him a plan of action—but I didn't want to escalate things between Grandel and Vincent. "Well, you do know that your so-called protestors are being paid, don't you?"

That made him sit up. "Really? By who? Vincent?"

"That's beyond me—you'll need a PI or someone who can trace the money to prove it. I'm also certain that Vincent is behind the online campaign against you. In fact, he's hired a media consultant named Yancey. The guy's pretty slick—has the protestors from the church filming this morning."

"Filming what?"

"When I saw them they were just singing a song, but Yancey likes drama, so don't be surprised if there's a repeat of yesterday's fainting episode or something like it."

He tapped his fingertips together in an irritating rhythm. "Any ideas what to do about it?"

"Preemptive strike. Get some video of the other protestors enjoying your hospitality and get that out there first—so it will be clear that Vincent's people staged it."

"Good idea. Security can grab the footage from their cameras. Anything else?"

"There are two reasons people around here don't like the plant—actually they boil down to one solution."

"What's that?"

I thought about the young couple I'd met with the protesters. "Jobs. Folks around here want a chance to make enough money to raise their families and keep them here. And that means jobs."

"But we've hired locally as much as we can. You can't exactly ask an out-of-work shrimper to man a nuclear reactor."

"I understand. But most of the people who do work here— where do they live?"

"Most, up in Beaufort. Houses are cheap there right now. A few of the supervisors live down in Hilton Head."

"Right. And that means a long drive either way." I stood and gestured to the large-scale map spread out on the wall beside him. He swiveled his chair to follow my finger as I traced the path of the river as it led to the sound. "Most of this land on the other side of the river is for sale—probably at pretty good prices given how old the FOR SALE signs looked. Now, if you bought several parcels and developed them together, you could turn it into a nice community. Views of the sound or river, forest, easy access to the highway."

"Ms. Palladino," he sounded affronted, "we're in the medical isotope business here, not real estate investment."

"Think about it. You could create homes for your workers as well as work for the folks who already live here. How much is that kind of long-term public satisfaction worth to your company?" Not only would it provide jobs, it might help to revive the community, and Lord knew, from what I'd seen, Colleton Landing could use all the help it could get.

He pursed his lips, considering. "This housing slump is bound to end soon. Might make for a good investment. Worth it if it got the community off my back." He nodded, a short jerk of his chin. "I'll have my people look into it."

"I also heard that you guys were supplying electricity to the surrounding area? Some kind of cooperative deal with the power company?"

"Morris set that up. We generate more than we can use. Could've sold it to Palmetto, but Morris got all soft-hearted and set this up— I was on the road, getting us capital, and he's giving away potential profits."

"Maybe it's lucky he doesn't have your business sense." Jeez, I was starting to sound like Elizabeth, practically stroking his ego. But it worked. "Again, think of the community relations windfall."

He nodded slowly. "Good work, AJ," he said, sounding half-surprised. "I'm going to call a press conference in time for the noon news. No sense waiting—I'd like to share some good news with my investors for a change. You'd better get changed."

"Me? None of this has to do with the environmental impact of the plant; you don't need me up there with you." I re-grouped. "I wouldn't want to steal the spotlight or anything."

"No worries there. You won't be saying anything. I just want everyone to know you're on my side."

I blinked, uncertain of how to get out of this. Because even though I was willing to take his money for helping him, I was most definitely not on Owen Grandel's side.

Then I thought about Floyd and Noreen and the other people I'd met like Elise and her husband. If it meant helping them, I could sacrifice a little self-esteem.

What could it hurt?

Totally demoralized after her conversation with AJ's parents, Elizabeth drove to her house three blocks away. Her own parents had divorced when she was young, and although they both doted on her when she was with them, she'd never really felt a part of either of their lives as consumed as they had been by their careers. She'd learned the lesson so well that she'd grown up emulating them, putting her career before everything until she dared to raise her head long enough to see Hunter for who he really was and make a stand for herself.

It occurred to her that maybe her parents and the Palladinos weren't so very different—different forms of obsession, maybe, but still so wrapped up in their own lives that they couldn't see the living, breathing family that required their nurturing.

AJ wasn't asking for much—and David wasn't asking for anything except the love of his grandparents, the chance to finally have a family. Yet it was too much for them to give.

No wonder she and AJ were friends. Despite their disparate social backgrounds, they had a lot more in common than it initially appeared.

She pulled into the driveway of her house. Although it had been in her father's family for generations, Elizabeth had never been here until after her father's death. It was a Victorian painted sky-blue with an inviting wraparound porch. Elizabeth smiled every time she saw it and realized that it was hers. It was exactly like the houses she used to pretend her dress-up dolls would inhabit when she was a little girl. The house of her dreams.

Today it looked more like a home than ever. Ty and Nikki sprawled across the front steps, talking to Jeremy, who was watering the plants hanging from the porch roof and suffering from neglect.

"You get settled in all right?" she asked Jeremy, joining Ty on the steps without even worrying about getting her skirt dirty. What was a little dry-cleaning bill when she'd just lost AJ's son for her? Nikki sensed her distress and rolled her head to one side so it slid beneath Elizabeth's palm.

"Yes, thanks." Jeremy seemed nervous, fiddling with the watering can even though he'd finished. "I don't know how to thank you."

"Just don't run off—this house is the collateral for your bond."

Whoops. She hadn't meant to remind him of that. It's just what was foremost in her mind—how much she'd risked on a person she barely knew.

He sank into the rocker beside the door, still clutching the watering can. His face collapsed as if the weight of his predicament had finally caught up with him. "It's bad, isn't it? They're going to crucify me."

"Don't worry. That's what you have me for," she tried to reassure him but couldn't muster the energy to lie convincingly.

"I know a few criminal attorneys," Ty put in.

Elizabeth doubted Jeremy had the resources to afford one. "Let's give it a day or so—the tox screen might help."

"But who's going to watch over Flora until then?" Jeremy asked.

"She's not coming home until tomorrow, the doctors said. In the meantime, I asked AJ's parents if they'd move into the summer-house. Judge Mabry won't let me care for David anymore—he thinks it's a conflict of interest." She explained about Masterson's fight for visitation and how it had evolved into an emergency custody battle.

"I can't imagine Frank or Edna leaping at the opportunity," Ty said.

Elizabeth hung her head, concentrating on her fingers kneading Nikki's thick coat. "They didn't. I'm not sure what to do."

"Maybe sending David to Masterson's isn't a bad idea," Jeremy said. "Kid figures out how horrible the old man is, he might beg the judge to deny visitation."

"I'm not sure how much stock the judge is going to put in a kid's testimony compared to Masterson's money."

"And AJ would kill you," Ty added. "She thinks Masterson is poison."

"What other choice do I have?"

"Call AJ. Get her permission for him to spend the night with his friends at my mom's house. Every kid his age goes on sleepovers during the summer vacation, why can't David?"

Elizabeth doubted if that was exactly what Judge Mabry had in mind, but it was worth a shot. She dragged out her cell phone and tried AJ. No answer; it just rang and rang, didn't even go to voice mail.

She hung up and was about to try again when Ty's phone rang. "David, slow down," he said after listening for a moment. "What? Mister who? Okay, we're on the way."

"What was that all about?" Elizabeth asked.

"David. He thinks he figured out what happened to Flora and Jeremy."

Jeremy leapt up so fast the rocker banged back into the window shutter. "Great. Let's go."

"You can't, Jeremy. Judge's orders. And neither can I," Elizabeth added with regret. She hadn't realized how quiet having a day without either AJ or David around could be.

"Well, no one can stop me," Ty said, climbing to his feet. Nikki did the same, ears perked with anticipation. "I'll call you as soon as I know anything."

"Keep an eye on David," Elizabeth said.

"I will." He and Nikki drove away but Elizabeth couldn't stop staring after them. AJ was the one who got premonitions, who trusted her gut instincts, but suddenly Elizabeth had a feeling that something very bad was coming.

Then she spotted Frank Palladino's pickup turning down her block. He pulled to the front curb, rolled down his window, and waited for her to come to him.

"I'll be watching over David tonight," he said once she was within hearing distance. "First time in thirty-two years of marriage that Edna and I been separated, I'll have you know. Tell the boy I'll be there end of shift."

His delivery was gruff, mitigating any sense of gratitude Elizabeth might have had. But she remained diplomatic—after all, it would be AJ paying the price once she was back home. "Thank you, Mr. Palladino."

Jeremy leaned out over the porch railing, head cocked up as he scanned the sky. "Do you smell smoke?"

# — TWENTY —

Grandel dismissed me, and I headed out to the parking lot to retrieve my travel pack with the dreaded power suit and heels stuffed inside. I was so focused on not looking forward to this damn press conference that I almost didn't notice the heat trying to broil me alive as I walked down the concrete path. No meandering around the riverside road this time—I wanted to grab my stuff and get back inside the air conditioning as fast as possible.

I'd just reached the second perimeter fence when I saw Morris, head down as he stared at his bright green handheld computer's screen, wandering along the inside of the fence.

"Hi, Morris," I said as I joined him. "What are you doing?"

He frowned and didn't look up, still squinting at the screen. Like me, he had no sunglasses, so he shielded his eyes with his hand. "Kermit says we got another perimeter alarm, but this one is different. It's moving."

"Moving? How can that be?" I glanced up and across the parking lot. The only movement I spotted came from the other side of the outer perimeter, where the protestors were congregated. "Could it be someone in the crowd?"

He shook his head. "No, the sensors triggered were on this inner fence. Over near the river, then they moved this way, then—I lost it." He kept walking until he hit the road on the outer boundary of the parking lot, then crossed over to where the fence followed the river. "Right here is where it started."

I looked at where he pointed. It was high tide, and the water came up past the fence, seeping into the mud on this side. The mud looked churned up, like something had been digging.

As I crouched down to get a closer look, Morris crossed the road back over to the parking lot, following his phantom signal. I heard a faint skittering noise and looked around.

There, edging out from beneath a pickup truck two rows in was a very large claw. Attached to an even larger leg.

"Morris, look out!" I sprinted across the road.

Before I could reach him, the alligator lunged at Morris. He backed up, toward me, slamming into the hood of a car, tried to put it between him and the gator, but the gator simply took the direct route below the car.

Morris ran across the road, back to the riverside, with the gator in pursuit. The gator almost caught him, its jaws snapping inches away. Then it suddenly stopped, its tail whipping back and forth, and just sat there making this strange hissing noise like a teapot boiling over.

Morris backed away until he ran out of room, his back to the outer perimeter fence, the gator facing him head on.

David had had an obsession with gators a few years ago and we'd watched every Animal Planet and Discovery special on them at least twice. Those TV gators hadn't acted like this one. They didn't chase after prey, they waited in the water for dinner to come to them. Maybe this one felt threatened?

"You're between it and the river," I called. "Try moving to one side, give it room to escape."

Morris gulped and nodded, sidling toward the corner of the fence that faced the outside where the protesters were. Worst came to worst, he could climb it.

At least I hoped he could climb.

The gator didn't head toward the water now that its path was free. Instead, as soon as it caught sight of Morris moving, it swung its head and lunged again, a weird uncoordinated lurch that was fast but still missed Morris, like the gator was drunk and not seeing straight.

Morris was pinned against the fence. There was no way he could turn his back to the gator long enough to climb it—it would be all over him.

"Stop," I called. "Don't move!"

Gators had two blind spots, I remembered. Directly behind them and directly in front of them. I crept up within a few feet of the gator.

It was bigger than I'd thought—at least seven feet long. Vicious claws gouged the grass as it lay there, its mouth wide open, teeth sharp and ready for dinner.

"Stay right in front of its nose," I told Morris, my voice dropping low—not sure why, as I doubted the gator cared if I was screaming or whispering. "It can't see you, especially with its mouth open."

Maybe the gator did hear me, because it snapped its jaws shut. Morris shuffled a bit so that he remained lined up in front of it, and it didn't move closer.

"What now?"

Wish I knew. I reached for my cell phone. Who to call, though? Owen. He could alert his security as well as the police and whoever dealt with rabid gators on a rampage. Because there was definitely something wrong with this gator—it couldn't seem to walk straight and it was acting way too aggressive.

I dialed. Owen's phone rang. Before he could answer, the gator twisted its head enough to spy me—and for some reason my presence only made it more furious. I decided it must be male, because I seem to have that effect on some men. Okay, most men.

It snapped its jaws again then sprang toward me. I jumped back, dropping the phone. The phone skittered across the black top, Owen's disembodied voice wavering as it bounced. The gator tracked the phone then pounced on it, crunching it between its massive jaws.

Then it lay there, still except for its gaze searching for me. I realized that its eyes were bloodshot—more than bloodshot, they were actually bleeding. Its snout, too, blowing snot-bubbles tinged blood-red as it hissed.

Gulping back my panic, I edged back into its blind spot, directly behind it again. Morris stayed frozen, now in clear view of the gator.

"Don't move a muscle," I told him. "Just stay still. I'll go get help."

"Please. Don't leave me." He was breathing so hard and fast I was worried he'd hyperventilate.

"You'll be okay." Even I didn't believe me. "I'll be right back."

"No. Don't go."

I hesitated. Big mistake. The alligator whipped its head around again, spotted me, and lunged forward.

◆

Jeremy pointed over Elizabeth's head from the porch. "I think I see smoke."

She shielded her eyes with her hand and looked. AJ's father was concerned enough that he opened his door and stood on the running board to get higher, also searching the sky. He must have seen something Elizabeth didn't, because his body jerked straight and he said, "Edna!"

He jumped back into the truck. Elizabeth still didn't see the smoke, but she opened the passenger side and climbed inside.

"Call 911," she shouted to Jeremy, who already had his cell phone out. "Tell them it's the Palladinos' house."

Frank peeled away from the curb before Jeremy could reply. He took the corner onto Main with two wheels in the air, leaving Elizabeth grasping at the door handle and bracing herself against the dash. One more sharp left onto Maple and she could see the smoke.

No one else had spotted it yet—too hot today to be outside if you weren't away at work, she guessed. She didn't see any flames, just smoke billowing from the rear of the house, silhouetting the Cape Cod's gables like a storm cloud. It didn't even smell all that bad—no worse than a trash pit fire, and folks around here were used to those.

Frank skidded to a stop and was out the door before Elizabeth could open hers. He had lung problems but seemed to have forgotten all about them as he raced up the walkway. Elizabeth followed behind, easily catching up as he collapsed, gasping, on the porch steps.

"Edna," he said weakly, one hand reaching out to the front door.

"I'll get her." Elizabeth knew it was crazy talk before the words escaped her lips. Who in their right mind rushed into a burning building without protective gear? But if she didn't, Frank would, and the way every breath was making his entire body heave with the effort, it would be the death of him for certain.

She took her suit jacket off and used it to muffle her face as she reached for the front door knob, testing it for heat. It wasn't hot to touch. That should be good. The fire seemed to be mostly smoke, but that could change quickly if she opened the door and fanned the flames with extra oxygen.

"Are you sure she's in there?" she asked Frank, who struggled to lift his head and nod.

"Go back to the truck, honk the horn, get some help," she told him, relieved when her voice emerged untainted by the terror pitching through her.

Then she opened the door.

# TWENTY-ONE

I'm no squealing girly-girl. I grew up hunting and running feral in the mountains of West Virginia, for goodness sakes.

But I have to admit, the sight of a seven-foot prehistoric throwback armed with fangs and claws coming at me had the grits and shrimp I'd eaten earlier scratching their way up my throat.

The only weapon I had was the knife in my boot—and suddenly I was thanking Mom for whatever crazy impulse had caused her to buy it and give it to me. I pivoted, took a second to reach down and grab the knife, then leapt around to the other side of the road, the side along the riverbank.

The gator didn't take the hint and slide back under the fence and into a nice cozy mud bath. Oh no. Instead he seemed fixated on me, although now that we were closer I could see that there was blood coming from his mouth as well from his eyes. Leftovers from breakfast, or was he sick?

The way he lurched, stalling then lunging erratically, made me think he was sick. Great. As if it weren't bad enough having a healthy gator whose movements I might be able to predict, I had to have the rabid gator from hell after me.

"What should I do?" Morris called, now safe on the other side of the road since I'd drawn the gator away from him. "Try to distract him?"

For a genius, that didn't seem like a very bright idea. Liable to get us both killed.

"Find something I can throw in his path. Maybe he'll go after it like he did my cell." Unless I stripped, the only things I had to throw were my belt and the nylon knife sheath.

I skidded the sheath at him first. He jerked his snout in to follow it but then was immediately back on me. Okay, maybe the smell of cowhide would interest him more.

Holding my knife between my teeth, I undid my belt and slid it free. I swung it so the shiny buckle caught the light, hopefully sparking his attention. It seemed to work. He stopped a few feet in front of me, his body heaving like he was short of breath.

I let the belt go, aiming it at the mud at the base of the fence, hoping he'd take the hint. It was obvious that given the tides and shifting mudflats, the fence worked better at keeping people out than gators.

The gator raised his snout, mouth open, sniffing the air as the belt flew past. His jaws snapped shut again—the damn thing had caught it!

I held my breath, hoping he'd settle down for a nice nibble, but no, he simply swallowed and then lunged back towards me again, like a hungry toddler wanting more.

And I had nothing.

Elizabeth braced herself for an explosion like she'd seen in the movies when someone opened the door to a burning building. No pyrotechnics here. Just a billowing cloud of smoke escaping.

Once it cleared, she saw that most of the smoke seemed to be coming through the cracks around the kitchen door. From there it curled up the staircase where the ceiling rose.

All the doors in the foyer were closed—thank goodness for Edna's compulsions. The bad news was that Edna was most likely upstairs in her office.

Elizabeth gathered her courage and jettisoned the voice of logic that kept telling her she didn't owe these people anything, that she was no hero, that she should wait the twenty minutes it would take the volunteer fire company from Smithfield to arrive, that her place was outside, watching, not in here doing . . . that she was no AJ.

The thought propelled her forward. In the few months that she'd known AJ, she'd seen AJ put herself in the line of fire— literally and figuratively—to protect total strangers time and again. Elizabeth knew she wasn't a hero like AJ, but she'd be damned if she'd let AJ's mother die, not if she had it in her power to do anything about it.

By the time her mind had processed all this, her body had already rushed halfway up the steps, clinging to the railing as the smoke obscured her vision, keeping her head down as low to the floor as possible. Finally, she ended up on her hands and knees in an effort to stick to where the air was fresh.

It wasn't hot—at least no hotter than outside—but her clothes were glued to her by a layer of fear and sweat. She wasn't sure the jacket around her face was actually helping much; every time she took a breath she inhaled a lungful of linen fibers and began coughing, but she kept it around her nose and mouth just in case. At the top of the steps she upset a pile of Edna's junk, raining boxes and unfolded clothing down on top of her.

Nothing heavy, that was good, but it slowed her down as she crawled through it, using her hand to guide her path as much as her eyes. The smoke was thicker up here, the fresh air quickly diminishing, even when she pressed her nose to the floorboards. The sound of a woman coughing carried through the smoke and the ringing in her ears. Her vision had diminished to a small circle directly before her, but she knew the sound wasn't coming from AJ's room, where Edna kept her office. It came from the opposite direction—AJ's dead brother's room.

Of course. Edna had preserved Randy's room as a shrine to his memory and all-too-short life. She'd never abandon it.

Elizabeth reached Randy's room. The door was shut. She reached up. Doorknob cool to touch. She turned it and pushed the door open. Less smoke in here. She dove inside the room and quickly shut the door behind her. Then she looked around.

Edna Palladino lay motionless on Randy's bed. Was she dead?

Lurching to her feet, Elizabeth took the three steps needed to reach Edna. Edna opened her eyes. "Leave me alone."

Not dead. That was good. "We need to get out of here. Now."

"I'm not leaving Randy." Edna closed her eyes again.

Well, hell, Elizabeth didn't have an answer to that one. More smoke seeped around the door, dark fingers grasping for a way in.

Elizabeth left Edna where she lay—Edna was petite but there was no way Elizabeth would be able to carry her down the steps. She wrenched open the window, hoping the fresh air would buy them some time. When she looked around, Edna still hadn't moved.

"You want to stay with Randy?" she asked, grabbing the wicker basket half-filled with the fifteen-year-old dirty laundry of a teenaged boy. "Then you'd better get moving."

She shoved the screen out of the window and emptied the contents of the basket outside as well. Socks and shirts and jeans and underwear fluttered through the air, landing in the shrubs below.

Randy's room faced the front yard, and she saw Frank sitting with his back against his truck's front tire, watching. He lurched to his feet, mouth open like he was shouting something but Elizabeth couldn't hear him.

She wasted no time. She swept the contents of Randy's trophy shelf into the basket. As she moved to throw them out the window, Edna launched herself off the bed to stop her.

"No!" she screamed.

It wasn't much of a fight. With one well-placed shove, Elizabeth pushed the older woman back and hoisted the basket high. "You want to save Randy? Then lead us out of here. Now!"

Edna stared, her eyes so dilated that Elizabeth could barely see any color left in them. She heaved in a breath and nodded. "Okay."

"Good." Elizabeth leaned the basket on the windowsill, judging their chances with climbing down. Not good—there were no handholds, and if they missed the shrubs they'd hit the sidewalk. She readjusted her jacket-muffler. "Take a pillowcase, wrap it around your face. Okay. Let's go."

They opened the door and crawled into the hallway. It was totally black with smoke now, and both women began coughing almost immediately. But the stairs weren't far, and going down was faster than going up. Within a few minutes they found themselves lying on the porch, gasping in the fresh air, each with one hand clinging to the laundry basket of memories.

◆

A loud jangling sound came from behind me. The fence at my back shook and swayed. The gator stopped his approach, and I dared to glance over my shoulder.

Morris stood on the other side of the road, a security guard beside him, talking into his radio. The protestors had gathered along the fence, watching my impending gator death match.

All of them except Liam. He'd thrown a piece of tarp over the razor wire at the top of the fence and was scaling it as easily as I walked up a flight of stairs. Like he did this kind of thing all the time.

The gator was close enough for me to smell its fetid breath, but it seemed as mesmerized by Liam's actions as I was. With every move Liam made, the gator let out a strange hissing noise like a steam engine getting ready to blow.

I took the opportunity to sidle to the side, then circle back behind it again. Now its focus was on Liam, who'd just reached the top of the fence and was carefully circumventing the razor wire.

"Don't jump," I called out, making sure I was in the gator's blind spot. "It'll be on you before you can stand."

He grunted his agreement. Then he jerked his head up and shouted to a guard who had drawn his pistol. "Are you crazy? You'll just make it angrier or you'll hit one of us."

The guard was a good thirty feet away. Liam was right, I wasn't about to trust my life to a stranger's aim. And I was too far from the fence now to climb it; there was no way the gator wouldn't get to me first.

"You know how to use that thing?" Liam nodded to the knife I held at the ready.

I realized immediately what I needed to do—use Liam as bait while I took out the gator. Hated to admit it but I was scared spitless by the thought of getting closer to the beast, much less having to kill it. But it was obviously sick, and better me taking it out fast than giving it time to attack someone else or let the guards use it—and us—for target practice.

Once, back home hunting with Ty and Cole when I was a kid, I'd shot a deer and hadn't made the kill shot I'd intended. The deer had run off into the woods, and we had to chase after it. The sound it made—that wounded cry—haunted my nightmares for months, not loud but such a sorrowful keening, it rattled my marrow. Ty finally caught up with the deer, me and Cole not far behind. I knew it was my responsibility to not allow that poor animal's suffering to continue, but I just stood there crying at the pain I'd wrought.

Finally Ty had done what I couldn't. With one quick motion of his knife, he put it out of its misery.

I never aimed at any creature again—not unless I knew I had a kill shot.

But that was with a rifle. This time it was me against a creature that wore its own armor, my only weapon a blade shorter than its claws or fangs.

The gator whipped its tail, gouging a furrow in the mud. Liam swung over to my side of the fence, clinging to the chain link just below the razor wire. The gator charged the fence, furious that its new prey hung just out of reach.

The crowd gasped as the fence bowed, the force of the collision almost dropping Liam into the gator's open, waiting jaws.

No time to think about being ready or to come up with another plan. I had no choice but to leap past the gator's writhing tail and onto its shoulders.

Raw, primal power surged below me as the gator whipped its snout back and forth, trying to dislodge me. I hung on, squeezing my thighs tight; I only had to last a second, just long enough to plunge my knife blade into its eye.

Liam jumped down from the fence and pushed the gator's lower jaw up, snapping its mouth shut, and holding it closed. The gator fought in his grasp, bringing him to one knee.

"Hurry," he said, muscles straining to control the beast.

I have to admit, I flinched and shut my own eyes at the last second, just as the blade pierced the gator's eye and sank into the goo beneath. I held the knife with both hands and pushed with all my might until I felt a crack like an egg bursting open. Then I pushed some more until the hilt stopped, unable to go further.

The gator writhed and twisted, and then, with a mighty heave, flipped over, doing a death roll.

Liam lost his grip as it whipped its snout around, aiming for my leg. I twisted away, its claws snagging on my jeans, tearing the fabric but missing my skin. It kept rolling, and suddenly I was trapped underneath its massive body, its weight squeezing my breath away.

It gave a final shudder then stopped, still on top of me.

I couldn't breathe. All I could see were the scales—gray greenish brown, slimy with algae and mud. A terrible stench filled my lungs as I fought to heave it off of me. I couldn't budge it.

Then the weight lifted and I saw the sky again and was able to breathe. Liam shoved the gator to one side and stood above me, a strange smile twisting his ragged features. He made a sound like a boar snorting when he extended his hand to me. It took me a second to realize he was laughing.

"What the hell's going on here?" Owen shouted from behind us. "Back. Everyone back."

I looked up to see reporters' cameras aimed at me and the dead gator. Then Liam pointed a finger at me. "Hey, your thingy there is beeping."

Thingy? I raised the dosimeter on its lanyard. Turned it around, and sure enough, there was a bright red light flashing and it was emitting a beep that was gradually growing louder.

Liam backed away. Pulling the dosimeter over my head, I held it out to Morris and Owen and the security guys and they backed up as well. The only people who crowded forward were the damn reporters on the other side of the fence—until more security pushed them back.

I had the sinking feeling that this couldn't be good.

Morris confirmed my suspicions when he said, "Call the health physicist and get the decon unit set up."

"I'm contaminated?" I shouted across the increasing distance between us. "But how?"

I swung my hand with the dosimeter down. The gator lay beneath it. The beeping grew more insistent.

"Drop it on the gator," Morris told me.

I did. The dosimeter landed beside the half-open jaw of the dead gator. The beeping crescendoed to a piercing wail like a smoke detector.

Just my luck. I wasn't attacked by a rabid gator but a radioactive one.

# TWENTY-TWO

Elizabeth watched as the firefighters brought load after load of junk out to hose down and rake through, searching for any stray embers or hot spots. There was no way Judge Mabry was going to let the Palladinos take even temporary custody of David, not after this. But hopefully he wouldn't know anything about it until tomorrow, after AJ was back.

Smoke burned her eyes and she finally turned away. Looked like almost the entire town had turned out to witness Frank and Edna's humiliation. Some just stared, others nodded as if they'd seen this coming, and a few even laughed and pointed.

One man leaned against his car, talking earnestly on his cell phone. He looked over the top of his designer sunglasses at her and did a finger wave before beckoning her to join him.

Elizabeth walked slowly over to Hunter—he looked entirely too pleased for this to be anything good.

"I agree, Judge, the best interests of the boy must be protected. No, I don't believe any psychological evaluation has been completed yet, but wait, here's Ms. Hardy, I'll ask her." He put the phone on speaker and held it out to Elizabeth. "Do you know if your client's parents have been evaluated by a psychologist, in light of this recent revelation?"

His tone was neutral but his smirk was downright nasty. Hunter at his best—and worst.

"No, they haven't." Elizabeth hated to admit it, but she couldn't lie to a judge. "Not to the best of my knowledge, sir."

"Mr. Holcombe is concerned about their ability to adequately supervise the child in question tonight."

"Actually, your Honor," Elizabeth dared a slight hedge of the truth—at least she hoped it was the truth, since Ty said he'd be talking to AJ. "Ms. Palladino gave permission for her son to spend the night at a friend's house. A sleepover with other children, supervised by responsible adults including a sheriff's deputy."

"That's all well and good if this was a normal day, your Honor," Hunter tugged the phone away from Elizabeth. "But the child has suffered several traumas in the past twenty-four hours. His mother abandoning him—"

"She left on a business trip. I'd hardly call that abandonment." Elizabeth was forced to yell into the phone when Hunter tabbed the speaker off and held it against his ear.

"He finds his great-grandmother near to death at the hands of a trusted employee—"

"Allegedly. We think—" Too late for the judge to hear what she thought about Jeremy's case, Hunter turned his back to her.

"And now he learns that his maternal grandparents are suffering from some kind of obsessive-compulsive hoarding that is so severe that it could very well have killed them."

Sacrificing all dignity, Elizabeth actually leapt into the air to snag the phone. "Your Honor, we can address all this tomorrow at the hearing—"

"I'm sorry, Ms. Hardy," the judge overrode her voice. "Until the hearing, I'm granting emergency custody to Mr. Kyle Masterson, the paternal grandfather. Mr. Holcombe, you may transport the child to the Masterson house at your earliest convenience. I'll see you both with your clients tomorrow."

"But, your Honor—" Elizabeth was pleading to a dial tone.

Hunter pocketed his phone and pushed his sunglasses up his nose with one manicured finger. "Gee, it's a good thing I happened to drive along when I did, saw this for myself. Of course, it was my duty as an officer of the court to report my observations to the judge immediately."

He cocked his head and smiled pityingly at her. "I'm sure you would have called him yourself if you hadn't been so busy dragging your client's parents out of their little"—again with the look over his sunglasses and down his nose—"fire trap of a house. See you tomorrow, Elizabeth."

He swung his car door open, then paused as if waiting for her to bounce back with a snappy rebuttal. Not today. She was too exhausted to waste time or effort on Hunter. She had bigger things to worry about. Like saving AJ's family.

◆

Ever wonder what happens after you've been contaminated by radioactive material, like, say, an alligator?

Abject humiliation. That's what.

It took the form of a stern-faced woman wearing full banana-yellow protective regalia who introduced herself via bullhorn as a "health physicist" and a pudgy, pasty-faced man who didn't introduce himself but his protective suit had "NRC Representative" written in letters big enough for me to read them from where Liam and I stood near the gator carcass.

Seems they were at an impasse. There were extensive decontamination facilities inside the plant, but to get us there (us, including the gator that was already beginning to stink in the heat—but that could have been my imagination) they had to figure out a way to transport us without spreading the contamination.

The health physicist, NRC guy, Grandel, and a bunch of other folks stood arguing—while Grandel's crew quickly screened the protestors and reporters for contamination, then ferried them away from the site, confiscating all the media footage in the name of security.

Thankfully Morris gave up on the debate, went to the inside guard gate where the tram was parked, and drove it up to us. By the time he arrived, several other workers had had time to don their protective suits—talk about roasting in a sauna, their faces were flushed red and beaded with sweat—and together they began to wrap the gator in lead blankets in preparation of hoisting him into a metal box they had wheeled out.

Morris loaded Liam, me, the health physicist, and NRC guy onto the tram.

"It's totally washable, easy to decon," he shouted to the two encased in their protective suits, waving an arm over the tram's plastic seats and metal walls.

I didn't notice the clouds growing black overhead or the wind picking up until we were speeding toward the rear of the plant in the rickety, overloaded tram. I craned my head out and glanced up at the sky, then back to the parking lot, where more workers were busily crouched over the black top.

"They need to finish before it rains," Morris told me. "We don't want to risk any contaminated runoff into the river."

"So how did the gator get exposed?"

"I have a theory on that," the NRC man spoke up. "I believe the gator drank from the puddle of contaminated water during the incident earlier this month. The timing would fit for his symptoms to be so severe."

"No, impossible," argued the health physicist. "The half-life—"

"All right then, perhaps the gator ate an animal who drank the water. That would concentrate the radiation in the animal's tissues prior to ingestion by the alligator. Similar cases have occurred at Savannah River."

The woman opened her mouth then snapped it shut.

"Hanford also had problems with that," Morris put in. "Rabbits. No matter what kind of fence they built, they couldn't stop the rabbits from getting into things. They've also had contaminated pigeons, squirrels, mud wasps, and once had an entire dumpster filled with contaminated fruit flies, which in turn contaminated some frogs and—"

"All right, all right. You've made your point," the woman said. "We'll see if your theory," she nodded to the NRC man, "holds true once we go to necropsy."

He jerked his chin as if accepting a challenge.

Liam and I exchanged glances. "What about us? Does that mean we're going to get sick, too?" I dared to ask.

"Heavens no. Once we get your clothes off, that will take care of a good 90 percent of the contamination," Morris said cheerfully.

"And a few runs through the shower will deal with the rest nicely," the physicist added.

I looked down at my boots. They were new, and I'd only just broken them in to where I liked them. "What are you going to do with our clothing?"

"Destroy it, of course. It's nuclear waste."

Exactly what I was afraid of. I glanced at Liam, who either had gas or the slightest hint of a smile cracking his stony features.

"Do we get to shower together?" he asked, surprising me.

I glared at him. "What would Reverend Vincent say?"

He shrugged. Definitely was smiling—in fact, his expression resembled the gator's right before he'd chomped my belt. "It will give us time to get better acquainted."

Right. Alone time with Vincent's pet gargoyle. I could hardly wait.

We pulled up to the loading dock, where workers had prepared a clear path to the decontamination facility. Just as I stepped off the tram, the skies opened up and it began to rain.

◆

David felt some of his dread lift when he spotted Ty's Tahoe coming up the drive. Ty would understand why he was so worried about Mr. X and since he was a police officer, he had the power to do something about it. Finally, someone who would take him seriously.

Ty and Nikki bounded up the steps. "Hey there, Champ. Hear you got a break in the case for me."

David showed him his timeline—now carefully copied on a blank piece of paper without the scribbles or doodles. Adult style. "So, you see that instead of trying to find evidence against Jeremy, you need to be looking for someone else."

"This Mr. X."

"Right. He'd be a man, probably military or law enforcement training—"

"Just because he knows how to apply a choke hold?"

David heard doubt in Ty's voice. That was okay, he'd done his research. "Because he knew how to do it without leaving any bruises or marks behind. That's not something you'd learn just by taking a martial arts class."

Ty nodded, his face turning grave. "Okay. I'll buy that. How else can we narrow him down?"

"He'd have access to whichever drug you end up finding in Jeremy's system—"

"Which might take weeks. If we can find anything. Some of those drugs are virtually untraceable."

Darn. David should have thought of that himself. "Well, he'd need a reason to do all this. Let's face it, anyone around here with a grudge against Jeremy would do the same thing they'd do back in D.C.—they'd cap his ass."

"Your mother know you talk like that?" Ty chided.

They both laughed—David's mom would never put up with him using street slang. "Seriously. If we can just figure out the why, then we should be able to figure out the who."

"Big first step there. Especially if Jeremy wasn't the end target but just the means to something or someone else."

That was an interesting way to look at the problem. But it opened up all sorts of parameters that complicated things. A lot. "Like who?"

"I wish I knew." Ty stretched his legs and got to his feet. "You eat lunch?"

"Yep. But I could go for another sandwich. Your mom bakes the best bread—don't tell Flora I said that, though."

"Don't worry, your secret is safe with me. By the way, they said Flora can probably come home tomorrow."

"So I can stay with her again tonight? Someone should be watching over her. Or are they going to let Jeremy?"

"No. The judge won't let Jeremy anywhere near her for now. He's staying at Elizabeth's house. And there's another slight wrinkle—"

"What?"

"Another judge said Elizabeth can't watch over you either. Seems like your Grandfather Masterson is taking your mom to court to mandate visitation."

"What's that got to do with Elizabeth?"

"It's complicated, but with your mom out of town, they're trying to see who'd be best to watch you. Probably gonna have some other folks for you to talk to as well. Like a counselor or social worker or the like."

David slumped back in his chair so hard that the front wheels bounced. "So I'm getting shuffled around like the kid no one wants on their team for dodge ball. No one wants me, do they?"

"No, just the opposite. They all want you, but that means a judge has to sort things out, and whenever you get the courts involved in this kind of stuff it gets complicated. But it's just for one more night until your mom is home tomorrow." Ty paused. "I'm trying to work it so you can stay here—would that be okay with you?"

Ty was the first one who actually bothered to ask David what David wanted to do with his life. That's why David liked him so much. He got it, he really got it.

"Yeah. That'd be cool."

"I have the night off, so Nikki and I will be here as well. Plus all the cousins—we can build a fire in the pit and camp out in the meadow if you want."

Now that sounded like fun. "Great. I'll have to go home and get my stuff first."

Ty's mom appeared at the door leading from the front of the house, accompanied by a strange man in a fancy suit. He must have come in the front door—the door that only strangers and guests used.

"I'm afraid we'll have to alter those plans a bit, young man," the stranger said.

David didn't like his tone. Neither did Nikki, who made a low rumbly noise in her throat and stood, planting herself between the stranger and David. Even Ty, usually the most laid-back and polite adult David knew, altered his stance so that his hip with the gun was aimed away from the man and his hand rested on it.

"David," Ty's mom said, "this is Mr. Masterson's lawyer. He's been ordered by the judge to take you to Mr. Masterson's for the night."

"Like hell he is." Ty surprised David with his sharp tone. "I have permission from David's mother to watch over him. I'm not relinquishing him to anyone unless I hear it from the judge himself."

The stranger smiled, but it wasn't the kind of smile that meant "of course, I understand." Rather, it was the kind of smile David had seen on bullies right before they launched a sucker punch. He wanted to warn Ty, but realized he didn't have to. Ty was already watching the man's hands even as they reached inside his jacket pocket for his phone. Nikki was at full alert as well.

"That can be arranged, Deputy." The man dialed. "And then the boy comes with me."

◆

Hutton watched the response to the Palladino fire from a perch in a kid's tree house across the street. Perfect. No collateral damage and exactly the outcome Masterson wanted.

It had been almost too easy given the state of the house. The biggest challenge had been in creating the opportunity for a fire that wouldn't get out of control and feed on all the fuel available. With all the crap shoved into the small house, he was surprised it hadn't burned down on its own long before he came to do his job.

He called Masterson. "You got what you wanted. They're homeless and humiliated. Happy now?"

"Good. Now that Edna's little personality quirk is a matter of public record, only one person stands between me and my grandson."

Jeez, why was it Masterson always had to talk like he was the villain on a soap opera?

Masterson thought that talking like he was God and everyone else was a peon to either do his bidding or get stepped on along the way somehow made him superior to the people whose lives he trampled.

Hutton had bought into it when he was a kid. Had kissed ass along with the others trying to secure their jobs, feed their families.

Not anymore. Now he understood the truth.

Like most of Hutton's clients, Masterson was just a narcissist, plain and simple. He didn't care about other people because he truly didn't see them as people—in his world there was only room for Masterson.

Usually it didn't bother Hutton too much—the money more than made up for suffering fools like Masterson. But for some reason, this job was starting to drag on him. Maybe he'd feel better when this was over.

"You ready to finish this?" Masterson asked, eerily in synch with Hutton's own thoughts.

"Yes sir."

# — TWENTY-THREE —

Here's how decon works. Everyone not glowing in the dark puts on funky yellow Tyvek overalls with hoods—like what you see in movies.

So they put on their overalls, then rubber boots, followed by two pairs of gloves, blue next to their skin and white ones on top. Then they go crazy with the duct tape—tape their boots to their pants, tape the gloves to their sleeves. Next, they put on goggles along with respirator masks and then pull their hoods up over everything.

It was our turn next. First, we got "frisked." We stood, palms up, arms out, while the Tyvek people slowly scanned us with a hand-held machine—they called it a GM, but it looked like a Geiger counter to me. They waved a little paddle close to our bodies and listened to the clicks.

Morris got off easy—barely any clicks, only slightly more than the background radiation, the guy scanning him said, so he got to keep his clothes.

Liam and I weren't so lucky. The clicks revved up to humming-bird speed on both of us—me a little more than Liam. So we were sent to open-doored cubicles and told to strip down to our underwear. Each article of clothing was packaged in a special biohazard bag and we were scanned again. Still too many clicks.

Next, they rammed Q-tips up our nostrils and dug around in our ears and mouths. Of course, all through this, all I could think about was David seeing footage of his mom skewering an alligator. I was putting the poor thing out of its misery, but you know the media, they don't always tell it like it is.

Morris assured me that wouldn't happen and that the security guys confiscated all the footage. Poor guy actually believed that. I know how reporters work. They don't give up a good story, not for anything. My only hope was to get out of here as fast as possible and call David.

But then they sent us to the shower, shouting instructions on how to wash our hair and rinse it away from our body, to work from the head down with the soap and disposable scrub brush they gave us, and they wouldn't let us turn the water hotter or colder, insisting on a tepid temperature that had me shivering anytime a body part escaped the water stream. I was in there so long my skin looked more wrinkled than Flora's.

They spread a pad out on the floor for us to stand on and gave us disposable towels to dry off with. Then again with the scan. Fewer clicks, but still not good enough. Back to the showers. Scrub, rinse, repeat.

After three cycles my skin felt raw and my hair literally squeaked, it was so clean. Another scan and everyone was happy, congratulating themselves on their good work.

Liam and I were given hospital scrubs and paper slippers to wear. Lovely. I wondered if Grandel would excuse me from his press conference.

No such luck—he arrived, huddled with the man from the NRC for a moment, then came over to me. "I was going to fire you for that stunt."

"Stunt? I didn't plan that. And by the way, you're welcome for saving your brother's life. Not to mention anyone else who might have gotten too close to that gator."

Two sheriff's men came inside and made a beeline for Liam.

"What are you doing?" he demanded.

"Arresting you for trespassing. Might throw in a federal violation, homeland security or the like, if your boss doesn't play nice," Grandel told him. I didn't like the smug expression he wore as the deputies clicked their handcuffs on Liam.

"Owen, he only jumped the fence to help me. You can't arrest him for that."

"Sure I can. But like I said, if Vincent backs down, removes his protestors and those Internet postings, I'll be happy to drop the charges."

Liam's glare was more terrifying than the alligator. "Vincent is the least of your problems."

"Really? Shall we add terrorist threats to the charges?"

The deputies began to haul Liam out the door, but he dug in his heels and looked over his shoulder at me. "AJ, we need to talk. Come to the station. It's important."

Wow, three complete sentences. At once. It must be important. I took a step to follow him when Grandel grabbed my arm. "Where do you think you're going?"

I shook free, tired of his attitude. "Home. My work here is over."

He didn't acknowledge my words and continued, "We have a media event to arrange. Now that we've demonstrated the efficiency of our decontamination response and the danger of Vincent's protestors, it's time to quiet the rest of the public's fears. And Hermes is giving us the perfect opportunity."

"Hermes? The hurricane?"

"It's going to hit in about twelve hours, give or take."

"Here? But I thought we weren't even in its path."

"Wind shear forced it to change course. Now we're smack dab in the bull's eye. And they're saying it's going to be at least a Category

Four storm when it does hit. You and I are going to make sure the public sees exactly how safe this plant is, even under the most drastic conditions."

"How are we going to do that?"

He looked surprised. "It was your idea, AJ. We're going to invite a film crew inside and ride out the storm right here."

◆

Ty had tried to call David's mom but hadn't been able to reach her. So after he talked with the judge—on speakerphone so David could hear it as well—he'd had to let the lawyer guy take him.

David spent the trip sulking in the back seat. Lawyer guy didn't seem to mind—he never even bothered to introduce himself, much less try to make conversation. They'd stopped at the summerhouse and David had grabbed his crutches and shoved a change of clothes into his backpack, then they'd driven straight to Mr. Masterson's house.

Well, not really a house. More like a mansion. There were iron gates at the front that you had to drive through after being buzzed in, which was kind of silly because the brick walls they were attached to stopped as soon as they hit the forest a few yards away. It was all just for show.

Once inside, a maid had shown David to his room. "Mr. Masterson is working from home today and will be joining you for dinner," she said after David refused to let her unpack his bag for him. "He suggested that you might want to take a nap beforehand."

A nap? He hadn't taken a nap since he was, well, a baby. Jeez.

She left him alone and he was free to explore. The room was huge—as big as the entire summerhouse but without any walls except between the closet and bathroom. The bathroom was wheelchair accessible, which was nice. And besides the big bed and matching dresser there was a whole living room area with a wide-screen

TV, gaming console, huge leather couch, his own refrigerator and snack bar, even a microwave to make popcorn in.

Okay, impressive. But David knew Mr. Masterson was trying to show off. Just like with the fancy gates out front. Instead of this fancy could-be-a-hotel type room, David would have much preferred a smaller room filled with his dad's old stuff. That way he could get to know him better, at least know what he was like when he was a kid growing up here.

"You settling in okay, son?" Mr. Masterson startled David. He was always doing that, walking in without knocking. And calling David "son" but never using his name—maybe he had a hard time remembering it?

Probably not. Not when he was running a company the size of Masterson Mining. David pivoted his chair around to face his grandfather.

"Thank you for having me, sir," he said, even though he'd rather have stayed with Ty or at the hospital with Flora.

Masterson nodded, seemed pleased with David's response. "You're welcome. If things work out the way I plan, you'll be spending a lot more time here. Won't that be nice?"

No, not really. But David didn't want to be rude. "Yes sir. Thank you."

They stared at each other across the vast open space of the room. David could tell that Mr. Masterson didn't know what to say either. He tried to think of common ground. "Do you think maybe I could see some of my dad's stuff? I'd love to learn more about him."

Wrong thing to say. Masterson's face drooped like a cloud blocking the sun, and his hands balled into fists like he wanted to hit someone. Not David. Maybe his mom. David figured Mr. Masterson still blamed her for Cole's death.

"It's all packed away." Masterson's voice came out in a rush, like the words tasted bad. "Why don't you get some rest now? I'll see you at dinner."

He left and closed the door behind him. David stared at it. What did Mr. Masterson want from him? Didn't he understand that David missed Cole as well? Maybe more so since he'd never gotten a chance to really know his dad?

Grownups. Sometimes they got all caught up in their own little worlds and never thought about anyone else.

Instead of napping or playing video games, David grabbed his crutches and hauled himself out of his chair. He needed to practice using them and felt cooped up after being in his chair all day.

During his last checkup at Children's, his doctors had tried a new medicine for the spasticity in his legs—the main reason why he had to use his chair—and it was really helping. He still sometimes got all tight and they'd scissor out of control, especially if he was tired or nervous. But the more he used the crutches, the fewer spasms and the stronger he got.

It was hard work, but to be free of his chair? Totally worth it.

He opened the French doors leading out onto his own private terrace and went for a stroll.

Halfway around the house he encountered another set of French doors and tall windows, all open to the afternoon breeze. It was shady on this side of the house and he was hot, so he leaned against the wall and took a break. A large planter with some kind of evergreen in it blocked most of his view inside the room, but he knew from his previous visits that it was Mr. Masterson's study.

He really didn't mean to eavesdrop, but when Masterson walked into the study and sat down at his desk, his back to David, David wasn't sure how to leave without making a scene. His crutches made too much noise on the brick pavers for him to just slip away. Plus, he had to admit, he was curious about how a man got to be as rich as Mr. Masterson—what better way to learn than watching him work?

Mr. Masterson made a strange sound, not the kind you'd expect from a rich businessman—it sounded more like the grunt a caveman might make when he lost the tug-o-war with a pterodactyl over dinner. Not that cavemen and pterodactyls coexisted in real life and if they did it would be the caveman who was dinner . . .

Flinging his stray imaginings aside, David concentrated on staying as quiet and still as possible. Not easy to do with his crutches jammed into his sides and his legs twitching with fatigue.

Masterson unlocked a desk drawer, pulled out a small cell phone, and lay it on the center of his desk blotter. All he did was stare at it.

Just take the damn thing and go, David thought, trying to ignore an itch between his shoulder blades. If he shrugged or moved to make it go away he'd make a noise, but the more he tried to ignore it, the stronger it got.

Finally, Masterson blew his breath out and pulled the phone to him. He dialed, put it on speaker, and set a small recorder alongside it.

"Hutton." The man who answered sounded young and mean. Like he didn't want to be bothered.

"Masterson here. It's a go. Time to finish what you started."

"I'm ready. But I still need her exact location."

"I just got it. Colleton Landing, South Carolina. The Landing Motel. Room Eight."

"Told you travel costs extra. Fifty thousand."

A long pause. David's itch had vanished, replaced by a trickle of sweat and an icy finger of fear.

Mr. X. That's who Mr. Masterson was talking to. And he was going after his mother next. The man on the phone was going to kill his mother.

"Deal," David's grandfather answered. "It has to be finished before three o'clock tomorrow. She can't make it to that courtroom. Do you understand?"

"I understand. Consider it done."

# TWENTY-FOUR

Before I could tell Grandel he was crazy—something Elizabeth would probably frown upon anyway—Morris bounced in. "I used the spare keys to get your stuff from the SUV." He beamed at me as he handed me my bag. "Now you can change into real clothes."

"Thanks, Morris. That's very thoughtful."

He flushed and bobbed. Grandel rolled his eyes at his older brother—I wanted to slap the superior look off his face, but restrained myself. Not for Elizabeth this time, but because Morris so adored his brother.

"I'm going to change now." I left them for the locker room next door that Morris directed me to and returned a few minutes later dressed in another pair of jeans and a Hardy & Palladino polo—my second to last one. On my feet I wore the pair of old tennis shoes I'd thrown in for emergencies or in case I ever actually did make it to the beach.

Morris was gone but Grandel was still there waiting impatiently. He frowned at my choice of ensemble. "Come on, we've got a lot of planning to do. We need to take the focus of the story off you and put it back on me and the plant."

"If you want, I can leave. Let you take the spotlight." I hoped he'd take that option, for I was really feeling like I needed to get home. Fast.

I wasn't certain if it was a mother's intuition or just the feeling that I'd already pushed my luck as far as it could go down here. After wrestling a rabid alligator, I wasn't sure if I was up to riding out a hurricane while stuck inside a nuclear reactor.

Grandel's secretary caught up to us just as we cleared the portal monitor and made it upstairs to the office level. "The front gate just called. They have Reverend Vincent and his people there. They'd like to speak with you. In person."

Grandel's face darkened. "Tell them—"

This time I was the one who took his arm. "Tell them to send them in. Thank you."

The secretary glanced at Grandel for confirmation. He opened his mouth, then closed it and jerked his chin into a nod. We arrived at his office. As soon as the door was shut he spun on me. "What the hell?"

"This is your chance. You and Vincent need to come to some kind of arrangement—and this storm gives both of you a perfect way to save face."

"How so?"

"It's an act of God, right? Use it."

He shook his head hard and fast as if shuddering down a revolting mouthful of some exotic dish that he was too polite to spit out. "That man wants to destroy my company. I'll be damned if—"

The door opened again and the secretary ushered in Vincent, Yancey, and Vincent's assistant, Paul.

"Be careful there, Owen," Vincent said. "I wouldn't tempt God any more than you already have."

"Hah. You're one to talk. What do you want?" Grandel marched behind his desk and stood with both hands flat, pressed against it, leaning forward.

"Paul, please wait outside for me," Vincent ordered. Paul frowned but then nodded and left to return to the secretary's antechamber. Vincent ignored Grandel's posturing and sank into one of the leather chairs, stretching his legs as if it were a beach chaise lounge. "You know what I want. A seat on the board. And 10 percent. I think that's fair."

"Fair? Is that what you call it? I call it blackmail, you sonofa—"

Yancey stepped into the fray. "Gentlemen, gentlemen."

I hoped that I was the only one who heard the undercurrent of self-satisfied sarcasm in his tone. If he could get Vincent what he wanted, then Yancey was in for a big payday. I couldn't really complain—stopping Vincent's protestors would go a long way to my getting paid as well.

Most important, it would allow the plant to succeed, which would mean more jobs and money flowing to the people of Colleton Landing.

"May I suggest a compromise?" Yancey said.

Both men were engaged in a staring match and neither seemed to hear him. Or neither wanted to acknowledge the possibility of compromise first.

"It's quite simple, really," Yancey continued. "We work a contingency deal. After all, no one wants to pay good money without results."

"What the hell is he talking about?" Grandel snapped.

"He means you guarantee me a seat on the board and I'll guarantee my people stand down."

"I think we can do better than that, sir," Yancey put in. "Use this hurricane to our advantage?"

"That's what she said," Grandel nodded to me.

"Yancey's right," the words practically choked me. Me and Yancey thinking along the same lines? Frightening. "The hurricane is an act of God, a sign from God, so to speak. Once the plant weathers the storm, Vincent can use that to convince his followers that the plant has been, I don't know, cleansed or something—"

"Purified by the wrath of God!" Vincent sang out in his tent-preaching voice. "It's good, I like it."

"You think that's worth a spot on my board?"

"I do. And once I help you convince the Japanese to invest, you'll sweeten the pot with a 10 percent finder's fee—payable in stock options."

Grandel slit his eyes as he thought. "Five percent. What about the other protestors?"

"I have no control over them, but Yancey here could probably help."

"She," Grandel nodded to me again. I was beginning to wonder if he'd forgotten my name. "She thought showing a few people how safe this place is would be a good idea. I thought with the storm, we could shoot a little film, invite a few civilians to weather it out inside with us—under close monitoring, of course."

Vincent nodded slowly. "Not a bad idea."

"I have some media contacts that would love a story like that," Yancey said. "Want me to stay and shoot the footage and voice-over?"

I should have been mad at Yancey co-opting my job, but instead I grabbed at the chance. It meant I could go home all the sooner—hopefully beating the storm—and I wouldn't have to deal with Owen Grandel or Reverend Vincent anymore. A win/win for all concerned. The plant saved, the town saved, along with my sanity.

"Yancey's very good at that kind of thing," I said, waiting for lightning to strike.

"What do you say, Grandel? I'm in for 5 percent. Is it a deal?" Vincent asked.

Grandel twisted his mouth but then nodded. "Deal. I'll draw up the papers, you get your people prepared. We can't afford any naysayers, so you'd better deliver or this whole thing could blow up in our faces."

"Don't worry, I can control my people."

Paul, Vincent's assistant, knocked and opened the door. He hesitated, then took a step forward. "Reverend? Shouldn't we just let God's wrath deal with this heathen and his infernal machine? Why waste our time here?"

Vincent leapt from his chair, grinning. "You're right, Paul. As always. We're above all these mundane enterprises."

He stalked out, leaving Yancey behind with me and Grandel. I rushed after them. "Wait, what about Liam?"

"What about him?" Vincent asked, as a security guard led us downstairs, where Vincent and Paul retrieved their cell phones and other personal property.

"Aren't you going to ask Grandel to drop the charges?"

Vincent's look of disdain made it clear that he wasn't going to waste any precious bargaining chips on Liam. "The Lord will provide."

Which translated to: Liam was stuck in jail. All because he tried to save me.

David remained frozen in place, trying to defy Einstein and push his own atoms into the vast subatomic spaces between the molecules of the brick wall beside him. On a strictly quantum mechanics level, it should have been possible, but all that he achieved was to shrink back into the shadow behind the plant a few centimeters more.

He had to warn his mom. But how? His cell phone was back in his room, and the last thing he wanted was to spend another minute here. Besides, with Mr. Masterson still sitting right there, he wasn't sure he could move anywhere without being caught.

His mouth went dry. Would Masterson kill him, too? Was this all some kind of revenge, killing everyone in Mom's family to avenge his son's death?

Maybe it wasn't even about Mom—after all, if he was totally honest with himself, he had to admit that he, David, was really the person responsible for Cole's death. He was the one the bad guy had been chasing when Cole got in the way.

He closed his eyes, the better to deny that those were tears making his cheeks wet, and pressed his cheek against the brick wall, trying to block out the image of Cole dying. His dad. Dead. Because of him.

The bricks gouged into his skin. It hurt. Even so, it couldn't compare to the pain he felt inside.

He'd only known Cole for a few days. No wonder Mr. Masterson had gone crazy after he was gone—and he must be crazy, trying to get nice people like Gram Flora and Jeremy and his mom killed. David tried to imagine the pain he'd feel if something bad happened to his mom.

Definitely enough to drive a person crazy.

The sound of a man's voice brought him out of his reverie. It was Ty! What was he doing here?

Mr. Masterson was asking the same thing. "The boy is resting, if that's why you came, Deputy Stillwater. Although I don't appreciate your barging into my home this way. I'm perfectly capable of caring for my own grandson. Certainly better than that mother of his."

David risked a peek through the plant's branches. Ty stood on the other side of Masterson's desk, looking down on the old man. He looked angry—you could tell because his face was a blank, like he'd wiped it clean of emotion and forced everything back. The only other time David had seen Ty look that way was when his dad died.

Mr. Masterson should have been scared by that look—David was—but he didn't seem to notice, instead kept his head down, fiddling with some papers on his desk like Ty wasn't even there.

"Actually, Mr. Masterson," Ty finally answered, "I'm here investigating an attempted murder."

"Really? I thought you'd already caught the man who tried to kill Flora—that gay nurse, right? What happened, did he slip away?" Mr. Masterson smiled as if he'd made a joke.

Ty didn't return the smile. "No. But we're still investigating. New evidence has come to light."

"Really? What kind of evidence?"

David frowned. There was no new evidence—Ty had as much as said so before the lawyer guy dragged David over here.

"Mr. Masterson." David could practically hear the fake-smile in Ty's voice. "Even though you're good friends with the Sheriff, I can't discuss an ongoing investigation."

"Then why exactly are you here, Deputy?"

"It occurred to me that there haven't been any unexplained accidents like this in Scotia since the night ten years ago when AJ Palladino almost died. I'm sure you remember that night. You were the last person to see her before she was forced off the road by one of your coal trucks."

A long pause. Masterson squared off the papers on his desk and leaned back, regarding Ty. "That's not what the authorities concluded at the time. The official cause of that accident was attempted suicide by a disturbed young woman. There was no evidence of any other vehicle, certainly none of mine, being involved."

As interesting as the conversation was, David realized that this was his chance to escape. While Ty kept Masterson's attention occupied, he could slip back around the house. Ty must have parked out front—or maybe better, near the rear of the house where there were lots of trees. He didn't have Nikki with him, which meant she must be with the Tahoe, so he would have wanted to park some-place where she could wait safely.

All David had to do was make it to Ty's car and he could get out of this place before Masterson knew he was gone. Then he and Ty could go save his mom.

Before it was too late.

# TWENTY-FIVE

I followed Vincent and Paul outside. The wind was blowing so hard that the rain had turned horizontal, slicing through the air like karate chops.

"Paul, would you kindly get the car?" Vincent asked.

The younger man nodded. Before he could head out into the storm, the door behind us opened. Morris rushed out, clutching his messenger bag as always. "AJ, great! You're just the person who can help me."

"What's wrong?" I had to raise my voice to be heard above the wind. And this wasn't even the hurricane, not yet. I had a hard time imagining how bad things could get when Hermes hit.

"The shelter I erected for the protestors collapsed. The guards are busy clearing the debris from the road. Can you help me get everyone to safety?"

"Of course."

"We'll help, too," Paul volunteered. "We can carry a bunch in the Escalade."

"Now, wait a minute, Paul," Vincent interrupted. "I'm not sure we should interfere—"

"Oh, it'd be a blessing, Reverend," I told him, enjoying his discomfort.

He glared at me, glanced at his fancy leather shoes, then finally nodded. Paul dashed out into the storm, down the path to the parking area. A few minutes later he returned. We all piled into Vincent's fancy SUV. It was big—like being inside a small school bus.

The guard at the inner checkpoint waved us through. Once we rounded the curve to the outer perimeter I saw that the guards there had their hands full.

The wind had torn the canopy and tarps from their poles and the entire structure had collapsed onto the road, along with the tables, chairs, fans, solar panels, and bales of hay. But the wind and debris wasn't the only problem—a large palm tree had toppled over, landing on one of the cars parked on the side of the road.

"Where will we take them?" I asked Morris.

"They can wait in the lobby until the weather breaks and it's safe for them to drive home."

"Isn't that against the rules?"

"We have security there, it's not like they can go any further. And it won't be for long." He glanced out the window at the black clouds whipping through the sky. "I hope." He took out his Kermit and began typing. "Satellite images show it should clear in an hour or so."

"So this isn't part of the hurricane? Is it still headed here?"

He chuckled and shook his head. "Sorry, but this is a routine summer thunderstorm around here. The satellite is showing some spots of possible tornadic activity, as well."

"Tornados?"

"Happens a few times a month this time of year."

I glanced outside. The palm trees were bending to the wind, the river obscured by wind-whipped waves and rain. "And the hurricane?"

"See for yourself." He handed me the handheld computer. The map showed the classic circular swirl of a hurricane, but when I compared it to the map's scale I realized that Hermes had grown massive.

You didn't need to be a meteorologist to realize that its course would bring it on shore somewhere between Savannah and Charleston—and we were sitting right smack-dab in the middle.

"The way its speed is picking up, we don't have much time," Morris continued. "Maybe eight hours or so."

Paul parked us just beyond the outer security checkpoint. Before he could shut the engine off, Elise, the young pregnant woman I'd spoken with in the morning, ran up and yanked his door open. "Please, help me. He's trapped, you've got to help me!"

◆

Once David made it out of earshot of the office, mainly by hugging the wall and not using his crutches until he was at a safe distance, the rest had been easy.

He found Nikki waiting beside Ty's Tahoe with her water bowl and a chew bone at her feet. He gave her a quick pat and let himself into the back seat. That was the easiest part—the Tahoe had a keypad lock for the doors and Ty used David's mom's birthday as the combination.

David lay down on the floor between the back seat and the front seats, covering himself and his crutches with Ty's windbreaker and bulletproof vest. The hard part was waiting—it was hot inside the Tahoe and his crutches were digging into his side.

Finally, he heard footsteps and Ty calling to Nikki. He opened the rear hatch, sending her into her protective crate in the back, then got into the driver's seat and started the engine. They began down the driveway. Once they passed the iron gates, David relaxed.

"You can come out now," Ty said.

David remained frozen, holding his breath. Surely Ty wasn't talking to him.

"You don't really think Nikki would let anyone into the vehicle without alerting me, do you? Come on out, David. It can't be comfortable down there under all that stuff."

Damn. Busted. David pushed the jacket and vest off him and poked his head up. Ty pulled the car over to the side of the road and then turned to look at him, stretching one arm across the back of the seat. Not like he was angry, more like he was disappointed.

"Do you have any idea how many people will be looking for you?"

David lifted his butt onto the seat. Nikki poked her snout through the grate and licked his cheek happily. "I need to go to South Carolina."

"Why? To see your mom? There's a hurricane coming down there. The last place she'd want you is anywhere near the storm."

"That won't stop him. Ty, she's in danger. He's going to kill her."

"He who?"

"Mr. X. I heard Mr. Masterson talking on the phone. He's paying someone to kill my mom."

Ty didn't even blink—almost as if he wasn't surprised by David's accusation. "And this person is heading toward South Carolina?"

David nodded, staring hard into Ty's eyes, trying to will him to get the car back on the road. "We have to hurry. He's already left."

"Hmm." Ty took out his cell phone, punched a few buttons. "No answer from your mom. Going straight to voice mail. Maybe the storm knocked service out. Let me try the local police."

"What can they do? We don't know his name or what he looks like. Please. We need to go get Mom. Now." David hated the way his voice cracked, but he couldn't help it. It was taking everything he had not to cry in front of Ty. Nikki produced a mournful plea in David's defense. One of the reasons he liked her so much—she always took his side.

"We know what your mom looks like and where she's at. Let me just find out who's in charge down there." He typed some on the laptop mounted on the console between the two front seats. "Looks like it's a county sheriff's substation." He raised his cell phone again. "Busy. The storm."

"Can't you use the computer to alert them?"

"I am," Ty said, resuming his typing. "But if that storm hits sooner than expected they're going to have their hands full—probably do already if they're evacuating."

"So, we need to go ourselves," David urged. "I googled it. It's only a seven-hour drive."

Ty frowned—something he almost never did. But then he turned the key in the ignition and put the car in gear. "I'll bet I can make it in six."

◆

I jumped out of the SUV and joined Elise. "What happened?"

She pointed to the river. "Nate, he went to get the truck and the tree blew over, he swerved and went into the water."

I had to look twice to make out the gray pickup truck obscured behind the swaths of blue nylon tarp caught on tree branches. It was several yards into the water. I couldn't see the front end of the truck at all, but the way the back end was angled, it looked like it was sinking fast.

"He didn't come back out," she continued. "Please, you have to help him."

"I will. Send the others," I told her. I sprinted across the road to the riverbank. The wind spun the torn tarp like a banshee, trying to tangle me up in yards of fabric.

Morris joined me, helping to fight through the nylon that blocked our vision. The truck had plowed past the foliage on the bank and was a good ten feet out into the water. The current was dragging it down and rolling it over onto the driver's side. The cab was already almost totally submerged—only the passenger side of the roof could be seen. "Can you see him? Did he make it out?"

"No." I'd already made up my mind as to what I needed to do; the problem was convincing my body that it was a good idea. After I nearly drowned after a car accident ten years ago, water and I haven't exactly been on speaking terms.

I plunged into the mud on the bank, my foot sinking several inches into the slime. I pulled free, leaving one shoe behind, and placed my next step more carefully onto a gnarled tree root. From there I leapt past the mud into the water.

The current immediately grabbed me and tried to haul me down. It was deep enough to swim, so instead of fighting to get my feet under me, I kicked toward the truck.

A splash came from behind me. I glanced over my shoulder, hoping it wasn't a relative of the rabid alligator I'd encountered earlier. Morris had shucked his messenger bag and waded in. He was also floundering in the uneven current. Wind whipped the rain into a frenzy on the water's surface, obscuring any object farther away than my fingertips into lumpy shades of gray and brown.

The current rammed me into the back of the pickup. It was canted at a dramatic angle. There would be no way to open the driver's side door, especially once it came to rest on the mud below.

Sliding one hand along the rim of the truck bed to keep my bearing, I half-swum and was half propelled by the churning water around to the passenger side. The door was still mostly above water, although tilted. I tried to pull it open, but there was nothing to brace against as the truck pitched beneath me.

Morris joined me, and together we were able to leverage the door open. Water poured into the cab.

It was hard to see inside, but I made out Nate's form crumpled against the steering wheel. He didn't have his seatbelt on and his body was already consumed by the water. Suddenly the truck lurched, the new water pouring in from the passenger side hastening its downward plunge. Nate's head was instantly buried in black water.

Nothing to do but go in.

Bile etched the back of my throat as my stomach revolted at the idea. Memories of that night ten years ago blackened my vision. I forced them aside and hauled in my breath.

Morris understood what needed to happen, taking my feet and securing me from the current as I dove headfirst into the water. At first all I could reach was Nate's hair. I tangled my fingers in it and hauled his head up. Then I pushed my shoulder under his, trying to leverage him up. His face broke through the surface, so at least one of us could breathe.

The water was a murky brown, dark, churning as it tried to suck me down as well. I wanted to vomit and take a breath and push my way back up to the light. Panic overtook me. Flailing for the surface, I kicked free of Morris's grip.

The current tore at me, gleeful, as if it knew that it'd almost killed me all those years ago and had decided now was a good time to try again. There was nothing I could do except kick and scramble, hitting the dash and steering wheel and seat back.

My chest was about to burst with the need for air. My vision had gone red—not that I could see much anyway—and my head felt light, as if it didn't matter anymore whether I lived or died.

David's face floated into my vision. I pushed down the urge to breathe.

Then I wasn't alone. Morris was there, wedged in beside me, pulling and pushing and straining, tugging at Nate. I fought him, grabbing, clutching as he hauled Nate's body past me.

I spun blind, my hands sliding along what I thought was the dash until I hit one of the truck pedals. Then came a hard yank on my ankles and I popped free from the truck cab, flying into Morris's arms.

Choking and sputtering, I grabbed all the air I could. Morris braced me against the hood of the truck with his hip as he wrapped an arm under Nate's arms. I spat out a stomachful of water and heard his voice over the pounding rain.

"Swim, AJ!" Morris grabbed my wrist and tugged me away from the truck.

The truck bed swung toward us as its nose continued its downward spiral to the bottom of the river. I kicked hard as Morris paddled backward, Nate in his arms.

The wave the truck left in its wake pushed us under for a moment. When we resurfaced, Nate was bobbing between us, linked in our arms, still not moving, but his chest was rising and falling and blood was seeping from a cut on his head, so at least he was alive.

"Kick, kick hard!" Morris shouted.

"Which way?" I shouted, completely disoriented as we treaded water. The waves had grown high enough that I couldn't see either shore. Then I saw what had gotten him so excited.

A huge whirling mass of wind and water had risen from the center of the river. A waterspout. It sucked up more water, then skipped across the surface like a massive blender looking for something to pulverize.

Headed directly toward us.

# TWENTY-SIX

Morris tugged us in a direction perpendicular to the oncoming spout. He was shouting, but I couldn't hear anything except the roar of the wind and water. It took everything I had to hang onto Nate and keep kicking.

The roar grew deafening and the waves churned so hard that I lost my grasp on Nate. Water sucked me under and I spun around below the surface, trapped.

The forces tearing at my body kicked the air right out of me. My vision turned from gray to black to red and I had no idea where the surface was. All I could do was kick blindly and pray.

I broke through the surface, gasping and crying, my throat raw. Thrashing to keep my head above water, I looked around. The waves were lower now that the spout had dissipated. A glimmer of sun broke through the clouds.

Typical summer storm? I'd stick to my mountains, thank you very much.

Faintly, I heard Morris calling my name. I spotted him—still supporting Nate—and swam toward them. We weren't far from the shore; I could see the bright blue tarp waving gaily in the wind, beckoning us to safety.

I joined them, took Nate's other arm, and we kicked toward shore. By the time we reached it there were a dozen people reaching out to help us haul Nate and our own weary, waterlogged bodies over the rocks and tree roots and back onto solid ground. They used a length of tarp as a makeshift stretcher to carry Nate up to Vincent's SUV.

"We can get him to a hospital faster than it will take an ambulance to reach us," Morris said as he offered a hand to help me to my feet. Paul was there with Morris's bag. Morris hugged it to his body like it was a security blanket, reminding me once more of his paradoxical nature: one moment an oblivious genius, the next a warm and sensitive man, and then he'd revert to childlike shyness. It was as if he knew how strange he was and that he didn't fit in, so he was constantly trying on new personas to see what might work best.

"I'm sorry I panicked," I told Morris, my throat still raw from choking on the water. "You saved my life. Thank you."

He pushed his hair out of his eyes and gave me a self-effacing smile. "Are you kidding? I would have never been brave enough to swim out there to rescue Nate if you hadn't jumped in first."

The men folded down the rear seats of the Escalade and slid Nate inside. "My fault," Morris muttered as he watched, his smile vanishing. "I should have sent them home."

"How could you have known?" I asked. Surely Morris couldn't blame himself for the local weather patterns.

He glanced at me, his face blanching, and said nothing.

We climbed into the rear of Vincent's SUV along with Elise, Nate's wife. Vincent didn't look very happy about playing ambulance or having his leather seats soaked in mud and water and blood. But with so many people around, there wasn't a lot he could say other than to direct Paul to drive.

"What's wrong with him?" Elise asked, holding his hand and rubbing it. "Why won't he wake up?"

"He must have hit his head pretty hard," I told her, mopping the blood gushing from Nate's temple with the hem of my shirt. Morris reached into his bag and took out a large handkerchief, which he handed me.

As I applied pressure, Nate's eyes wobbled open. "What happened?"

"Oh honey," Elise cried, hugging him hard.

The roads were clogged with people fleeing the hurricane. Mostly out-of-state plates. Tourists, Morris explained.

Paul turned on the car radio. The announcer was reading a list of closings and updates, detailing evacuation routes and explaining that they still had no mandatory evacuations because they weren't sure where the storm would hit—its course was too erratic to predict. He did say it was expected to make landfall somewhere along the South Carolina coast by midnight.

We reached the hospital in Beaufort and the rain stopped, replaced by blinding sunshine. The sky quickly cleared except for a faint band of gray in the distance. The hospital was in chaos with hurricane preparation efforts, so everything took longer than expected. By the time we helped get Elise settled, made sure she and Nate were in good hands, and left, the sky had filled with ribbons of red and gold as the sun set.

Paul hadn't said a word the entire time. I couldn't help but wonder what was going on behind those blue eyes of his. Probably he was worried about our heathenness rubbing off on him. Yet, he'd been the one to volunteer Vincent's SUV in the first place.

"We'll drop you off," Vincent said when we arrived back at Colleton Landing.

While we were gone the debris had been cleared and the fallen tree moved out of the road. The car it had damaged still sat there, but otherwise it was hard to tell anything had happened here just a few hours ago.

"You're not staying in your RV during the hurricane, are you? You need to evacuate your people before it hits. How long do we have?" I asked Morris, still hoping to borrow one of Grandel's cars and head west before the roads got blocked. After seeing the reaction of the folks in Beaufort, I'd decided to take Hermes seriously.

Morris went to consult his Kermit. He rummaged in his bag. "That's funny. It's gone." He glanced out the window toward where we'd gone into the water. "I must have dropped it."

Paul turned the radio up. "Sounds like they're still saying some-time around midnight."

"That gives me a few hours," Vincent said. "I'll be back. Tell Grandel to be ready to keep his end of the bargain."

Somehow he made it sound like a threat.

But what did I care? I was going to be on my way home just as soon as I grabbed my bag.

◆

Ty was as good as his word, and once they made it to the interstate, they were zipping along in the fast lane, making good time, muscling slower drivers out of their way as they noticed the light bar and sheriff's decals. Best road trip ever—or it would have been if they weren't in a race with a hit man.

Or if Ty had let David at least sit in the front seat. Maybe work the siren or lights. But no, David had to stay in the back. At least he had Nikki to keep him company. Ty had unplugged the computer from the center console—David wasn't sure why, but he had a sneaking suspicion that it was to keep anyone back home from tracking them.

"Are you going to get in trouble because of me?"

"Because I'm a K-9 officer, I'm allowed to use my vehicle for personal use," Ty answered. Or rather didn't answer. The look he gave David in the rearview mirror pretty much said: the less you know, the better. Probably the same reason why Ty handed his cell to David and told him not to answer it.

"You sure I shouldn't call Elizabeth?"

Same look. "No, let's give her the night off."

David tried to call his mom again. Still no answer. And she hadn't opened any of the texts he'd sent either. "What if the guy already found her?"

"Don't see how he could. Unless he has his own plane, it'd take longer to fly commercial than drive it. And a small plane flying into a hurricane? I don't think so."

Ty's phone rang. "It's Mr. Masterson again."

Ty sighed. "Put it on speaker. Don't make a sound."

David leaned forward, holding the phone close to Ty's face over the seat. He was surprised Ty didn't pull over to take the call—just went to show how seriously Ty was taking all this.

"Ty Stillwater," he said cheerfully.

"Deputy Stillwater," came Masterson's voice. He sounded angry, like he was fighting hard not to shout. "I know you have him. You'll return my grandson to me at once."

"David? Excuse me, sir, I don't understand. I'm taking some personal time, headed to North Carolina, so I might have missed something. Is David okay?"

"Don't play games with me. I'll destroy you and your entire family. Now turn around and bring me what's mine."

"I'm not on duty, sir, but if David is missing, I'm happy to put in some calls, facilitate a missing persons report and Amber Alert. Or did I misunderstand your meaning?"

"No. You understood exactly what I meant. And you'll live to regret not listening to me and doing what I asked." Masterson hung up.

David lowered the phone, still analyzing the conversation. "You didn't lie. Not once."

"Didn't have to."

"Is he going to call the police? Are they going to be chasing us?" As exciting as police chases were on TV, the last thing David wanted was to get Ty in trouble.

"I doubt it. Not if it means letting folks know he couldn't keep track of a nine-year-old kid. What judge would give him custody then? Plus there's nothing Masterson hates worse than being made a fool of."

"Is that why he hates my mom so much? That and my dad dying?"

"He hated your mom way before you were even born, David. Don't waste too much time or energy trying to understand a man like Masterson because there's less there than you think."

"I don't understand."

"Men like Masterson aren't complicated at all—they're not evil masterminds like the bad guys in the movies. They're just selfish, pure and simple. To them the entire world is about what they want. No one else exists."

David thought about that. About how many times his mom or Jeremy or Gram Flora had gone out of their way to help him or do something nice for him. Ty and his family. Elizabeth, too. Even his dad before he died.

But the only thing Mr. Masterson had ever gone out of his way for, put any effort into, was to get his own way. Even now—fighting to get David to visit had nothing to do with David or taking the time to get to know his grandson better. It was because someone else had something he wanted.

And Mr. Masterson just couldn't stand that.

"The judge won't let him keep me if I tell him what I heard, will he?" David shivered even though Ty had the window cracked and the AC off. "I mean, I get to stay with Mom, right? They can't take me away from her."

"We're not going to let that happen." Ty paused, met David's gaze in the mirror. "I promise."

That made David feel a little better, but he still wished they'd already found his mom. She would deal with Masterson—it couldn't be any harder than stopping those greedy corporations out to rip folks off.

They passed a sign saying they'd just entered South Carolina. David leaned forward. "Ty? Could we hurry a little more? Please?"

Ty said nothing, but the muscle at the corner of his jaw gave a jump. The speedometer edged up as they plunged into the night.

◆

The tram still wasn't in service, so Morris and I had to walk from where Vincent dropped us off. Morris stopped to check his bag again but still couldn't find his Kermit and wandered off to search the riverbank. I wasn't sure what he was so worried about—I lost phones all the time, and not just to rampaging alligators, and it was no big deal. David had taught me how to synch stuff so nothing was ever lost.

Since I'd lost my shoes in the river, I walked barefoot along the path from the outer gate to the front of the plant, admiring the beautiful sunset as the sky darkened from indigo to black. You'd never know a hurricane was getting ready to hit.

The guard at the front door looked askance at my bare feet and directed me to the security desk where they were holding my bag. I retrieved my fancy black pumps.

The front lobby of the plant had totally changed. Instead of the upscale modern hotel vibe it'd given off earlier, it suddenly felt like a neighborhood block party. The protesters were all still gathered there—in fact, if anything, their numbers had swollen.

Floyd and Noreen from the Landing Motel had joined them and were setting up a buffet table in front of the security desk. Others unrolled sleeping bags and blankets, while workers on the promenade level carried computers from their offices, placing them on a wheeled cart overseen by a security guard with a clipboard.

In the middle of it all stood Yancey, both directing and filming the operation. "What's going on?" I asked him.

"AJ! So glad you made it back. This is going to be my best work ever. I convinced Grandel to remove any sensitive items from the offices and we're converting them into a storm shelter for the night."

"I'm surprised he agreed to let all these people in. I thought it would be just a chosen few."

"I explained how much more bang for his buck he could get by opening his doors—and that the value would far outweigh the costs of the extra security guards." He looked down from his camera's viewfinder for a moment. "Where's Vincent? We need to get some shots of him and Grandel making nice together and all that jazz."

"He went to see to his own people. But he said he'd be back." I looked around. Hated to say it, but this crazy stunt could very well solve all of Grandel's problems now that his feud with Vincent was over. "Seems my work here is done."

"Oh, but you can't leave. The party's just starting."

Morris came in the door behind me, looking upset.

"Just a few loose ends and I'll be on my way."

Yancey nodded absently and wandered through the crowd to interview Noreen. I caught up with Morris before he passed through the portal monitor. "Hey, can I talk with you for a minute?"

He looked around and nodded. "Sure, let's go to my office."

Morris's office was in the operational area, so I had to go through the portal monitor one more time, get a dosimeter, and be pronounced "clean" before we could proceed. He led me inside, dropped his bag on the floor, and sank into a comfortable rolling chair that sat in the middle of the floor.

His office was in the center of the building—one door led to the observation deck and one into the control room—and there were no windows, only large monitor screens lit up with a steady stream of information. There was no desk, but as he swiveled in the chair with its wireless keyboard attached to one arm, I could see he didn't need one. Everything was right on the screens before him.

"You really can run the whole place from here."

"I don't use this office very often," he said, scowling at the empty space. "I programmed my Kermit to run the whole place from anywhere. It meant I could get out, talk with folks, not be cooped up inside here all day." He made a complete circuit in the chair, gaze raking over the readouts, then turned back to me. "What's up? You're not leaving, are you?"

"Yes. I need to get home. But before I go I wanted to let you know that your secret is safe with me."

He stopped, planting both feet on the ground, the chair swinging to a halt.

"Morris, I know you were paying the protestors from town. I'm not going to tell Owen, I just want to understand why."

At first I thought he was going to try to deny it—but it would have been useless. His face was so easy to read. "I thought it would keep Owen here. Stop him from moving to Japan." He scuffed his foot against the carpet and looked up with a rebellious expression. "That's all."

I blew my breath out. I'd thought it would be something like that. "You know you can't keep him here forever."

"I know. I guess." He looked down, his hair falling into his face, reminding me of David.

"Morris. Look at me." He glanced up, finally meeting my gaze. "You didn't arrange those accidents did you?"

His eyes went wide with surprise. "No. Of course not! I couldn't do that, someone might have gotten hurt."

He was telling the truth. "Okay, good. That's all I wanted to know. Good-bye, Morris."

"AJ—" He stopped me just as I reached the door.

I turned back. "What?"

He stared past me at the monitors on either wall beside me. "Nothing. I guess. Thanks."

"You're welcome." I closed the door behind me and headed out through the portal monitor one last time—still "clean," thank goodness.

One final stop and I'd be out of here—with plenty of time to beat the storm as long as the roads weren't too clogged with traffic. But hopefully most of the evacuees were long since gone.

"Can I use your phone to call long distance?" I asked the guard. He nodded and dialed an outside line for me. No answer at the summerhouse or Flora's, but Elizabeth finally picked up.

"Where have you been?" she answered, not bothering with hello. "I've been calling and texting and e-mailing all day."

"No phones inside the plant," I took the easy way out, not giving her the play-by-play explanation. "Can you put David on?"

A long pause. Too long. "That's why I was calling."

My stomach plummeted. I *knew* there was something wrong. Why hadn't I listened to my gut? "What happened? Is he okay?"

"David's fine. But he's not here. The judge wouldn't let him stay with me or your parents. He sent him to Masterson's for the night."

"Old Man Masterson has my son?" A few people in the lobby turned my way as I raised my voice. I put my back to them, leaning on the countertop. "Elizabeth, how could you?"

"It's only for the night. He'll be fine."

"I'm calling him. Telling him to bring David back immediately. He has no right—"

"You might want to calm down and just let things run their course. The judge wants us all in court tomorrow. Three p.m."

"To decide visitation?"

"That's what you need to stay calm about. He's going to decide custody. AJ, you have to be there. And you need to play nice with Masterson; he could really screw you over."

My teeth ground together so hard I thought I was going to break a filling. "Tell me everything."

By the time she had finished, I had managed to stop hyperventilating, although I was far from calm.

"So, your folks are at Flora's, David's fine for the night, and there's really nothing you need to worry about except getting home in time for court," she summarized.

"I'm leaving now." I hung up and turned to the guard, who'd been listening in and looked highly entertained by the drama that was my life. "Is Mr. Grandel in his office?"

"Yes, Ms. Palladino. He said for you to go on up."

# TWENTY-SEVEN

Hutton hadn't counted on this. Tracking AJ to her motel only to be told by the owners that he'd have to leave. And now trapped at a slumber party locked up inside a nuclear reactor with her just across the room, only he couldn't touch her—couldn't even follow her when she left to go into the secure area, where he might have had a chance to get her away from this crowd.

Definitely not what he'd bargained for. This is why he never let others call the shots for his jobs. When he set the time and place, when he was in control of all the parameters, things went perfectly.

Between Masterson, Mother Nature, and AJ herself, this was turning into a disaster.

He climbed to the promenade at the top of the stairs to get a different vantage point and assess his options. AJ returned through the monitors and made a phone call at the security desk. He watched her walk across the marble floor. She wasn't very steady in those heels—given what he'd seen of her, they either weren't her shoes or she wasn't used to wearing heels.

Maybe he could use that as an advantage. He grabbed a bottle of water from a woman who was handing them out to the refugees.

By the time AJ started to climb the steep, curved staircase with its slick polished wood treads, he had a plan.

He started down, drizzled water on the step behind him, stopped and waited for her to pass him going up. It wasn't a very high fall, but if he pushed her just right, there was a good chance he could snap her neck against the steel railing while making it look like he was trying to catch her.

He mentally rehearsed the moves he'd have to make. He'd never tried anything like this, out in plain view of dozens of people, before. The adrenalin rush was like nothing he'd ever experienced with his previous jobs.

She stepped past him. He fumbled his bottle, dropping it to draw her attention toward him. She put her weight on her top foot, the one on the wet tread. He nudged her with his hip while scrambling for his bottle, throwing her off balance. She began to topple, the whole scene playing out like it had in his mind, her arm flailing for the railing but her body aimed in the wrong di rection to catch it since she'd turned to watch him retrieve his bottle.

All he needed was to reach out for her and propel her neck-first into the railing before toppling her down the steps—hands grasping for her body as if he was working to save her.

He spun up to make the move. But AJ was too fast for him. With cat-like balance, she fought the natural instinct to reach for the railing and instead flung her body back and down. As he swung up, she landed on her butt on the lower step.

"Ouch," she said, untwisting her leg from beneath her body. "Darn heels."

"My fault," he said, helping her up—what else could he do with everyone watching? "I spilled my water. I'll grab something to clean it up."

She smiled her thanks, stepped around the water, and was gone.

He had no choice but to watch her go.

Grandel wasn't too happy about my leaving. I reminded him of his promise to get me home by tomorrow and how now, with the storm hitting, it would be impossible for him to keep. He reminded me of the large fee and bonus he'd offered. We met in the middle— he agreed to my leaving tonight in one of his vehicles if I agreed to return on Sunday and help him prepare for the Japanese visit next week.

It meant a lot of driving, but I was determined to get home.

I had to get to David before Old Man Masterson did irreparable damage. I knew firsthand how Masterson loved to play his mind-games, and I wasn't about to let David be any part of them.

The elements seemed determined to keep me in South Car-olina. By the time I left the plant, the winds had picked up and it had begun to rain again. If I thought this afternoon's storm was bad, it was nothing compared to the rain that tore through the skies now.

I turned onto the road leading to Highway 170. The only good news was that I was the only car in sight. Most sane folks were keeping off the roads, waiting for Hermes to deliver his message from the gods.

Wind tore across the two-lane road, making the car's steering wheel buck. Rain slashed against the windshield as thick tendrils of fog choked the headlights. I was almost to the turn-off that led to Vincent's revival tent—six whole miles in almost eighteen minutes. At this rate I'd be driving all night before I even made it to the interstate.

I swerved to miss a fallen tree branch strewn across the road. Since I was the only one crazy enough to be out here driving in this mess tonight, I had the entire two lanes to maneuver in.

A half-mile down the road, I rounded a curve when the high beams from a car coming from the opposite direction blinded me.

Panic set in as I realized he was in my lane. I yanked on the wheel, skidding over the yellow line.

A sickening thud reverberated through the car. Not the mechanical kind like something's broken. No. The kind of thud where you just hit something large and fleshy.

Even as I registered it, I slammed on the brakes, swinging back into my lane, behind the other car, and onto the shoulder. The other car was motionless, I realized. Parked on the road, headed the wrong way. What had I hit? Was it some poor slob changing a flat?

My stomach spiraled down in a whirlpool of panic. I set the emergency brake and my hazard lights, and then ran out into the storm to retrace my path. Despite the heat, the rain was freezing against my skin—sharp daggers that sliced through my cotton shirt. I was soaked through and through before I made it the twenty feet back down the road.

The other car sped off, its brake lights vanishing in the fog. What the? Maybe I hadn't hit anyone? I staggered a few more steps, the wind and rain pushing me back as if trying to protect me from something awful.

Then I saw the man's body.

# — TWENTY-EIGHT —

The wind had grown so fierce that it almost pushed me off my feet as I struggled to reach the man. He lay face down, and in the darkness I couldn't tell if he was breathing or not. I finally got to him, my stomach clenching from both effort and fear, my fingers chilled when I stretched them out to check the pulse in his neck.

Nothing. When I pulled my hand back, it was sticky with blood.

I don't usually panic. But kneeling in the rain and wind and dark, alone on an empty road, no help in sight, knowing that I may have just killed a man—my mind spun out of control with options and re-criminations and fear and rescripting my entire life from a peaceful existence spent with my family to one spent behind prison bars.

In an instant, I might have lost everything.

No time to worry about me. I had to try to save the man. Cautiously, supporting his neck, I rolled him over. Rain quickly washed the road grime and blood from his face. But I didn't need the extra seconds. I recognized him instantly.

Reverend Vincent.

He was cold to the touch—much too cold, a small voice in the back of my head whispered. I tried CPR for a minute or two but got no response. He needed more than I had to offer.

I had no cell phone, and no other cars had driven by—so, feeling like a thief, I searched his pockets. His cell had a cracked screen but still lit up when I turned it on. Two bars—hopefully enough. I dialed 911.

It took a while to get through—or maybe it just felt like forever. Wet to the bone, sick to my soul, confused and frightened, I heard "9-1-1, what's your emergency?"

"There's a man in the road. I hit him—he was in the road. He's not breathing. I need an ambulance. Come fast." The words tumbled out in such a jumble that I wondered if she understood me or if it sounded like gibberish.

To my relief she said, "Ma'am, can you give me your location?"

"I'm about six miles north of the entrance to Colleton Landing."

"And you're on the road? Not a side street or residence?"

"The side of the road. My car has its hazard lights on."

"Okay, ma'am. Help is on its way. Do you need me to walk you through CPR?"

"I've already started it. He didn't have a pulse when I found him, but I thought I should try—"

"You did the right thing. Can I have your name?"

"AJ, AJ Palladino."

"And where do you live, AJ?"

"I'm from West Virginia. I'm just visiting here."

"Can I have your address and home phone number? Just in case we need to contact you?"

I wasn't sure if she was collecting the information to calm me down or to build a case if it ever came to that. Who was I kidding? Of course it would come to that.

Except . . . who had been driving Vincent's Escalade? That had to be the car I saw right before I hit him.

"There was another car." My teeth were chattering and I felt nauseous—my blood sugar plummeting from the adrenalin rush. "I think the driver pushed Vincent out right in front of me."

"Who's Vincent?"

"The man I hit. I recognize him. Reverend Richard Vincent. The other car drove off, I couldn't see, but I think it might have been his assistant driving."

The operator was amazingly patient—I'm not sure I could have untangled all the directions my thoughts were spinning in. "The assistant's name?"

"Paul. I don't know his last name."

"But you said he was driving the victim's vehicle?"

"I think so. It was a black Escalade."

In the background I heard her typing and the muffled sounds of her talking to someone else. "Okay, AJ. You're doing great. Our deputy says he's only a few minutes away. Now, can you tell me what direction the other car drove?"

"South. Toward Colleton Landing."

I heard sirens before I saw the flashing lights of the deputy's cruiser coming from the north. He pulled up across from me, angling his car so that I was pinned both in his headlights and by a spotlight aimed from the driver's window. I tried to block the light with my hands, but was blinded for a moment—his intention.

"Ma'am, could you please stand up, keep your hands where I can see them?" he asked in a calm, polite tone.

The Southern accent made him sound cordial, but just like when Ty spoke, there was an underlying current of command. I did as he asked, then obeyed him when he instructed me to turn my back and interlace my hands, after which I let him pat me down. He escorted me to his car and locked me in the back while he examined Vincent. I could see him checking the pulse, heard him through the car's radio calling in to dispatch about the ETA of the ambulance.

A few minutes later the ambulance arrived along with a second police unit. Two men got out of the second cruiser, both wearing long, yellow rain slickers with "Police" written on them. They huddled with the first officer, who turned and pointed at me.

One of them broke away and jogged over to me. The wind whipped his ball cap away and I was surprised to see that I knew the man.

Reverend Vincent's assistant, Liam.

◆

Jeremy had insisted on cooking dinner for her, but as soon as they'd finished, Elizabeth barricaded herself behind her law books in her office. She couldn't believe Hunter had been able to out-maneuver her and that she'd let AJ down so badly.

She had to come up with some way to get David back and make sure AJ never had to worry about Masterson again.

Unfortunately, the more she dug into West Virginia case law, the more she realized that any wiggle-room in the statutes wasn't designed for lawyers to manipulate but rather to give judges discretion. Which meant it was all up to Judge Mabry.

Given that he'd initially ruled in favor of her request for the Palladinos to watch David, she was hopeful. But having Edna's secret revealed in such a public manner had probably destroyed most of her credibility with him. Still, Elizabeth wasn't ready to give up hope.

Not until she went online and found the many photos of Masterson and Mabry together at charity golf outings, community dinners and fund raisers, and even at their church picnic.

Great. Just great. She didn't know anyone here, had no influence. And AJ? Most of the folks here in her hometown blamed her for everything that had happened five months ago—it wasn't like they'd find many character witnesses around Scotia.

Burying her head in her arms, resting on the tabletop, she tried to explore her options. That's when she made the mistake of closing her eyes and drifted in a limbo short of sleep where her mind was whirling like a hamster trapped on a wheel but no answers came.

She was awakened by pounding on the front door.

She and Jeremy arrived at the door at the same time. She turned on the porch light and looked outside. Before she could reach for the door, it burst open. Hunter rushed in.

Jeremy immediately stepped in front of Elizabeth, shielding her, hands raised.

"Lay one finger on me and you'll be back in jail," Hunter told Jeremy. "This is between me and my wife."

Elizabeth sighed. Hunter didn't scare her—not when he was like this. An outraged Hunter acting like a two-year-old was a Hunter she could control; it just took patience and energy. Both of which she was short on tonight. "It's okay, Jeremy."

Jeremy didn't move for a long moment. He looked over his shoulder at Elizabeth and she gave him a weary nod. Finally he left, but he made a point of not going far, standing in the open kitchen door a few feet away.

"Hunter, why are you here?" To gloat, she imagined. But instead, he seemed upset.

"You think you're so smart. I'm here to tell you that you won't get away with it."

"Get away with what?"

Hunter's scowl turned deadly. "I can't believe you'd stoop this low, Elizabeth. Really, just to get back at me? You couldn't stand to see me win. Well, it's going to cost you. Everything. Your license, this house, your pathetic new career. Kiss it all good-bye."

"What the hell are you talking about?"

"You think using Stillwater to do your dirty work is going to protect you or your client? Forget it. We're going to bury you all.

See you tomorrow. In court. Tell your client if she's not there, she's going to prison for a very long time."

Elizabeth shook her head, trying to puzzle through what he could be talking about.

"You really expect me to buy that innocent act? Well, if you're so innocent, call Stillwater. He'll explain everything." Hunter stalked out of the house, slamming the door behind him, without saying another word.

Elizabeth puzzled over his words for a few minutes, then returned to her office and tried to call Ty. No answer.

A few minutes later she heard a loud knock at the door. She rushed to the hall, wondering if Hunter had returned.

"Sheriff's department. Open up!"

Jeremy hurried out of the kitchen, holding a wooden spoon aloft as if it would make a useful weapon. She looked outside. Two deputies and one man in a suit stood there. Not looking happy at all.

"Are they taking me back to jail?" Jeremy asked.

"No. It will be okay." Elizabeth said the words automatically as if they were scripted. In all honesty she had no clue what had brought the police to her door. Probably something to do with whatever Hunter had been raving about.

They pounded again and she opened the door. "What can I do for you, officers?"

The man in the suit did the talking. "Do you have any knowledge of the whereabouts of David Palladino?"

"Yes, sir, I do." To her surprise, the men all tensed, one even rested his palm on the butt of his gun. "He's with his grandfather, Kyle Masterson."

"No ma'am. Mr. Masterson has informed us that the juvenile in question has gone missing. He believes that he was taken by Ty Stillwater—and that it was at your behest."

Elizabeth straightened, folding her arms across her chest as she absorbed the barrage of information. David gone? Taken by Ty? Ridiculous.

"And what proof did Mr. Masterson offer for these outrageous claims?"

"Deputy Stillwater was at the Masterson estate immediately prior to Mr. Masterson becoming aware that the juvenile was missing."

"Hmmmm. . . ." Elizabeth stalled for time, trying to make sense of this. If Ty had David, then David was fine, but if Ty didn't— "How long?"

"Excuse me, ma'am?"

"How long between the time Deputy Stillwater was there and when Mr. Masterson notified you?"

The detective shifted uncomfortably. "Approximately three hours."

"So, there's a good chance Deputy Stillwater is innocent. And since I haven't seen him since around noon, I'm not sure why you all are here instead of searching for David."

The uniformed deputies looked away, as if studying the gingerbread on the porch.

"Ma'am," the detective said, his voice dropping as if asking a favor. "I'm sure you understand that we would like nothing more than to clear Deputy Stillwater of these allegations. And I'm sure you also understand Mr. Masterson's position in the community."

"Sounds like you all are in a pickle," she said, trying to keep the amusement from her voice. Hunter was behind this, she was certain. But why? She couldn't see what it bought him. And why that dramatic stunt, accusing her?

"Could we search the premises, verify that the juvenile is not present?"

Elizabeth thought about it. They had no probable cause, no exigent circumstances, but allowing them to search would show good faith on her part. She stood aside and gestured for them to enter. "Certainly, gentlemen. I assume that you've already searched Mr. Masterson's residence?"

"Yes, ma'am, we did."

The two deputies strode past Jeremy and Elizabeth and split up to begin searching any nooks or crannies in which a nine-year-old in a wheelchair could be hidden. The detective stayed with Elizabeth in the front foyer.

It didn't take the deputies long to come up empty. The detective slumped his shoulders.

"So, good night, then." Elizabeth opened the door for them.

"Just a minute ma'am," the detective said. "The judge asked me to call him as soon as we were done here."

"Judge Mabry?"

"Yes. Apparently Mr. Masterson's lawyer informed him of the juvenile's disappearance." He stepped out to the porch, talking into his cell, then returned a minute later. "Ma'am? The judge requests that you and Mr. Holcombe meet him at his residence to discuss this matter." He wrote down an address and handed it to Elizabeth. She didn't move. "Ah, I think he meant sooner rather than later, ma'am."

"Thank you, detective. I'll head right over."

They left and Elizabeth closed the door, collapsing against it. David missing? AJ was going to kill her.

"What can I do?" Jeremy asked.

"Get on the phone and don't you give up until you reach either Ty or AJ," she told him. "As soon as you do, call me on my cell." She glanced down at her shorts and tank top. At least she'd showered and no longer smelled of soot from the Palladinos' fire. Well, not much, anyway. "I need to go see a judge."

❖

To my surprise, Liam opened the door to the police cruiser I sat in.

"How did you get out?" I asked him as he offered me his hand and helped me out.

"Come with me. We'll take your car." He waved to the deputies and led the way through the rain to my borrowed SUV. I wasn't too surprised when Liam took the driver's seat. He stared at me through the open door when I didn't move.

"I'm not going anywhere with you until I know what's going on," I told him.

I wasn't sure if he actually smiled or if it was just a trick of the light reflecting off the rain running down his face.

"Does this help?" He reached inside the slicker and pulled out a black wallet, flipped open to reveal a set of credentials. I leaned forward to read them.

"FBI?" Okay, maybe that did explain a lot—but not everything.

"That's what it says. Hop in. Now."

I trudged around to the passenger side, my nice leather pumps hopelessly ruined in the mud. I climbed in, and he had the car rolling before I had the door shut. He stretched his arm across my seat back, looking behind him as he quickly reversed the car's direction.

"Where are we going?" I asked.

"I'm taking you to the station so we can talk."

"I didn't mean to kill Vincent. There was no way I could avoid—"

He shook his head and surprised me by touching my arm. "You didn't kill Vincent. The paramedics found a gunshot wound. Said it looked close range."

Relief that I hadn't killed someone rushed over me. I took my first deep breath since hitting Vincent's body. "It had to be Paul."

"How do you know that? I didn't put everything together until today, myself."

"You suspected he wanted to kill Vincent?"

"No. We suspected Vincent or someone in his organization of plotting to commit an act of nuclear terrorism. Someone with computer skills was creating the false alarms at the plant and using them to attack their security system. They came damn close to penetrating it, too. Why did Paul kill Vincent?"

"He found out Vincent was a non-believer. Vincent was using his congregation to put pressure on Grandel to give him a share of Colleton Landing."

"So it was all about money."

"Not to Paul." I was guessing now, but it felt right. "He really does believe."

"That's what makes him so dangerous." We were making slow progress, dodging debris blown at us, with almost no visibility. Liam didn't seem as distressed by the weather as he did by Paul being on the loose.

We rounded a bend, narrowly avoiding hitting a car stopped in the road. A downed tree blocked its path, and a man was struggling to push the tree aside enough that he could avoid getting its branches tangled in the vehicle's undercarriage.

"Liam, that's Vincent's Escalade." Of course, as soon as I said it, Paul spun around and saw us. He gave the tree one last yank, moved it just enough that he might get past it, and ran back to the Escalade.

Liam pulled a gun from beneath his raincoat and opened his door. "Wait here."

"Shouldn't you call for backup?" Too late; he was gone.

Paul had made it to the Escalade's driver's door and was half inside. No way I was going to sit helpless, watching. I slid over to the driver's seat, hunched over and watching through the space between the rim of the steering wheel and the top of the dash. Not that I could see much in the blinding rain, even with the wiper blades going full tilt.

A flash of light came, aimed right at me. Then I heard the sound of a shot. And another, not as loud as the first. I craned forward, trying to see if Liam needed my help or if I should try to escape or what the hell was going on. Couldn't make out anything helpful. Finally I rolled down the window and looked out without exposing too much of my body.

"Stop where you are!" Paul's voice rang through the night. He held a pump-action shotgun in one hand and a small, bright green object in the other. "I can blow it anytime I want!"

I ducked as he shot in my direction. The SUV shook but the engine never faltered. The Escalade pulled away, sending a spray of mud and water cascading behind it.

I ran out into the rain. Liam lay in the road, his gun clenched in his hand. He pushed himself up to sitting, and by the time I'd reached him he was talking on a cell phone.

"I'm okay," he gasped. His color sure didn't make it seem that way. "Got my vest. He's headed toward the plant."

That's when I figured out what that green object in Paul's hand was. Morris's Kermit. The handheld computer that he could run the entire plant with—including bypassing the security.

"I've got to stop him," I told Liam. In the distance I heard sirens. Liam would soon be in good hands. But if Paul got inside the plant and locked it down, then no one would be getting out alive.

# — TWENTY-NINE —

Paul had a good head start on me. I couldn't stop thinking about how I, with Yancey's help, had convinced Owen to invite all those people inside to weather the storm.

*Safest place around.*

As each mental nail of guilt hammered down, my foot lowered on the gas pedal. By the time Paul made the turn into the plant's entrance, I had narrowed the gap between us to only a hundred feet.

He plowed through the outer security checkpoint, flinging the guard to the side. I didn't have time to stop and check him. All I could do was hope that Paul would forget about the tram path and turn down the winding road instead.

No such luck. He sideswiped a line of cars parked in the lot, gaining me another few feet, then bounced onto the paved path. It was barely wide enough for him to squeeze past the inner perimeter— sparks flew as he scraped the metal fence pole—but he didn't slow down.

Not enough for me to catch him, anyway. He skidded to a stop at the entrance and hopped out. A security guard ran from the checkpoint, but Paul whirled and opened up with the shotgun in one swift motion. The guard staggered and fell.

By that time, I was on his tail and was going to ram him with the SUV—couldn't think of any other way to stop him—but he turned toward me and fired.

The windshield cracked and I ducked instinctively. My SUV hit the side of the Escalade and spun out of control. My seatbelt tugged at me as gravity tried to pull the SUV into a roll and two wheels left the pavement. I yanked the wheel hard, and the car bounced back down before sputtering to a stop.

By the time I caught my breath, Paul had yanked my door open and was aiming the shotgun at me. "Welcome to the end of the world, AJ. Come on inside."

◆

Judge Mabry lived in a modest two-story stone house that looked like it'd been standing since the Revolution. He opened the door himself, waving Elizabeth inside. The house behind him felt empty.

"I'm so sorry to disturb you and your family," she said.

He led the way into a large paneled study where Hunter waited. "No worries. I'm all alone. My wife died eight years ago now."

The judge took a seat behind the desk. The only other chair in the room was already occupied by Kyle Masterson, leaving her and Hunter standing.

"I'm sure you two appreciate the gravity of this situation," the judge started. "I'm not sure if you appreciate exactly how tired I'm becoming of this case."

Hunter spoke up. "Your Honor, we believe Sheriff's Deputy Tyrone Stillwater may be aiding and abetting Ms. Hardy in preventing my client from exercising the rights you granted him earlier today."

"That's a serious charge. What makes you think a sworn officer of the law would be involved in what you have described as a kidnapping, counselor?"

"Boy's been sweet on AJ since they were kids," Masterson burst out. They all stared at him, especially the judge.

"Excuse me, Mr. Masterson?"

The judge's tone managed to penetrate Masterson's shield of self-involvement. "Er, sorry, your Honor. I tend to call anyone my son's age 'boy.' No disrespect intended, I assure you."

"I should hope not. Deputy Stillwater's record is exemplary, and it troubles me that he is not here to answer to these allegations."

"That's the whole point. He's run off with my grandson."

If they'd been in court, Elizabeth was sure the judge would have banged his gavel. Masterson obviously had the mistaken idea that because he was inside the judge's home, he could speak candidly.

Hunter put a hand on Masterson's elbow and whispered something in his ear. Elizabeth watched, enjoying how Masterson was torpedoing his own case.

"Where is Deputy Stillwater?" the judge asked.

Elizabeth answered. "I spoke to his mother, your Honor. Apparently it's Deputy Stillwater's weekend off. She said that to the best of her knowledge, her son had gone on a fishing trip."

The judge nodded. "So no one has been able to reach him to verify that he has the child in question?"

"No, your Honor," Hunter admitted, his grip on Masterson's sleeve tightening when Masterson opened his mouth. "But if your Honor would grant a warrant to access the deputy's GPS on his phone or vehicle—"

The judge frowned. "I'm not going to violate anyone's rights based on a guess. However, I will issue an order to track his county-issued vehicle's GPS."

"What about AJ? Can't we track her?" Masterson persisted.

"Ms. Hardy." Elizabeth jerked her head up when the judge called her name. "You've been awfully quiet. Any word from your client on when she'll be returning?"

"The hurricane is hitting that area hard, your Honor. I haven't been able to reach Ms. Palladino. She doesn't even know her son is missing."

"Doesn't need to," Masterson muttered. The judge pretended not to hear, but Elizabeth caught it. "She's arranged all this."

"This whole thing is a mess. I've been told that the police are doing everything in their power to locate him and have issued an Amber Alert."

Masterson outright scoffed. "They'll protect their own. C'mon Stephen, just issue a warrant for Stillwater's arrest. We all know he did it."

The judge stood. "Mr. Masterson." Masterson jerked his head up at that, surprised by both the judge's tone and his formality. "You need to understand the severity of the charges you are bringing against a man who to the best of my knowledge is an exemplary officer of the law. And without any proof, at that."

"But Stephen—" Hunter nudged Masterson hard. "Er—I mean, your Honor—"

"No *but*s." It was clear the judge's patience was at an end.

Hunter turned to stare at a framed photo on the wall beside him. Six Marines in desert camouflage. He bent forward and read the caption below it. "Your Honor, is the Stillwater in this photo related to the deputy in question?"

The judge glared at Hunter, but he was too busy examining the photo to notice. "It's his older brother. He's the leader of my youngest grandson's unit in Afghanistan."

Hunter straightened, a calculating look on his face. Elizabeth knew that look, knew it well. It was his bold move look.

Do it, she urged silently. Ask the judge to recuse himself. It's exactly what Hunter would do back in Philly where there were a dozen family court judges to take one's place. But here in Smith-field County? Implying that a judge couldn't remain impartial? She doubted that would go over very well.

"Before you say anything, counselor," the judge faced Hunter head on. "You should know that there have been Stillwaters leading the men of this area to war for generations, so you'll be hard pressed to find anyone around here who hasn't had family serve with them."

Hunter paused, then nodded, heeding the judge's warning. "I'll keep your grandson in my thoughts, Judge."

Disappointment washed over Elizabeth, but she could tell from the judge's expression that Hunter hadn't won any points.

"That's all," he said, making a shooing motion with his hands. "I'll see you all in court tomorrow."

David couldn't believe that after escaping Mr. Masterson, driving all day and night, fighting a hurricane—well, not quite a hurricane, but the radio said it would be here soon, said no one should be out on the roads—after all that, they'd missed his mom and were now stuck here until the hurricane passed. He didn't even want to think about his mom out there on the roads, could only hope that she'd gotten enough of a head start that she'd be out of the danger area before Hermes made landfall.

Although, he had to admit, if he was going to be stuck any-where, being stuck here in a nuclear power plant was pretty darn cool.

Ty didn't seem to agree. Instead he wore that worried face that he usually tried to hide. The same one he got whenever Mom was in trouble.

David helped him feed and water Nikki and then, while Ty let the younger kids who were scared of the storm pet Nikki, he went to ask some of the folks who worked at Colleton Landing about their jobs.

He'd just finished talking to a guy about radiation exposures from animals and their contaminated droppings—apparently the plant had had an incident with a radioactive alligator, how cool was that? He wondered if his mom had gotten to see it—when there was a crash from the front of the building.

Ty and Nikki were caught at the back of the room where the kids were gathered, but from where David sat on the steps beside the physicist from the NRC, he saw Ty tense. The parents with the kids shepherded them back into the corner while Ty and Nikki made their way to the front of the building. They'd just taken up a position behind one of the steel pillars when the doors burst open.

David looked over. His stomach catapulted past his toes as his body went numb with shock.

It was his mom. And there was a strange man with her. Holding a shotgun to her back.

# THIRTY

Paul propelled me toward the plant's front doors. No one inside seemed to have noticed anything, but it was hard to tell with so many people crowded in the lobby. My doing, I couldn't help but think. Delivering all these innocent targets into the hands of a madman.

"Paul, you really don't want to do this," I tried to reason with him. Hard to do with the muzzle of a shotgun nudging your spine.

"It's God's will," he said. "Nothing I tried worked, but then today He gave me the means to bring forth His glory." He wagged Morris's Kermit. "He has anointed me and I shall not disappoint Him. Now, open the door."

I did as he instructed, and he pushed me inside. The crowd was buzzing with conversation. I raised my hands over my head in the universal sign of surrender. Slowly people began to shut up and back away, their faces confused—like this was some kind of strange, strange joke.

I glanced over the crowd, hoping that if Morris saw Paul with his Kermit he could figure out a way to disable it or block it or something. Even better would be a security guard ready to tackle him—preferably without getting me blown in two.

Instead my eyes came to rest on the one person I most did not want to see.

David.

I pulled up short, my feet unable to move, cemented to the floor with horror. Paul rammed into me. Then someone screamed.

Riotous noise bounced from the steel and glass surrounding us. I pivoted to face Paul. If David was here, there was no way in hell I was going to let this man take one step closer to him. I didn't care if I had to tackle him myself.

"What are you doing?" he said, a puzzled expression on his face. "You must obey me."

The sounds of the people around him grew shrill. He waved the shotgun in the air, pulling the trigger. The noise so close to my ears was deafening.

But the next instant was silence. Followed by the sound of buckshot pinging from the glass and steel above us.

Before anyone could blink, a blur of brown appeared to my side. Then Paul was down, pinned to the floor by 110 pounds of pure canine muscle. Ty kicked the shotgun to one side. I was more interested in Morris's Kermit. Paul's left hand was closest to me and he still hung on to the small computer.

I threw myself at him, clawing at his fingers. He resisted at first, then relaxed. His face was turned toward me and he smiled. "Too late."

David pushed himself to his feet and grabbed his crutches. Some security guys came and restrained the man with the gun while the people below pushed back away from the scene. Ty released Nikki and praised her, then Ty and his mom were talking. It must have been something important because his mom's whole body was bouncing like she needed to go somewhere fast. She glanced up at David once, but her face was angry—although not at him, he hoped. Looked like she was upset with Ty.

David made his way down the steps, not ashamed about using his crutches to push through the crowd. By the time he'd reached the spot where he'd last seen her, she was gone.

Ty and Nikki were following a security guard hauling the man with the gun—now in handcuffs, the shotgun safely in Ty's hands—into a small room behind the security desk.

"It's our designated holding area," the guard was saying, "but we use it as a coat room. Honestly, things around here are always boring, nothing going on. At least not until Ms. Palladino arrived."

"Yeah, that happens," Ty said.

The guard left to join his comrades who were now weaving through the crowd, directing people out into the storm. What was up with that?

David went into the room that held Ty and the man. Ty had cleared a spot on the floor where there were no potential weapons the man could reach and sat him there. He stood over him, the shotgun resting in his hands, Nikki at full alert at his side.

"Where's my mom?" David asked. "What were you two talking about?"

Ty didn't take his eyes off the prisoner. "David, you need to leave. One of the security guards will give you a ride."

"I'm not going anywhere without my mom." David planted his crutches and prepared to make a stand.

The man on the floor smiled like he had just gotten his birthday wish or something. "AJ Palladino is your mother?"

"Yes. What did you do to her?"

"Not me, child. The will of God."

David wanted to hit the man, kick him in the balls, anything to wipe that smile off his face and get him to tell the truth. Ty lay a heavy hand on his shoulder before David even realized that he'd gathered his body, ready to lunge.

"Shut up," Ty told the man in a calm voice—so calm that it infuriated David further. Why wasn't anyone taking this seriously?

"No, I want to hear what happened to my mom," David insisted.

"No need to worry anymore, child." The man inhaled deeply, then exhaled and smiled wider. "It's begun."

"What?"

"The Rapture."

"I don't understand."

The man looked at David with pity. "You wouldn't; you haven't been saved. I'm ready to sit at my father's right hand. I'm one of the chosen."

"Chosen to do what?" Ty asked.

"Bring forth Armageddon."

David inched back, suddenly frightened for more than just his mother's safety. The man was so certain, so matter of fact. Talking about the end of the world.

"How?" Ty asked, matching the man's tone.

The man's smile widened—his mom called that kind of smile a smirk, and now David understood why she was always telling him to wipe it off his face. It wasn't a pleasant smile. Instead it was ugly, ugly, ugly.

"I used Satan's own hell fire against him. Their own technology— they think they're so smart. But they weren't smarter than me."

"Of course not," Ty nodded in agreement. "So you—"

"I took over their computer systems and used it to start Armageddon and no one can stop it."

"Armageddon?" David blurted out.

"You mean the reactor?" Ty said, somehow his voice still calm. "You're going to blow up the reactor?"

"No," the man said, his voice almost dreamlike. "It's going to blow us up. Everyone. The world ends today. And I started it. The Rapture begins here and now with me." He raised his face to look at the ceiling. "I'm ready, Lord! Ready to be bathed in your glory!"

As if in answer, alarms began to shriek, and everything went black.

# THIRTY-ONE

I reached Morris's office just as the lights went out and alarms began to blare. Low-level emergency lighting came on, enough for me to see Morris and Owen arguing. Morris stood beside his control chair, turning in a circle. His face looked haggard.

"It's all my fault," he was saying.

Owen pounced on that. "You? You did this? Coddling those damn protestors. Were you working with him? Did you give him the security codes, Morris? Are you trying to kill us all?"

"No," Morris stammered. "Of course not. I—I never—it's not my fault! I only wanted—" Tears choked his words and he turned away.

"He just wanted you to stay," I interceded.

Owen spun toward me and stared for a long, hard moment. Then he lunged for Morris, slapping him so hard that Morris's body snapped back a step.

"You stupid sack of shit!" Owen slapped him again, sending him reeling against the wall. "All my life you've held me back and now I finally get a chance and you—"

"Stop it!" I pushed myself between them. Morris was cowering,

232

arms held over his head, trying to protect himself, refusing to fight back. "You stole everything from him—his designs, his chance at a career. You used him all your life."

"Like hell I did. He'd be nothing without me, nothing! No one would have ever seen his fancy designs because he'd be too scared to let them. This place would have never been built without me, and you know it!" He aimed another blow at Morris, who scurried sideways along the wall, dropping to a crouch, whimpering, but still not defending himself. "To hell with you! All of you!"

"Wait, you can't go. Who's going to fix this?" I gestured at the darkened computer screens.

"He broke it, he can fix it." He stormed out.

I ran after him. The claxon's alarm changed to a more ominous pitch. "You can't be serious. Grandel, there are lives at stake here—"

He shook me free so hard it wrenched my arm. "Yeah, my life. And I'm not hanging around to let it get fucked up any more than it already has been."

He pushed through the door. It slammed shut behind him. I ran to Morris, who had staggered to his feet. "Are you okay? What's going on? How do we stop this?"

I followed him from his office into the control room. Dozens of different-pitched alarms sounded, adding to the confusion and sense of chaos.

The controllers were all scrambling, some futilely punching their computer keyboards in the dim light, others working manual instruments. Morris ignored them, running from work station to work station, taking in the analog readings.

Finally, he hit a button, silencing all the alarms, and stood in the middle of the room. Everyone around him stopped, looking to him, hope shadowing their faces.

"It's no good," he said. "He knew what he was doing—the one

combination that could never happen. I underestimated one thing when planning: how devious a human mind could be."

"Morris, stop beating yourself up and tell us what to do," I said, yanking on his arm, guiding him to a work station.

"We've lost secondary and tertiary backups," his voice held a hint of amazement. "He's shut down the pumps, closed all the coolant system valves."

"Can't you open them from here?"

"No. He's circumvented all the overrides."

"What about those control rods—the ones you said could shut down a reactor? Scram it?"

"They're locked into place. He put them in maintenance mode before he killed the power." His face focused on one last indicator. This one was now lit up in red, making his face look like it was covered in blood. "We'll have to manually lower them as well."

"Just show me what to do."

His face cleared as determination crowded out his guilt and confusion. "Not you, me."

He clapped his hands. "I need everyone working on the same page. We'll be working protocol eighteen—this guy pulled the ultimate Stuxnet on us, so remember you can't trust any of your readings. Every valve must be checked and if need be, opened manually."

"Do you have any idea how many miles of pipe we're talking?" someone called out.

"Twenty-six," Morris answered. "And nine hundred twenty-eight valves." A groan went up but no one stopped working. "We don't need all of them, though. Just the emergency coolant lines."

A few workers were handing out walkie-talkies. "We have the turbine and coolant crews," one operator said, listening to his radio.

"I've made contact with the containment crew," another put in.

"Good." Morris took a radio and began speaking into it. "What's the situation?"

A voice over the radio answered him. "The sudden spike in pressure—" There was a sputter of static. "Catastrophic failure . . . reactor pressure-overflow relief valve blew."

The entire room tensed at that. I had no idea what a pressure-overflow relief valve was, but I could tell it was bad.

Morris was the first of us to regroup. "I need Team One working on manually bypassing every valve in the emergency coolant system, get it flowing a.s.a.p. Team Two, you get the generators back up and running—and remember, go manual, we can't trust any system that he might have had access to." He paused. "What's the situation with the control rods?"

"Not good. He used some kind of random sequence when he locked down the system. If we try to reset them all together we're only resetting some and actually freezing up the others."

"You'll have to do them one by one, then." Morris's voice was grim. "In the meantime, I'll be going in to pull the plug on the quench tanks manually."

Everyone froze and stared at him.

"All four reactors?" one man asked.

"What's a quench tank?" I asked the operator closest to me.

"A tank of gadolinium nitrate that will smother the core. They sit above each reactor in case of a direct hit from above like a jet or missile strike."

"Morris, you can't," someone protested. "With the relief valve blown, it's suicide."

"Not if you all move fast enough and get those rods down before I need to go that route." He began to leave and I scrambled to follow.

"What about your robots, can't they do it?" I asked, envisioning C3PO walking into the reactor. Better than Morris.

He didn't slow, merely shook his head.

I caught up with him. "What can I do to help?"

He paused. I thought for a moment he was going to order me to leave.

"With communications out, I'll need someone to relay information via a handheld—these guys are all gonna have their hands full. Come on, we don't have much time."

This entire day was not turning out the way Hutton had expected, and that frustrated him to no end. He should have had AJ on the stairs—he'd never failed like that, not when he was that close. It just shouldn't have happened.

Of course, the whole impending nuclear meltdown thing wasn't exactly on his agenda either.

He knew he should have joined the stream of people racing to their cars, but he couldn't resist one last look at AJ. She fascinated him.

From the plant manager's empty office, he watched her join the workers in the control room below. There was a speaker on the wall, so he listened in shamelessly. It was pretty obvious that things were dire and that there wasn't much time. One guy, apparently the guy in charge, had just signed up for a suicide mission. And AJ was joining him.

Maybe this day would end as planned after all. Of course, if AJ died in a meltdown that meant there was a good chance Hutton wouldn't be around to collect his paycheck. But it wasn't like he could do anything to help the situation. His best bet was to make sure the kid made it to safety—Masterson had been very clear about that in his instructions. No harm was to come to the child.

Hutton left the office when AJ left the control room. He went back downstairs, reaching the security office just in time to see Ty Stillwater, the deputy with the impeccable timing, usher his prisoner outside. He followed, hanging back out of sight but within listening range.

"The sheriff's station is twelve miles up 170," one of the security guys was saying as two more joined the prisoner in the back seat of a black Yukon. "We'll meet you there."

"I'll be right behind," Stillwater said.

Hutton noticed a sheriff's vehicle marked *Smithfield County* with West Virginia plates parked not far from the two crashed SUVs. He ducked back into the shadows just as Stillwater, his dog, and the boy exited the plant and headed to their vehicle. Time to blow this pizza joint.

AJ Palladino's life he'd leave in the hands of fate.

For now, at least.

◆

I followed Morris into the locker room. The plant was now empty except for the men and women working furiously to save it.

Morris no longer acted like the congenial absent-minded professor I'd met yesterday. Instead, he radiated an intensity that made me give him more room than usual, afraid to crowd out any important thoughts.

I understood that kind of focus—it was exactly how I got when I was hard at work and felt "in the zone." Never with the fate of thousands in my hands, though.

While he donned his own suit, he talked me through putting on a heavy-duty radiation suit. Instead of the flimsy yellow ones I'd seen when I was decontaminated, these were made of a heavy black material. Demeromn, Morris told me, as if knowing the brand name would reassure me. It didn't.

We put on headsets and microphones along with full-face masks, another departure from the respirators that the health physicist and NRC guy had worn earlier. Funny how I hadn't seen them rushing to help. I wondered when they'd abandoned us.

"Because of the shielding near the reactors," Morris explained as we hurried down to the containment area, his voice surprisingly calm, "my radio may not transmit all the way to the control room. You're my failsafe. You'll be standing outside the containment area, so you should be shielded from any radiation. All I need is for you to repeat everything I say to the control room and then relay any information they have for me."

"Redundancy," I muttered, a little frustrated that my job was to stand there and play Whisper Down the Alley.

"Failsafe," he corrected. "There's a window that you'll be able to see me through. If my radio totally fails, you'll have to use the whiteboard to send me messages." He pulled a small whiteboard with a pen attached from a pocket on his pants leg and pointed to a duplicate one on my suit.

It was hard enough moving in the heavy suit, which was way too big for my frame. I wondered if I'd be able to write anything legible with the thick gloves I wore. Hoped it wouldn't come to that. The suit's interior was hot, my hands and face were sweating, and if I breathed too hard the facemask fogged up.

We passed through several thick doors, the last two painted magenta with large yellow radiation warnings printed on them. I remembered Morris's lecture about the importance of redundancies. Finally we reached the containment area. No one else was here. Morris steered me to a narrow horizontal window.

"I'm going inside. I need to climb up to the upper level and manually open each tank." He pointed to a narrow steel ladder fastened to the concrete wall, barely visible in the emergency lighting.

All along, the other teams had been reporting in their failures and successes, transmitting through our headsets. Morris took it all in stride, occasionally contributing a new idea or alternative, but for the most part he trusted his people to get the job done. But knowing that he was about to go inside an area that the others clearly thought he wouldn't emerge from alive, I felt the need to make absolutely sure.

Toggling my mike clumsily with my gloved finger, I broke in and said, "Morris is entering the containment facility. Do you guys have any reason why he shouldn't go?"

Silence met me. Guess nuclear engineers aren't really into chatter—or saying good-byes. Then an anonymous voice sounded. "Good luck" was all he said.

Morris didn't even act like he'd heard. He was hunched over the door's manual controls. It was designed like an air lock, but as soon as hc opened the first door an alarm sounded and a red light began flashing through the darkness. He turned to close the door behind him, and our eyes met.

Mired in helplessness, all I could do was wave good-bye.

# — THIRTY-TWO —

The radio chatter continued in my ears, frustrating me even more because I didn't understand most of what was being said. Just as Morris entered the chamber through the second air-lock door, the lights came back on.

I got my first look at the heart of the plant. It was a large concrete-walled dome riddled with colored pipes headed in every direction. The actual reactors sat inside a second dome, this one made of stainless steel. It sat in the center of the room, the maze of pipes emerging from it.

"Status," Morris's voice cut through the others, interlaced with static.

"Generators online."

"Control rods?"

"Still working on them. It'll go a little faster now that we have juice."

"Core temperature?"

A pause. "Rising fast. Do you have a count in there?"

"Low enough to give me a few minutes. Let's make them

count." Morris began climbing the ladder. The platform he was aiming for was a good forty feet over his head.

I couldn't resist, I had an idea and I figured it couldn't hurt. "Couldn't you release some of the pressure by having the robots open the isotope extraction chambers?"

A pause in the chatter. "Wait, she has a point. It could buy us some time."

"We'd have to—" The conversation drifted back into technical jargon that I couldn't interpret. But at least I'd contributed something.

Morris kept climbing. At one point he stopped and tapped the top of his head.

"Morris, can you hear me?"

No answer, but he nodded his head. "Can you hear the others?"

Now he shook his head. Great. It was up to me to relay the information that was bombarding me like waves in a hurricane.

"Guys," I cut into the chatter once more. "Morris has lost you. I can't repeat everything to him—there are too many conversations going on, so could you let me know when you have something he needs to hear?"

"Nothing good on this end," a voice replied. "Coolant pumps still off-line. We're trying to track the problem—our readings say they're all open."

That sounded familiar. I remembered reading—"Three Mile Island," I interjected. "Didn't they have the same problem?"

"You're right. A false reading led them in the wrong direction. We'll manually inspect and open each of them."

"How long?" I asked, watching Morris's slow progress. He still had ten feet to go before he even reached the platform.

"I've put everyone on the emergency coolant line, maybe four minutes if we don't run into problems."

"Is that enough time? Should I pull Morris out?"

He paused. "No. We're past the point where the emergency coolant will stop things. It will only buy us time."

"AJ?" came another voice, this one a woman's—the health physicist. So she hadn't abandoned us after all. "Are you at the observation window?"

"Yes."

"Now that the power is back on, you should be able to see a monitor on the wall next to the air lock. It's encased in a red box and has a color reading as well as a digital one."

"I see it. It's too far away from me to read the number, but the needle is just at the top of the yellow, verging on the red." Even I could figure out that wasn't good. "What is it measuring?" I wasn't sure I wanted to know but had to ask.

"The radiation inside the chamber."

"So how long does Morris have?"

She didn't answer. Instead, a man did. "Long enough to get the job done."

His words were hopeful but his tone was anything but. I refocused on Morris—if he could still hear my end of the conversation he hadn't shown any sign. "Morris, they say they'll have the emergency coolant going soon. And that your radiation levels are okay, you should have time."

He jerked his head in a nod, never pausing in his climb. He reached the top catwalk and hoisted his body up onto it. I could tell he was exhausted, but he hauled himself upright and, hanging onto the railing, stumbled across the catwalk to the first quench tank control.

It was a big metal wheel like what you see in submarine movies. There was a control panel beside it and Morris tried that first, then pounded his fist against it. Obviously despite the emergency power being back on, Paul's sabotage of the electronics had done irreparable damage.

He leaned his body against the wheel and began to turn it to the left.

"The controls wouldn't work. Morris is opening the first quench tank manually," I reported to the others.

"We're almost there on the emergency coolant," someone piped in.

Whatever Morris was doing must have worked because suddenly someone shouted, "Reactor One down!" and there was a cheer.

Morris turned around, raising his hands questioningly.

"You did it!" I shouted. He made no sign that he could hear, so I gave him a thumbs up and he nodded. Then he shuffled to the next control area.

"He's opening tank two," I reported. Morris was struggling now, leaning hard against the wall, his grip slipping as he worked.

"Good. We just got emergency coolant and have most of the control rods down in Reactor Four."

"Two's down!" someone cut in.

Morris collapsed.

"Morris!" I shouted. "He's not moving. What should I do?" There was no way I'd be able to go in and carry him down from the catwalk.

"We have control of Number Three!" a voice trampled my words. "We've done it! We're clear!"

"Morris is down," I cried into the radio, trying to break through the cacophony of jubilant noise. "Someone tell me how to help him!"

I pounded my fist against the window but the glass was so thick that I couldn't even make a thud. Standing there, helpless, my mask fogged with tears of frustration and sorrow.

The red lights stopped flashing, cheers filled my helmet. But Morris never moved.

◆

Hutton spent the night with the other refugees at the sheriff's station. He wasn't too surprised when the news came that not only had
AJ survived but she'd also helped to prevent a nuclear catastrophe.

He wasn't a religious man, but even he could see when the universe was aligned against him.

Masterson didn't agree when Hutton called to cancel the job.

"I'm tired of your excuses. You need to stop her before she gets
here."

"Or what? You'll tell my mommy?"

"Or recordings of your transactions will be forwarded to the
FBI," Masterson snapped.

"You can't do that. You'd be implicating yourself."

"I didn't say 'our' transactions, I said 'yours.' I've kept tabs on you
since you first got started in your new trade years ago. What? Did
you think I was just going to trust you to vanish and not try to
blackmail me?"

Silence.

"Okay. I'll take care of Palladino. But then you and I are long
past due for a face-to-face meeting."

"Fine. As long as she doesn't make that court hearing." Masterson hung up.

◆

The sun was coming up the next morning when I finally got a
chance to see David again. Hermes hit just north of Colleton
Landing, but inside the plant, we barely noticed. Everyone was too
busy cleaning up the mess Paul's sabotage had wrecked.

Everyone except me, that was. I had plenty of time to think
about the damage I'd done—had I been too greedy, seeing Grandel's

job as an easy way out for my family? Too ready to quit because I wanted to go home? What should I have done differently?

Comfort came, of all places, from Yancey. He'd gotten left behind in the evacuation and had spent the night in one of the offices filming a self-documentary of surviving a possible nuclear disaster.

Once the crisis was over, he'd found me sitting on the stairs. I'd been pronounced "clean" of any contamination, but felt anything but.

"Wrong place, wrong time," he said, sinking down beside me and offering me a Snapple left over from the refugees. "You can't blame yourself for that, AJ."

Easy to say. That's the drawback of being a control freak—when things go wrong, you can't help but blame yourself.

"At least your client will be happy," he continued, holding his camera up for me to view his footage. "Give me an hour of editing time and I'll have a piece that will make any investor leap at the opportunity to buy into this technology."

"You mean Morris's technology." I choked a bit on Morris's name. I'd only known him for a day, but his death was still painful. I couldn't stop thinking about his smile—so innocent, all he'd wanted was to save his family. Just like me.

Yancey nodded, looking sad himself, and gave me a hug. Must have meant it, too, because he didn't even try to cop a feel.

When Ty arrived at the plant with David just after sunrise, I was treated to a barrage of questions about the near-disaster, peppered with David's account of what it had been like to ride out the storm at the sheriff's station.

I barely got two words in—just kept hugging my son, embarrassing him in front of the plant workers who had gathered to pay their respects as the emergency crews were finally able to retrieve Morris's body. Everyone stopped and bowed their heads as the metal container holding Morris—identical to the one used for the alligator a day earlier—was rolled out to a waiting van. Even the NRC guy had a tear in his eye.

"You know this would have been a real disaster in a conventional plant," he told me as he followed the container out. "Morris's design saved us all."

"He was a true hero." I shook his hand. He left, and I turned to see Yancey filming. Almost smacked him, but it wasn't worth it.

Owen Grandel didn't show up until Ty and I were transferring my stuff from the wrecked SUV into Ty's Tahoe.

Grandel had brought a gaggle of media types with him. I ducked my head and jumped into the front seat, locking the door, before he could spot me. But that didn't block out the sound of his speech from the front steps. A memorial tribute to his brother, he called it, but it really was a thinly veiled announcement of four new foreign joint venture partners investing in Grandel Reactor Technologies.

Ty loaded Nikki into the back, I checked to make sure David was secure, and we drove away before Grandel finished. The glass dome sparkled in the early morning sunlight, washed clean by the storm. As it flashed in my side view mirror I couldn't help but think of the flash of Morris's smile. That's how I wanted to remember him.

I prayed that I wasn't the only one.

# THIRTY-THREE

David was so exhausted that he slept most of the drive home. But he'd wake every now and then to the warm voices of Ty and his mom talking. About him, about his dad, about when they were kids, about their work—even arguing about Ty bringing David to South Carolina, which started out with both of them talking in that rapid-fire muffled-loud whisper adults think kids can't hear and ended with them holding hands over the center console.

He liked that. A lot.

Closing his eyes as the hum of the tires sang him back into slumber, he decided that sometimes grownups weren't so very smart after all. Otherwise his mom and Ty would have figured things out a long time ago.

◆

After listening to Ty's story about his and David's journey, chasing after some phantom hit man targeting me, I'd been ready to take David and run away to a desert island where Masterson could never find us.

Eventually Ty's logic prevailed, although I was still angry at him for bringing David into all this. But he was right, there really was no one else I could have trusted David with—if Ty had taken him back to Scotia, Masterson might have found some other way to get to him.

Once we finished arguing we started talking, and my jangled nerves smoothed out. For the first time in days, I was able to relax. Something about the hypnotic monotony of the interstate. Or maybe it was the man beside me.

I tried not to think about that. About anything.

We'd just settled into a congenial silence when Ty's phone rang. Elizabeth. I answered. "It's me."

"You would not believe the night I've had," she started, her voice pitched with excitement. I stifled my laugh. "I hope you guys are on your way back, because the judge wants to talk to David in chambers at two."

"I'll tell Ty."

"Tell him the judge wants to hear from him as well—and he'd better be ready to do a bit of tap dancing. Masterson had everyone up in arms, practically accused Ty of kidnapping David."

"He's not in trouble, is he?"

"I think I smoothed most of it. But you all need to get here on time. Don't piss this judge off."

"Okay, thanks." I hung up. "Elizabeth said the judge is expecting David there at two."

Ty inched down on the accelerator. "We should just make it."

"What do we tell the judge about what happened since yesterday?"

"Couldn't we just lie?" David asked from the back seat.

"No!" Ty and I said together. I twisted in my seat to make sure David got the message loud and clear, only to find him grinning.

"Just kidding," he said.

"You're in enough trouble, young man," I lowered my voice to my most fierce mama-bear growl. "You might want to just sit back and be quiet, let the grownups think in peace."

He squinched his nose at me, knowing that I wasn't as angry as I sounded—how could I be? I was so relieved he was okay. And even more worried about what to do about Masterson and this invisible hit man he'd sent.

I mean, really, a hit man? Is this what my life had become, a Tarantino movie cliché?

"I still think we should have gone in separate cars," I told Ty.

"No. We stick together."

There was no way I was about to waltz into that courthouse with a target on my back, a hit man on the loose, and my son in the line of fire.

But I couldn't say that, not with David within hearing distance. Instead I jerked my thumb back at David, rolling my eyes at Ty until he scowled and finally got the message.

"I don't want to risk David being late for his meeting with the judge," I said, covering our real, silent conversation. "Drop me at your place and I can take your truck to the courthouse after I get cleaned up. That way no one will be able to track me."

Ty didn't like my plan. But we had no choice. Neither of us would risk David.

"You get cleaned up at my place," he suggested. "I'll drop David off and come back for you."

I knew what he was feeling—wanting to be in two places at once. I'd felt that way my entire time in South Carolina.

"No." Ty was the best person to keep David safe. "You stay with David."

He gripped the steering wheel tighter but grudgingly nodded.

"What did you tell your boss when you talked with him this morning?" I asked, glad to change the subject.

"Just that I found David hidden in my vehicle and that it was late, he was asleep—which he was at the time—and I'd make sure he got to court on time."

"Pretty much the truth, then."

"Except for the part about being five hundred miles away in the middle of a hurricane."

David popped his head forward between the seats. "Why can't we tell the judge about what I heard Mr. Masterson say on the phone? Can't you just arrest him? He's a bad man, shouldn't he go to jail?"

It occurred to me that David read way too many books that had happy endings. After everything he'd been through in his real life, he knew that good guys didn't always win. Yet somehow, he still believed that we—me and Ty—could make the world right again.

I only wished I was up to the job—I never, ever wanted David to feel powerless like he had been when he'd seen his dad killed. I wanted him to believe in a world where justice did triumph, where everyday folks like me and Ty could be heroes. Where men like Masterson got what they deserved.

"We have no proof," Ty finally said the words aloud.

David flopped back into his seat. "I thought that's what you'd say. And nobody would believe a kid like me, right?"

"It's not that they wouldn't believe you," Ty continued, somehow knowing just the right thing to say. "It's that our legal system requires more evidence than only what one person says before they send someone to jail. Otherwise anyone could say anything about anyone and lie, right?"

"Yeah, I guess." David blew out his breath. "So, what do I tell the judge? He'll ask me why I ran away and if I tell him the truth about what happened, Ty will get in trouble."

I had little faith in the legal system to give us justice. And whatever happened today would decide the fate of my family. But I couldn't ask David to lie.

I squeezed Ty's arm. His muscles tensed enough to stretch the seams of his shirt sleeve. "I know how much your job means to you. But he has to tell the truth."

Ty nodded. "Of course he does." Then he did that half-joking, half-serious lop-sided grin of his. "Isn't that what I said like an hour ago? Trust me. It'll be fine."

"Yeah, Mom. You should just listen to Ty. He knows what he's doing."

Nikki made a sound of agreement—or maybe she was simply happy because David had found a good spot to scratch between her ears. But I knew when I was out-ranked and out-numbered. Even if I had a very bad feeling. Not because I didn't trust Ty and David with the fate of my family, but because there wasn't one damn thing I could do about it.

I was the one powerless. And I didn't like that at all.

◆

Ty and David dropped his mom off at Ty's cabin up the mountain behind Ty's mother's house. Ty hadn't wanted to leave her, but she'd out-stubborned him as usual.

"The hit man is five hundred miles away—how could he know where I am?" she'd argued. "You just concentrate on getting David to the judge on time. Don't worry, I'll be right behind you."

David thought they might kiss through Ty's open driver's window, there was a strange moment where they both seemed to want to, but it passed and Ty pulled out of the drive once Mom was inside with the door locked.

As much as David wanted them to stay together, he was glad to have a few minutes alone with Ty.

On the way to the courthouse David tried his best to straighten the creases from his clothes. At least he'd be walking into the judge's chambers on his crutches instead of sitting in his wheel-chair. He wanted the judge to see him as someone worth listening to, not just a little kid dependent on others.

"What's he going to ask me?"

"Probably just what it's like living with your mom, how you like it here compared to D.C., stuff like that."

"He'll ask me about D.C.?"

"He might. Why, is that a problem?" Ty glanced back in the mirror.

David swallowed. He wasn't supposed to know about their being evicted or the few nights when his mom had miraculously allowed him to spend the night at a friend's house and he'd realized the next day that she'd slept in the car. She always found a place for them. But sometimes things got a bit scary.

"Is it a lie if you tell part of the truth but not everything you know? Like what if you told what happened but not why it happened?" What if he got his mom in trouble by talking too much? Maybe he shouldn't say anything, act like he was just another dumb kid.

"David. You know the answer to that. You need to tell the truth. No matter what happens, it won't be your fault. And your mother won't ever stop loving you."

Nikki stuck her nose through the grate and licked David's ear. He giggled, feeling better. Then he turned to the other subject on his mind. "You love my mom, don't you?"

Ty made a sputtering noise that turned into a laugh. "You got me. Guilty as charged."

"So how come you two—I mean—"

"Well, when we were kids she and your dad were together. And then she was gone. And then your dad died."

"But what's stopping you from telling her now? You're not chicken, are you?" David knew he was playing dirty with that last, but damn it, he knew Ty could make his mom happy, and wouldn't that be the best thing for everyone?

Because if David had both a mother and a father, no judge could separate their family and neither could Mr. Masterson.

It was so very simple. And obvious. Why couldn't the grownups see that?

To his surprise, Ty didn't answer or make a joke of it. Instead he grew thoughtful, gave a little nod. "You know what? I think I am chicken. Sometimes when you want something so bad for so long, it's easier to let it slip away than to reach out and grab it."

David leaned forward, enjoying this change in the power balance. Here he was, giving advice to a smart guy like Ty.

"Hey, Ty." He made his voice go low like the older kids at school goofing around in the locker room. "Grow a pair, why don't cha?"

◆

I waved to Ty and David. Then I kicked as much mud as I could from my shoes before stepping into Ty's impeccably kept A-frame log cabin. Now that I knew David was safe, all I could think about was a long, hot shower and clothes that weren't so stiff with mud and sweat that they could walk on their own.

"You made good time, AJ," a man's voice came from the living room beside me.

I whirled. A man, medium built, mid-thirties, medium brown hair and eyes, stood holding a semi-automatic pistol on me. Time felt like it was spinning out of control as I caught my bearings.

"I've seen you before," I stammered, surprised that I was speaking my thoughts aloud. In my head, this was all happening in ultra-slo-mo, but out here in the real world everything seemed spinning way too fast. "You were at the plant. You dropped your water."

"Almost had you there." A smile curled his lips, revealing his upper teeth. "No worries. Once I knew where you were headed, I just made sure I got here first." He glanced past me out the window. "I'm glad David is going to make it to court on time."

"How—" I stopped myself, trying not to sound too slow. "You had a bug in Ty's car."

"Yep. Technology. So very helpful in my line of work." He waved the gun. "Let's go, we'll take Ty's truck. Just like you two planned. Only we're going to make a little stop along the way."

# THIRTY-FOUR

Ty and David arrived at the courthouse just in time for their appointment—but were told Judge Mabry was busy. While they waited, David leaned against his crutches, soaking in the nineteenth-century architecture: so many small details, like the scales of justice, carved into the cornices. But Ty paced, more nervous than David had ever seen him.

"You want something to drink?" Ty asked.

"No thanks. I'm fine."

Ty made another circuit of the wide corridor. Finally he seemed to make up his mind, coming to a stop before David. "Would you be okay waiting by yourself?"

"Sure. Where are you going?"

"I thought I'd go pick up your mom, give her a ride to court myself."

David fought an eye roll. Grownups were so oblivious.

"And—" he prompted Ty. "Are you going to tell her how you really feel?"

Ty looked down at his shoes as if checking to see if they were tied. "Uh, sure, maybe, you know, we could talk." Ty straightened, and David knew that was the best he would get.

"Ty. My mom needs more than a ride to court. She needs to know that this," David waved his hand at the marble and wood and solemnity of the courthouse, "could never happen again. The best way to do that is if I have a father."

Ty jerked his chin up in surprise, blinked, then sank down onto the bench beside David. "You mean," his voice broke, "you want me to ask her to marry me?"

David slumped against his crutches, his body feeling heavier than ever. "Gee, don't sound so excited." He tried to bury his disappointment in humor and failed. "Not like I actually need two parents or anything. We're doing pretty good just like we are."

"No. David. I didn't mean—"

The judge's clerk opened the door, beckoning David inside. "Never mind," David muttered. "It was a stupid idea."

The judge's chambers were behind the courtroom, the clerk explained as she led David down a long corridor with pews on either side, then around an area walled off by a waist-high wooden wall, and through two heavy wood doors.

"Here he is, Judge Mabry," she called out, giving David a little wave, as if he might get lost if she didn't send him in the right direction.

David took his time, keeping his head up high as he maneuvered his crutches. He wanted time to study the judge and for the judge to see him as strong, independent. Not a fatherless cripple or a kid too young to have a say in his own future.

Judge Mabry wasn't very tall and didn't have much hair left. What little there was grew in long scraggly strands that he'd arranged around a liver spot on the top of his head. David wondered why he didn't just shave it all off, but he didn't ask.

"David, it is very nice to meet you." The judge stood and came around his desk to motion to two adjacent leather chairs.

David took one, carefully arranging his crutches beside him so they wouldn't fall down and hit one of the many photos that stood on the table between them. Tons of photos of smiling kids, family picnics, birthday parties. David tore his glance from them, hoping the judge wouldn't be expecting him to produce any such evidence of his own familial bliss.

The judge wasn't wearing his robes; instead, he had on gray slacks and a short-sleeve plaid shirt—the kind old men wear golfing. His shoes were slip-ons, nothing to tie, and he didn't wear socks. David suddenly felt overdressed for the occasion.

"You aren't nervous, are you?"

"No sir." David was relieved when his voice didn't crack. "Well, maybe just a little. I've never met a judge before."

The judge smiled and sat back in his chair. "Well, we're just people like anyone else. Except we've been given a very serious job to do. Do you know what that is?"

"Yes sir. You're going to decide who gets custody of me." David wasn't sure if he should quote the West Virginia code, Chapter 49, Article 6 on child welfare or not. He didn't want to show off or insult the judge.

"That's right. And this case has turned out to be much more complicated than expected."

David decided it was time to confess. "I suspect that I'm the cause of that, sir. I should have respected your wishes and not run away from Mr. Masterson."

The judge nodded but didn't look too angry. "Is that what you call your paternal grandfather, Mr. Masterson?"

"Yes sir."

"What do you call your maternal grandparents?"

"Grandma and grandpa. And my great-grandmother is Gram Flora." David realized he hadn't had a chance to call Flora; he hoped she was doing okay. Maybe the judge knew. "Do you know if Flora is out of the hospital? Someone needs to be monitoring her diabetes, it's very difficult to control."

"She's fine. Going home today, I was told. You took care of her the other night when she got sick, didn't you?"

"Sure. Jeremy, er, Mr. Miller, her personal care assistant, taught me how. He's very good at his job and a good teacher."

"I imagine you're an excellent student. I've read your school files."

David wasn't sure what he could say to that without sounding like a show-off. So he just nodded and waited for the next question. It was obvious that the judge was being very careful about what he was asking. David wondered if he was worried about somehow hurting David's feelings by making him say something bad about someone he loved or if the judge was trying to protect someone else.

"And what happened in March—your quick thinking helped save lives then as well."

David didn't really want to talk about what had happened when his dad died, so he shrugged one shoulder and looked away.

"Which leads me to believe," the judge continued, "that you're an extremely bright and capable young man with a promising future. So, you tell me, who do you think would take the best care of you and provide you with the most opportunity for your future?"

Finally, a grownup treating him like an adult. David turned to the judge. "That's easy, sir. My mother."

"Really? But Mr. Masterson has all that money—think of the potential."

"I don't want my future handed to me bought and paid for," David declared. "My mother has always taught me that everyone can be their own hero if they just find the courage to fight for what they believe in. I want to grow up to be just like her. I think sometimes you have to learn things the hard way and make mistakes and work hard for something before you discover what really matters and what you really believe in." He ran out of steam, worried that he'd gone on too long, so quickly added, "Sir."

The judge stared at him for a long moment. Then he gave a quick jerk of his chin and patted David on the shoulder. "Very well said, young man. Have you considered a career in law?"

◆

The gunman made me drive Ty's F-150. We didn't see anyone as we left Scotia and headed toward Smithfield. At first I was worried he was taking me to the courthouse, conjuring up all sorts of doomsday scenarios where he used me to get to David, but then he made me pull off at the scenic viewing area overlooking the New River Gorge.

The place was empty—usually was; hardly anyone came here except for teenagers looking for a make-out spot at night. Once we left the parking lot and walked down the path to the rock ledge, the trees hid us from sight of the road.

"Don't you love this view?" he asked, heaving in a breath, his chest stretching the button-down shirt he wore. "No wonder so many choose to make it their last."

I froze, digging my heels in on the gravel path. He took my elbow, effortlessly forcing me past the observation area into a boulder-strewn meadow that ended in a sheer drop-off. It was at least a thousand feet down to the bottom of the gorge.

"No one would ever believe that I'd kill myself," I tried to reason with him. "You won't get away with it."

"Well, now, I admit it's not as nuanced as my usual methods," he drawled, "but the beauty of it is that it doesn't matter if people believe it or not. You'll be dead and I'll be gone, and no one will ever be able to prove what really happened here today."

I had no idea what to say to that. We'd reached the last line of boulders. I dropped my weight suddenly, twisting free of his grasp for one short moment, and ran. Of course the damn heels slipped on the long meadow grass, landing me smack on my face.

At least he didn't laugh as he hauled me to my feet. "You really are something, AJ Palladino. I'm almost sorry to see this come to an end."

"At least tell me who hired you," I pleaded. "It was Masterson, wasn't it?"

He merely shook his head like I was asking him to do something naughty and spun me in his grasp until he held me with one arm around my throat, not quite choking me but definitely able to control my movements.

"He's after my son, David," I continued. "Please, if you've met the man, you know what he's like, you can't let him take my son. I have a ten-year-old son, he's a brilliant, wonderful boy—did you know that?" I was babbling, sobbing, saying anything that came to mind. I clawed at his arm but couldn't loosen his iron grip. "Please, just tell me that you won't hurt David, that he's safe."

"I don't kill children," he said, his voice a low growl as if I'd offended him. "David is safe."

He tightened his grip and my vision blackened. Too late I realized his plan—choke me unconscious, then toss my body over the edge. No sign of a struggle that way.

He dragged me onto a boulder and leaned back so I couldn't reach any part of his body as I flailed—I even tried going for his groin but hit the boulder instead. I fought like I'd never fought for anything before, reaching for his eyes to claw them out, craning to bite him, anything to fight free. It was all useless.

Just as my head thundered with a roar of blood and I knew it was all over, I heard a dog bark.

The man loosened his grip. Slowly my vision returned. Ty stood at the edge of the meadow, his gun aimed at the man's head.

"Drop it!" Ty shouted. Nikki circled in front of us to one side of Ty, not crossing his line of fire, her teeth bared.

Ty was so focused that for a moment I wondered if he even saw me. Of course he did. But Ty was good at his job.

Thank God. Because that was probably my only way out of this alive. My body half lay, half sat on the boulder, the gunman behind me.

Ty kept moving forward as the gunman yanked me back, forcing me to sit up and shield him.

"Stop," the man called. "Drop your gun or I'll kill her."

That wasn't going to happen. Ty always scoffed at hostage scenes in movies where the cops gave up their guns. "All you end up with is a dead cop along with a dead hostage," he'd said. When David had asked him what a real cop would do, he'd shrugged. "You do the best you can. Sometimes you can't save everyone. But a good cop always makes sure he makes it home alive so he can save someone else the next day."

Which meant I was probably going to die.

But right here, right now, all I could think about was what an easy target Ty made, standing there out in the open. I tried to remember if he'd put his vest on—he'd worn his uniform during the long drive from South Carolina, but I had a sudden, terrifying image of his Kevlar vest lying on the back seat of the Tahoe.

If I could find the strength to shout I would have told him to leave, but when I opened my mouth it was all I could do to drink in the oxygen the choke hold had deprived me of.

The gunman was no dummy. He crowded his body behind mine so that there was no way Ty would be able to hit him without shooting me.

"I said, drop your gun," he shouted at Ty. "Don't push me, Deputy. I mean what I say."

"I know you do, Mr. Hutton."

The man jerked suddenly. "Then you also know that I need to finish what I started."

"What the hell are you talking about?" I finally managed to ask. My voice was a scratchy whisper but Ty heard.

"Mr. Hutton here was an employee of Masterson's," Ty answered, edging closer. "Until the night ten years ago when he vanished. Same night you almost died, AJ."

He was stalling for time. I played along. "You mean, he—"

"There's been no trace of him since. No employment or tax records." Ty paused. "I'm guessing that's because people like Mr. Masterson pay him in cash. But before then he worked for Masterson driving a coal truck. Just like the one that ran you off the road ten years ago."

The gunman froze. Then laughed. "Okay, so you can add two and two. Even if it did take you ten years. All the more reason for me to kill you both."

Ty kept walking. "Really? Because you might shoot me, but not before my partner gets you." He gave Nikki a whistle and she stalked closer to us. "Or you can let AJ go and testify to the truth of what really happened ten years ago and who hired you now to make sure Masterson got custody of David. We can arrange protection if you're frightened of him."

Damn, Ty was good. He was hitting all of the gunman's vulnerabilities. I could tell because I could feel Hutton's muscles tighten, plastered against his body as I was.

"I'm not afraid of Masterson!"

"Then why are you letting him call the shots? I'm sure targeting frail old ladies and the mentally ill isn't your usual MO." Ty paused, frowning, while from the side, Nikki crept closer, her gaze locked onto Hutton. "Maybe I have it all wrong and you're not a professional?"

Hutton's teeth ground together, the cracking noise echoing through my skull, his face was so close to my ear. Another bull's-eye for Ty. I slanted my gaze, noted that Nikki had inched even closer. Unfortunately Hutton saw her as well.

"Call the dog off!"

Ty whistled to Nikki and she froze, waiting for his signal. Still at full alert, poised to pounce. She was about twenty feet away—but I'd seen her cover that much ground in a flash.

"Shoot that dog or I'll shoot the girl!"

"No, Ty, don't," I shouted.

But almost as if he hadn't heard, Ty pivoted, whistled a command to Nikki, and, when she turned to him, fired.

Nikki flopped to the ground. The meadow went silent as the gunshot echoed across the gorge and faded into oblivion, then Nikki gave out a painful whimper.

Unable to restrain myself, I broke away from Hutton's grip and lunged toward Nikki's motionless body. To my surprise he didn't just let me go, he gave me a hard shove that sent me tumbling directly into Ty's line of fire.

Once more I did a face plant flat into the dirt. Ty rushed to me, gathering me into his arms. By the time I looked up, the gunman had vanished.

An engine's roar and the screech of tires on pavement sounded in the distance.

"You shot Nikki," I cried, fighting his embrace. "Ty, how could you?"

In the past, I'd been a little jealous of Ty and Nikki's partnership—he'd take a bullet for her, he often said. How could he kill his partner just to save me? Betray a partner, a loved one? It was totally unlike Ty—the person or the lawman.

He only hugged me tighter. Once I stopped struggling I realized he was laughing. I looked up at him, stunned.

His whistle shrieked through the trees. An instant later, Nikki bounded to her feet and was streaking toward us, uninjured.

"You bastard, scaring me like that!" I punched him hard in the arm, then turned to embrace Nikki, giving the dog all the loving she deserved. "I can't believe that you'd even pretend to shoot Nikki."

"Well, the whole point was that Hutton didn't."

I turned to look at him, puzzled.

"If he'd really wanted to kill Nikki, she was in his sights. But he couldn't. Just like if he really wanted to kill you, he would've done it before I even got here, much less had the chance to get the drop on him."

"Maybe I'm harder to kill than you give me credit for."

He hugged me hard, squeezing the breath out of me. "I sure hope so."

"What were you doing here, anyway?"

"I didn't want you going to the courthouse alone. And something David said—" His face flushed as he stuttered to a stop. "Anyway, I saw my truck and knew you'd never stop here, not with the judge waiting, risking everything if you were late."

"So you risked everything on a hunch? I thought you always said cops relied on logic and training."

"It's three-twelve." Ty avoided my question. "Aren't you late for court?"

I bounded to my feet. "David—the judge is going to take David away from me."

"Not if I have anything to say about it. How'd you like a police escort?"

As he drove us in the Tahoe—his truck had of course vanished along with Hutton—he filled me in on how he'd discovered who Hutton was. "I still have no proof, of course, so we can't use it against Masterson. I wasn't even sure myself until I saw him with you. But maybe someday—"

"Someday? What if Hutton comes after us now that he knows we know who he is?"

"That's just the point. He won't. He'll go underground."

"And what about all the other people he might kill in the future?"

"If he's smart, he'll find a new line of work. Because I'll make sure every law enforcement agency in the country is looking for him." Ty said the last with such determination that I couldn't help but believe him.

Besides, sometimes you just have to do the best you can.

Elizabeth checked her watch again and looked over her shoulder toward the heavy oak door at the entrance of the courtroom. Still no AJ. "Your Honor, if I could beg the court's indulgence—"

"Your Honor," Hunter interrupted her, "we've already been waiting forty minutes for Ms. Palladino. I move for an immediate decision on behalf of my client."

"But, your Honor—"

The door burst open and AJ rushed in, followed by Ty. To Elizabeth's dismay, AJ was dressed in torn jeans, black heels, and a muddy polo top that had the collar half ripped off. There was dried blood on one arm, and her hair was a tangled mess that she was trying to comb with her fingers.

"I apologize, your Honor," AJ said as she jogged down the aisle to join Elizabeth, slipping on the marble floor in her heels. She leaned over to adjust them, using the motion to slip a piece of paper onto the table in front of Masterson.

"Ms. Palladino," the judge's tone was a cross between a sigh and a scold. "You do understand this hearing was to begin at three o'clock?"

"Yes, your Honor. I'm afraid I was unexpectedly detained." AJ took her place beside Elizabeth.

Across the aisle, Masterson was reading the note AJ had passed him, the color on his face draining until it was the same dingy gray as day-old dishwater.

"Your Honor, we would love to hear what was so important at

Ms. Palladino's job that she made it a priority over her son's well-being and this court." Hunter puffed his chest out as if the judge had already ruled in his favor. He didn't seem to notice that Masterson had sunk low in his seat beside him.

Elizabeth wondered what the hell was in the note AJ had given Masterson. Masterson wouldn't even look at AJ. Instead he leaned into Hunter and whispered something behind a cupped hand into Hunter's ear. Hunter's eyes went wide and his lips tightened as if he didn't like what he was hearing.

"Actually, work had nothing to do with it," AJ said. "I was detained because an employee of Mr. Masterson's tried to kill me."

◆

Things moved pretty fast after AJ's dramatic announcement. The judge waved Hunter down before he could protest or object.

"Ms. Palladino, you do have some evidence to back up your allegation, I presume?"

AJ glanced at Elizabeth, jerking her chin at the courtroom door and mouthing "Ty." She didn't need to bother with the charades, it was obvious what the next move was. "Your Honor, we would like to call Deputy Tyrone Stillwater to the stand."

Again the judge motioned to Hunter to not bother objecting. Masterson hunched over the table, concentrating on something he was doodling, not making eye contact with anyone. Judge Mabry, no fool, took it all in and leaned back as if ready to hear a damn good story.

Elizabeth had no earthly idea what Ty would testify to, which scared the shit out of the lawyer side of her, but the side that was AJ's friend was curious to hear the whole story, so she simply asked Ty what events had transpired that made them late for court.

Ty took it from there, giving the details about the attempt on AJ's life, identifying the man responsible as a previous employee of

Masterson Mines, Robert Hutton, who was the same man suspected of trying to kill AJ ten years ago. As Elizabeth led him
through his testimony, he was quick to infer that Hutton had also
been behind Flora's "accident" and the Palladinos' arson.

Despite the fact that Elizabeth had no real evidence to point at
Masterson, by the time Ty was finished, the judge was looking at
Masterson with narrowed eyes. Hunter was smart enough not to
cross-examine Ty.

"Before the witness is excused, I have a few questions for him,"
the judge said just as Ty was starting to stand. Elizabeth felt AJ
tense beside her, but she knew better than to ask anything. "Deputy
Stillwater, did you knowingly remove the minor in question from
the custodial care of Mr. Masterson yesterday?"

AJ blew her breath out as Ty answered, "No, your Honor. I discovered the minor hiding in my car after I'd already driven off and
was heading south."

Ty was smart. He'd answered the judge's question with just
enough details to obfuscate the truth. He could've been a lawyer.

"And why did you not immediately return the minor to Mr.
Masterson's care?"

"Your Honor," Hunter jumped to his feet. Masterson appeared
pale and was tugging at Hunter's sleeve, urging Hunter on. "We re-
spectfully withdraw our petition at this time."

The judge jerked his head up, looking disappointed and highly
suspicious. "Hmm. Let's get it on the record. Mr. Masterson, am I
correct that you are no longer contesting Ms. Palladino's ability to
adequately supervise and maintain custody of her child?"

Masterson stood beside Hunter. He swallowed hard enough
for his Adam's apple to jump. "Yes, your Honor. Now that Ms.
Palladino is home, I'm sure David will be, er, raised in an appropriate manner."

From his grimace it looked like every word was like swallowing
glass. Elizabeth wondered what Ty had to say that Masterson was

so frightened of. She glanced at AJ, who was grinning and bobbing in her seat in her excitement.

The judge pursed his lips. He glanced at Ty, who appeared terribly composed and in control, then at Masterson, who squirmed under his scrutiny. Finally he banged his gavel. "Very well. This matter is dismissed. Ms. Palladino will retain full parental rights and custody of the minor, David Palladino. We're done here."

AJ let loose with a whoop. The judge hid his smile while the bailiff shook his head at her sternly. Elizabeth gathered her papers, trying to think of an appropriate remark to put Hunter in his place.

She glanced sideways. Hunter was thrusting papers and notepads into his case without any order, bending and crushing them. More than angry, he was furious—and a bit frightened. Masterson was speaking to him in a tone too low to hear, but whatever he was saying obviously made things worse. Neither noticed the tiny bit of paper AJ had given Masterson swirling to the floor.

Finally, Hunter straightened and turned his back on his client. Which brought him face to face with Elizabeth. Who still didn't have the one-liner she wished for.

He glared at her, pivoted on his foot, and walked away, his shoulders slumped enough to put a crease in the otherwise perfect drape of his suit jacket.

She watched him go, wondering when the man she'd fallen in love with had vanished. There was no trace of him left. And thus, no need to try to hurt the empty shell that now wore his face.

It had been Hunter who'd felt the need to salvage his pride by coming all the way from Philly to humiliate her. She had nothing to prove to him—what mattered most was that she'd been able to save AJ's family.

Surprised by her smile, she reached for her briefcase, snagged the note as well, and strode down the aisle. She caught up with AJ outside and opened the note.

*AJ gets custody or Hutton talks.*

Elizabeth quickly shredded the note and threw it in the trash.

"I can't be a party to extortion," she told AJ, who watched with a smile dancing across her lips while they waited for David.

"You weren't. You were party to a bluff."

"You're kidding. You risked everything—"

"Hey, it worked, didn't it?"

# THIRTY-FIVE

"My friend Larry called," Elizabeth said as we counted out forks and plates for David's birthday cake. "Remember? The radiation oncologist? He saw you on TV. Was wondering why you didn't call him."

"Hello—I didn't call anyone. Alligator ate my phone, remember?"

"Yeah, I tried to tell him that, he wasn't buying it. If you're ever in Philly you might owe him dinner." She was grinning—of course, she hadn't stopped grinning since she'd convinced the DA to drop the charges against Jeremy.

"No, no," Flora said in that voice that made everyone shut up fast and listen. "I say presents first. Then cake."

I pulled my finger out of my mouth, hoping she wouldn't notice the missing glob of chocolate icing from the base of the cake. My present wasn't even wrapped yet. I'd been counting on sneaking off to the summerhouse while everyone was eating. I couldn't wait to see David's face when he opened it—an Apple iPad that I'd gotten a good deal on because it was refurbished. Now he could read and listen to his books all with one device.

"David would like to do something special this year," Flora

continued. I turned and eyed David, who was smiling so wide I thought his ears were going to do a jumping jack right off his head.

"Mom, you need to leave for a few minutes."

Good. I could go wrap his present. "Okay. Holler when you're ready for me." I headed out and turned toward the summerhouse but Ty intercepted me.

"We need to talk," he said, sounding way too somber for my liking. "Walk with me."

I tried to protest, but he seemed so upset that I didn't press it. Instead of going to the summerhouse, he steered me up the path toward the wishing stone. "What's wrong?"

"We can't find anything to tie Masterson to Hutton."

"Nothing at all?"

"No e-mails, no phone records. Nothing. Other than the fact that Hutton worked for Masterson ten years ago, there's nothing to suggest they ever knew each other."

"Still, it's an awfully big coincidence that an ex-Masterson employee would try to kill me, much less burn down my parents' house and try to kill Flora and frame Jeremy."

"Other than his attack on you, we can't prove anything. There's not one shred of evidence. And no trace of Hutton resurfacing either. But we have a BOLO out for him, and I'm going to keep poking around, maybe talk to Masterson again."

"Be careful. Last thing I want is for Masterson to target you next."

Ty made that snuffly grunting noise that meant he heard me but was politely ignoring me. We reached the wishing stone—usually my favorite spot in the universe. The limestone outcropping that perched over the valley made anything feel possible. Usually.

Ty joined me as we faced the endless vista of green and blue beneath our feet. For the first time ever, the view made me feel dizzy. Then I realized it was because I was holding my breath.

"Masterson wins," I whispered, my words snatched by the wind almost before they left my lips. "What's to stop him from trying to take David from me again?"

I hated feeling so bitter, not to mention helpless. Especially on a day that should be reminding me of the joy David brought into my life. I tried to turn my words and feelings into a joke. "Short of hiring another hit man, of course."

Ty was silent, his face without a trace of a smile. Stupid to joke about hit men with a police officer. I started to apologize, but he surprised me by interrupting.

"I know one thing that can stop Masterson," Ty said, taking my hand and turning me to face him.

Before I realized what was happening, he was kissing me. A kiss filled with promise . . . and passion.

By the time it ended, I was breathless. I wanted more—much more. But I held back, terrified at leaping into an emotional abyss. For so many years I'd guarded my heart, sharing it only with David—and David, what would he think?

Ty waited, his breath caressing my face. My stomach twisted like it was trying to escape. Who knew it would take an act of supreme courage to kiss a man I loved?

How could my life have come to this?

Ty had been right all along. My priorities had been totally screwed up.

Time to fix that. I gathered my courage and kissed him.

"Woohoo! About time, you two!" David's shout of glee startled me so much that Ty had to tug me back from the edge of the cliff.

"David—how?" His face was beet-red. Sweat glistened from his hair and dripped from his nose. I rushed forward, took him in my arms, not caring as his crutches fell to the ground. "My God! You did this? All by yourself?"

My words were so jumbled together I doubted he or anyone could understand me. Ty joined us, pulling David up into a bear hug.

"I'm so proud of you," I heard him whisper to David.

David's face filled with an expression I could never put there, as much as I tried: a son's joy returning a father's love and pride.

Flora, Jeremy, Elizabeth, and my parents came huffing up the path bearing cake and utensils. I stood, still stunned by what David had done, by what Ty had offered, by the fact that I was actually thinking of risking my heart . . .

Elizabeth brought me back to earth. "Yancey called. Said he has a lead on a job for us. Right up your alley, he says."

I rolled my eyes. "You know what? I need a vacation."

A smile crinkled her eyes as Ty came up behind me, wrapping his arms around my waist. Pure reflex had my body relaxing back into his, fitting perfectly. "At least this time you won't be going alone."

David bobbed up, using one crutch to balance himself as he offered a piece of cake to Elizabeth. "What are you guys talking about?"

"How'd you like a trip to the beach?" I asked him.

"Sure." Then he looked at me suspiciously. "Wait. Are you sending me away?"

"No." I rumpled his hair—and with his hands full he had no defense. "I'm talking about a trip for the family." I intertwined my fingers with Ty's. "The whole family."

◆

Masterson almost made things too easy, Hutton thought as he watched through his binoculars. Unless he was hosting a social function, Masterson's staff had weekends off, and this weekend was no exception. Just as Hutton had suspected, Masterson's ego had gotten the better of him and he hadn't hired any security. Typical.

Masterson had spent the day working at his desk and then had relaxed with a steak on the grill and a bourbon—Bookers. He'd sat out on the patio for a while, looking old and alone, Hutton thought, before changing into swim trunks and doing fifty laps in the Olympic-sized indoor pool.

Hutton used the time Masterson spent swimming to move into position. And, just like always, Masterson climbed out of the pool, threw a towel over his shoulders, poured himself another bourbon—a double this time—and headed into the sauna.

Usually he'd spend just ten minutes or so in there, then either go back to get more work done or go to bed.

Not tonight.

Hutton followed him inside, closing the door behind him just as Masterson stood, surprised enough that he spilled some Bookers from his glass.

"What the hell are you doing here?" he demanded. "We can't risk being seen together. You need to leave."

Hutton said nothing. Simply stood, enjoying the moment. Masterson didn't realize it yet, but they'd come full circle from the master-employee relationship that had begun ten years ago.

Masterson's gaze dropped, and he took in the skin-tight gloves Hutton wore. Ah, that's what Hutton wanted. To see the fear, the panic swallowed in a single heart-galloping gulp before acceptance set in.

He rarely indulged himself in showing himself to his targets—if they truly were surprised by their deaths, they tended to appear all the more accidental.

But this time he was very happy to make an exception. "Sit down."

Masterson started to take a step forward, unaccustomed to being ordered around, but Hutton drew his pistol and that squelched any rebellion before it started. "Rich man like you, living alone, a robbery gone bad works just as well as any other scenario."

Masterson nodded and sank onto the bench. "How are you going to do it?"

He'd never had a target ask that before. Hutton wondered if it was a bit inhumane to answer. But if knowing how he was going to meet his maker was Masterson's last request, he'd honor it.

"Dosed your bourbon. It's a plant extract similar to digitalis but untraceable. I'll swap out the bottles before I leave, of course. Just in case. But a man your age, drinking in a sauna, falling asleep in the heat after all that exertion—"

"It will appear like a heart attack."

Hutton nodded. "Less painful than a real one, if that helps any."

Masterson met Hutton's gaze, raised his glass with a challenging quirk of one eyebrow, and downed it all in one gulp. He carefully set the glass down. "How long?"

"Not long at all. Just relax."

"You do realize that when I die, they'll find everything. All those secrets out in the open."

"I'm willing to take the risk. Besides, I'm not that easy to catch." He didn't add that he was planning to retire—everything, the travel, the job, the name. Canada might be a nice place to settle. After all, he was still young, might just start a family—especially if he could get lucky enough to find a girl as smart as AJ Palladino.

Funny how his first failure had been his last. Full circle. He liked it when things balanced out that way.

Masterson's face grew flushed and his breathing rapid. His eyes slid to half-mast as his body slumped to one side. Hutton sat down beside him, holding his wrist, his fingers on his pulse. Seemed only fitting to keep him company. After all, Hutton did owe the man a lot.

Masterson had created Hutton. Now it was time for Hutton to become his own creation.

The pulse became fainter, then vanished all together. Masterson went still. Hutton waited several minutes, checking for breathing and a heartbeat. Silence.

Without saying good-bye, Hutton left as silently as he had entered.

Be sure to read

*Rock Bottom*

by Erin Brockowich with CJ Lyons

Turn the page to read an excerpt from the book.

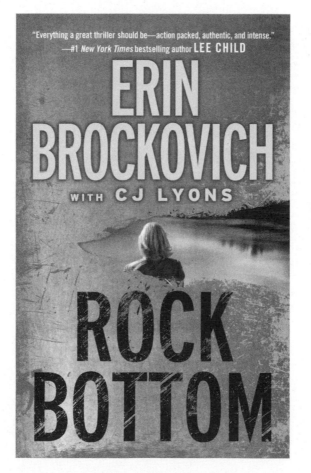

MASS MARKET EDITION
AVAILABLE IN NOVEMBER 2011

# ONE

"Hi, you're on the air with AJ Palladino, the People's Champion." I couldn't help but cringe every time I chirped the greeting, but the station manager insisted on using the title foisted on me by *People* magazine, so I had no choice.

Unlike my freelance research work, this radio gig kept food on the table and a roof over our heads. Small price to pay. Didn't mean I had to like it.

"AJ, hi again!" came a woman's voice. Happy, unlike many of my callers. "It's Martha. Martha from Pennsylvania."

The computer screen in front of me lit up with Martha's history and her previous calls. But I didn't need to read the details. As soon as I heard her name and voice I remembered. "Martha from Deercreek. You were having some problems with a fish kill in your stream, if I recall?"

"You remember! Thanks to you, we've been able to finally get things put right."

"We found you a contact with your state Department of Environmental Protection, and I think the local Ag-extension was going to help set up monitoring for your well?"

"The Ag-extension folks were so helpful. Turns out we weren't the only property affected. Two more farms downstream were as well. And the DEP, well, there was some hassle there at first, but I did what you said, I kept calm and just insisted that they do their jobs and investigate. And you know what? Turns out it was a dry cleaner from in town. Too cheap to pay to safely dispose of all those chemicals, he thought he could come out here and pump them into our creek! But they caught him, red-handed. And now he's paying to clean it all up—him and the state. Anyway, I wanted to thank you for all your help. It means the world to me and my neighbors."

It wasn't often that people took the time to call back and say thanks, so of course I smiled and gave my producer a double thumbs-up. "Thank you, Martha. Without people like you being willing to take a stand for what's right, guys like your dry cleaner would get away with destroying our environment and our communities just to save themselves a few bucks. You're a real people's champion."

My producer cued the cheers, applause, and celebratory sound effects. We signed off from Martha and took the next call. "Hi, you're on the air with AJ Palladino, the People's Champion."

"You're the one who took on Capital Power, won all that money for those folks?" This guy didn't sound near as happy as Martha.

"I helped. It wasn't about the money, though. It was about helping the people whose families suffered after their water was contaminated by Capital Power." I chose my words judiciously. The court case was famous, over and done with for four years, but every day someone just had to remind me of it—and of how far I'd fallen since.

Cinderella, the day after the ball. When she learned the prince didn't put the toilet seat down, the royal horse stalls needed mucking, and glass slippers weren't the most practical attire when running your ass off all day long in a palace with marble floors.

"What about helping all us people out of work now that Capital declared bankruptcy? You gonna go to court for us? Fight for our right to feed our families?" His words skidded together, building momentum like a NASCAR driver spotting the checkered flag.

"Sir, I'm not a lawyer—"

He drowned me out before I could finish my routine disclaimer. "No, you're just the bitch who took my job and my house, and now I can't even look my wife and kids in the eye. We're living in a tent. A goddamn tent! All because of you—"

I signaled my producer to record and trace the caller's location. Sitting up straight, I pressed my headset hard against my ear, as if I could channel the intentions behind his words.

"Sir, tell me more. How many kids do you have?" I tried in vain to engage him. Some were like that—they'd phone in to rant and vent and call me names that had the producer tapping the bleep button faster than a telegraph key. Those shows always made the station manager grin as ratings spiked. Usually I gave as good as I got. But something about this guy. . . .

"What do you care? The People's Champion, my ass. This is all your fault. Remember that, bitch. All your fault."

A blast thundered through my headphones. I tore the headset off, my ears ringing so loud I didn't realize I was shouting. "Sir, sir! Are you all right? What happened?"

The ON THE AIR light faded to black. I climbed off my stool, my balance wobbly. "Did you find him? Is he okay?"

"We've called nine-one-one. There's nothing more I can do." My producer was calm as he switched out PSA spots to fill the dead air.

"That was a gunshot."

The switchboard lights danced like firecrackers. He ignored them. We wouldn't be taking any more calls. Not today. Maybe not ever.

Sinking into the chair beside him, I cupped my ears, trying to muffle the screeching echo still rattling my fillings. "He's dead, isn't he?"

The direct line rang. He answered it, listened, then said, "Thank you," and hung up.

"Tell me." I wanted to throw up, needed to throw up, just to have an excuse to curl up alone in a bathroom stall, but instead I hung on to the arms of the vinyl chair, squeezing all my hope into their faux-leather padding.

"You can't blame yourself," he said in a tone meant to be kind.

I squeezed my eyes shut, blocking out the sight of his lips moving, letting the echo of the gunshot stampede through my brain.

"He's dead."

*Four months later . . .*

The tug-of-war in my stomach was a tractor pull pitting an eighteen-wheeler against a Panzer tank. My blinding headache as I hunched over the steering wheel of the van and peered through the equally blinding rain didn't help. Once we'd left the concrete tangle of highways surrounding D.C. and made it over the West Virginia border we were on two-lane switchbacked highways crossing through the Appalachians.

Home. The word filled me with dread—and yet also offered a tantalizing feeling of anticipation. Maybe this time. . . .

When we were kids, we used to whine that Scotia, West Virginia, was the town where dreams went to die.

But I'd escaped.

I'd lived my dreams. Lost most of them. Except the most important one, the one sleeping in the backseat, his corduroy snores harmonizing with the beat of the windshield wipers.

David. Almost ten years old and going to meet his grandparents for the first time. Not to mention his first trip to the mountains. First time leaving D.C. since he was an infant in my arms.

Was I crawling back, a failure, a fool for returning to the town that had tried so hard to assassinate my dreams? Or was I really still just a kid myself, coming home at twenty-seven to be healed?

Lord, how I wanted it to be the latter, that Walton's Thanksgiving special where John Boy reunites with his father and everyone ends up safe and sound, wrapped in a crazy quilt of love. . . .

I passed the WELCOME TO SCOTIA, POPULATION 867 sign and noted the bullet holes that had blown out the center of every "o" and dotted every "i." Nothing changed. Good-bye, Walton fantasy—hello, Scotia reality.

With all the finesse of a roundhouse punch, that reality hit home when I pulled up in front of my parents' house and saw that the only light on was upstairs. Last week, when I'd called to let her know I was coming home, my mom had been so excited by the idea of getting to know her only grandchild that she'd insisted I stay with her and Dad instead of with my grandmother, as I'd planned.

She'd gushed about preparing a room for us to share, said it would be no problem to accommodate David, none at all. Of course, she'd also poured on the guilt about me keeping David from her for so long—as if it'd been my idea.

Goes to show how low I'd fallen that I'd taken her at face value. Of all people, I should have known better. Usually I'm the biggest skeptic in a crowd, too guarded, barricaded even, but she'd suckered me into trusting her. And stupid me, I'd told David about it.

"Is the ramp around back?" he asked, his voice still ragged from sleep. "If they don't have it ready, I could use my crutches."

David was so excited about making a good impression on his grandparents—he'd changed clothes three times before we left D.C. I glanced in the rearview mirror and saw that he had his face pressed against the window. A kid on Christmas Eve, searching the sky for Santa.

And I was about to give him a lump of coal. Courtesy of my folks, Frank and Edna Palladino.

"No crutches. Not in this rain and mud."

"Mo-o-om." He dragged it out to three syllables. "I can do it. You're not going to carry me." The horror!

"Let me run in first, see what's going on." See if I could salvage anything, protect him from having all his familial fantasies crushed.

I jumped from the van before he could protest and dashed through the rain to the front porch of the only home I'd ever known. The doorknob was icy cold. I stopped myself before turning it. Going on ten years since I left—should I knock first, like a stranger?

The doorbell echoed through the darkened downstairs. After a few minutes the hall light came on, and my father came tromping down the steps. He looked surprised to see me, but long experience told me he was faking it. Denial, our family's drug of choice.

"Angela, what are you doing here?" He opened the door. He didn't invite me inside but instead stood there filling the doorway with his broad shoulders, barricading the entrance.

"Did you forget we were coming today?" For David's sake, I didn't lash out the way I wanted. Instead, I played along with his delusions. "That's okay, we can sort things out in the morning. Mom said she'd have the downstairs bedroom ready for us." It was a tiny room, called the "maid's room" back ninety years ago when the house had first been built, but it had its own bath and wouldn't need a lot of work to accommodate David's wheelchair.

"Well, see, we just didn't realize how much work it would take. . . ." He peered over my head to the van, trying to make out David's face. But the windows had steamed up, and all you could see of David was a black blob bouncing in anticipation. "It's just not fair to your mom, asking her to care for a crip——, a handi-capped child. And not fair to you or David," he added, as if he was doing us a favor.

As much as I'd have loved to punch him in the nose and take David away from this town, we had nowhere to go. If there was one thing I'd discovered in the years I'd spent away from Scotia, it was that as long as I had breath in my body, I'd do whatever it took to protect my child.

Didn't matter if it meant facing down a grizzly with its tail caught in a hornets' nest or groveling to my parents. David was my heart and soul—everything I did, I did for him, so he'd have a future better than any I'd ever dreamed of, so he'd have a present that was the best I could give him, so he'd never look upon his past with dread and anger and fear like I did.

I dug in for one last try. "Is Mom around?"

"She's having one of her spells." Pain shadowed his face as he shifted his weight from one leg to the other, still blocking the doorway.

It was Mom he was protecting. The "spells" started after my brother died, fifteen years ago. Our family secret. As if grief was something to be ashamed of. He stepped forward, forcing me to step back.

"Okay. I guess we'll spend the night in the van." I wasn't serious, of course. But venting some of my anger made me feel a little better.

He actually nodded, his gaze not quite vacant—I gauged it as a two-thirds-of-the-six-pack-consumed stage. His own nightly trip into oblivion.

Then he got this wistful smile that made me remember swinging off a rope into a pond, his strong arms stretched open to catch me. A younger me, trusting him, making the leap.

"Does he have your eyes? Those green Costello eyes? You get that gypsy blood from your mom's side of the family, that's why you couldn't stay put here."

Memories unearthed themselves like zombies clawing their way out of a freshly dug grave. I held on to the door, the wood gouging my palm, and fought to bury them once more. I couldn't "stay put" in Scotia because I'd been LifeFlighted out ten years ago, half-past dead. Me and David—although he hadn't been born yet. That had been another rainy night.

"Try your gram. Edna said something to her about your coming back." I noted that he didn't say "coming home."

With that, he turned and climbed back up the steps, turning the light off when he reached the top, leaving me standing just outside the threshold, in the dark.

A familiar dread and uncertainty roiled over me, making me feel off balance, unable to remember the life I'd built for myself as an adult, feeling dwarfed, diminished. Meaningless. Nothing.

I was definitely back home.